The Cookie Crumbles

"I'm surprised you're not fat," Olivia teased her brother.

"I'm surprised you're not in jail," Jason said, just before forcing another half of a sandwich into his mouth. He closed his eyes in ecstasy while he chewed, which left him unaware of the sudden silence. Only when he opened his eyes and reached for the last of the food did he notice the confused stares from his nearest and dearest. "Wassup? Do I have a piece of bacon up my nose?"

Ellie frowned at him, a rare occurrence. "That was an unusual statement you made about your sister," she said.

"What? About her being in jail?" Jason looked from his mother to his stepfather and finally to Olivia. "You really haven't heard, have you?"

"Heard what?" Allan's tone was clipped, no nonsense.

Jason wiped his mouth with his napkin and scraped back his chair. "Sam Parnell was rushed to the hospital, unconscious. I guess he finally got too snoopy for his own good and somebody tried to kill him."

Olivia was first to break the stunned silence. "How do they know it was a murder attempt?" she asked. "And even if it was, what could it possibly have to do with me?"

Jason started to laugh, but the dangerous look on Olivia's face sobered him quickly. "I don't have the inside scoop or anything, only what's going around town."

"Which is?"

"Well . . . Look, Livie, don't kill the messenger, okay? What's going around is, Sam was eating a cookie when he collapsed, and he didn't choke or have a heart attack or anything. He had a bag from your store, and there were still cookie crumbs and icing bits inside. All I'm saying is, it doesn't look good."

Cookie Dough or Die

VIRGINIA LOWELL

BERKLEY PRIME CRIME, NEW YORK

THE BERKLEY PUBLISHING GROUP
Published by the Penguin Group
Penguin Group (USA) Inc.
375 Hudson Street, New York, New York 10014, USA
Penguin Group (Canada), 90 Eglinton Avenue East, Suite 700, Toronto, Ontario M4P 2Y3, Canada
(a division of Pearson Penguin Canada Inc.)
Penguin Books Ltd., 80 Strand, London WC2R 0RL, England
Penguin Group Ireland, 25 St. Stephen's Green, Dublin 2, Ireland (a division of Penguin Books Ltd.)
Penguin Group (Australia), 250 Camberwell Road, Camberwell, Victoria 3124, Australia
(a division of Pearson Australia Group Pty. Ltd.)
Penguin Books India Pvt. Ltd., 11 Community Centre, Panchsheel Park, New Delhi—110 017, India
Penguin Group (NZ), 67 Apollo Drive, Rosedale, Auckland 0632, New Zealand
(a division of Pearson New Zealand Ltd.)
Penguin Books (South Africa) (Pty.) Ltd., 24 Sturdee Avenue, Rosebank, Johannesburg 2196,
South Africa

Penguin Books Ltd., Registered Offices: 80 Strand, London WC2R 0RL, England

This is a work of fiction. Names, characters, places, and incidents either are the product of the author's imagination or are used fictitiously, and any resemblance to actual persons, living or dead, business establishments, events, or locales is entirely coincidental. The publisher does not have any control over and does not assume any responsibility for author or third-party websites or their content.

COOKIE DOUGH OR DIE

A Berkley Prime Crime Book / published by arrangement with the author

PRINTING HISTORY
Berkley Prime Crime mass-market edition / April 2011

Copyright © 2011 by Penguin Group (USA) Inc.
Cover illustration by Mary Ann Lasher.
Cover design by George Long.
Interior text design by Kristin del Rosario.

ISBN: 978-0-425-24067-0

BERKLEY® PRIME CRIME
Berkley Prime Crime Books are published by The Berkley Publishing Group,
a division of Penguin Group (USA) Inc.,
375 Hudson Street, New York, New York 10014.
BERKLEY® PRIME CRIME and the PRIME CRIME logo are trademarks of Penguin Group (USA) Inc.

PRINTED IN THE UNITED STATES OF AMERICA

10 9 8 7 6 5 4 3 2 1

For my father and for Marilyn

Acknowledgments

Writing a book may be a solitary pursuit, but most of us need plenty of help and support to reach the end. I'm no exception. It has been a delight to work with Michelle Vega, a talented editor who provided great ideas, as well as understanding at crucial moments. Many thanks to my longtime writing buddies: Mary Logue, Pete Hautman, Ellen Hart, and K. J. Erickson. I am grateful to the members of the National Cookie Cutter Collectors Club for their enduring passion and for their newsletter, *Cookie Crumbs*, which inspired many a detail in this story. Marilyn Throne has saved my life more than once with her depth of knowledge about the writing process and her no-nonsense support. Thank you, Marilyn. And, of course, my deep gratitude goes to my father and sister and to my husband, my loving cheerleaders.

Chapter One

Olivia Greyson's eyes popped open to darkness—and to the sense that someone was downstairs. Her little Yorkie had heard something. Spunky hadn't barked, but he was watching the bedroom door, ears perked.

Olivia's beloved store, The Gingerbread House, occupied the entire first floor of her small Victorian home. In a town like Chatterley Heights, no one bothered with fancy burglar alarms, but Olivia—who had, after all, lived a dozen years in Baltimore—kicked herself for not knowing better. On the other hand, Chatterley Heights barely managed to provide enough crime for two officers, so what were the odds?

It must have been a dream. "That does it," Olivia said. "No more chocolate-iced shortbread before bed. And that includes you, young man. Don't think I didn't see you lap up those crumbs." Spunky objected with a whimper.

Olivia's head dropped to the pillow, but her eyes stared into the darkness as she mentally ticked through the contents of her store—cookie cutters, first and foremost, but she locked the valuable antiques in the safe each night, along with the day's receipts. Some of the glossier cookie cookbooks, designed for coffee table display, carried hefty price tags; however, they were too heavy to steal. The more expensive aprons, hand-appliquéd with decorated cookie designs, drew sighs only from the few customers who understood the skill it took to create them.

Olivia left only one costly piece of equipment on permanent display in the cookbook alcove, a bright red mixer set with a stunning array of attachments. It was worth stealing, but even a desperate thief might think twice. Try explaining *that* contraption to a pawnshop clerk.

Spunky curled into the curve of her knees, relaxing the tension in Olivia's body, but her mind kept bouncing around the store downstairs. Luckily, she had a fail-safe method for falling asleep. She closed her eyes and imagined herself snuggled in a fleece-lined canoe, drifting along a river of chocolate sprinkles. She smelled the rich, sensuous aroma of chocolate melting under a warm sun. Soon she felt a gentle drop as her canoe glided down a waterfall of colored sugar crystals. Sparkling cascades of violet, red, and blue splashed all around her. A soft landing in a pool of frothy icing, and she'd be asleep.

Instead, she crash-landed awake as Spunky jumped to his paws and barked at the closed bedroom door.

Olivia dragged herself up on one elbow. "What is it, Spunks?"

Spunky stiffened and growled.

Reaching over the tiny dog, Olivia patted the top of her bedside table to locate her alarm clock, also known as her cell phone. She pushed the center button to wake it up. The lit numbers at the top read four a.m.

So far, Olivia hadn't heard a sound in the house, at least nothing besides the usual creaks or the furnace kicking on. Spunky had excellent hearing, though, so perhaps someone really was trying to get into the store—someone who didn't realize the pricy items were locked away.

Olivia started to punch 911, then hesitated, remembering an incident the previous autumn. An extended family of hungry mice had invaded The Gingerbread House kitchen and settled down for the winter in brand-new sacks of flour and sugar. Spunky had heard them through the floor vents upstairs. It would be a shame to rouse the town's limited police force, only to confront a band of unarmed mice. She'd never hear the end of it.

Olivia slid her feet from under the covers and into a pair of battered tennis shoes she used for slippers. Ears erect and ready for anything, Spunky hopped off the bed and trotted toward the bedroom door. His right-front paw, injured in puppyhood, twisted inward a bit, so he had a limp. Still, he moved as fast as any five-pound dog alive. He had no awareness of his size; he would protect Olivia to the death. She had no intention of allowing him to do so.

Using her firm alpha-dog voice, learned in puppy school, Olivia said, "Spunky, stay here and guard the inner sanctum."

At the word "stay," Spunky tilted his head sideways. A curtain of silky hair fell across his face, covering one eye. The other eye pleaded for a chance to do battle for her. Olivia reached down to smooth the hair back over his head.

"Nice try," she said. "I'll be right back." She cracked open the bedroom door enough to squeeze through sideways, blocking Spunky with her foot, then snapped the door shut behind her. Spunky had a frightening habit of exploding through doorways as if escape were his only salvation. A holdover from puppyhood.

In the hallway, a nightlight made from a cookie cutter cast a glowing teakettle shape on the wall. Olivia decided to leave the overhead light off, just in case, though she still hadn't heard any alarming noises.

At that moment Olivia heard a faint scraping sound, and it hadn't come from the bedroom behind her. It might have been beneath her feet. Olivia knelt down, put her ear to the floor, and listened. There it was again, a scrape, like a stuck door being yanked open. The door to the supply cabinet in the kitchen made a sound like that. She kept meaning to ask Lucas Ashford, owner of Height's Hardware next door, to stop by and sand it down. Now she was glad she'd forgotten. That telltale scraping sound told her someone was downstairs in The Gingerbread House kitchen, opening cupboard doors.

Olivia had left her cell phone by her bed, but she could use the wall phone in her small upstairs kitchen, two doors down, at the rear of the house. She bolted to her feet and reached the kitchen in seconds, panting more from anxiety than exertion. Her hand shook as she grabbed for the phone.

The noises were much louder now that she was in her own kitchen, right above the store kitchen. Olivia hesitated, listening. Surely not even a battalion of mice could make such a racket, let alone any self-respecting intruder. The sounds downstairs had become way too familiar—the clatter of metal pans, the rhythmic clink of a spoon hitting a porcelain bowl, the oven door clunking shut. Either the mice were baking cookies or . . .

"Maddie." The name came out as an exasperated groan, as Olivia collapsed on a kitchen chair.

Madeline Briggs was her best friend, had been since they were ten years old. In the intervening twenty-one years, Maddie had brought much to Olivia's life, including fun, a shoulder to cry on, and the occasional murderous impulse. The latter had become more common in the past year, since she and Maddie had become business partners. Olivia's fun quotient had increased, too, but this was not one of those moments.

Olivia had dawdled at bedtime and, so far, had achieved only four hours of sleep. The last fifteen minutes had worn her out. The thought of crawling back under the covers brought her to her feet. She'd have to remind Maddie that she wasn't in her own kitchen. After more sleep.

At that moment, the Chatterley Heights Gospel Chorus erupted into deafening four-part harmony. Except Chatterley Heights didn't have a gospel chorus, and it was barely past *four o'clock in the morning.*

This was vintage Maddie. Her aunt Sadie, who'd raised her, used to complain that Maddie would awaken with a masterpiece in mind for the school bake sale, pay no attention to the time, run down to the kitchen—oblivious to the absence of sunlight—and jump headfirst into her project. Never mind that someone might be in hearing distance, trying to complete an adequate night's sleep. Only she'd never before pulled this stunt in The Gingerbread House.

On the plus side, Maddie was responsible for several wildly creative ideas that had already made The Gingerbread House a shopping destination for customers from DC and Baltimore. Everyone loved her, and she was fun to work with. Most of the time.

Olivia grabbed her keys from the kitchen wall hook and draped them over the waistband of the sweatpants she'd worn to bed. She would simply explain to Maddie that most people don't find loud music conducive to slumber, they would come to an agreement, and Olivia could enjoy another few hours of sleep.

First, she stopped at her bathroom to splash some cold water on her face. It didn't help. The woman she saw in the mirror had sleep-crusted bluish gray eyes, one creased cheek, and serious bed hair. She consoled herself with the thought that she looked terrifying.

Olivia's laceless sneakers flopped as she trudged down the stairs to unlock her front door, which opened into the house's original entryway. A wealthy Baltimore family had built the little Queen Anne in 1889 as a summer getaway. During the following century, new owners had transformed the house into a duplex by blocking off the staircase and adding two inner doors inside the entryway. One led upstairs, the other opened into The Gingerbread House. This double entry had sold Olivia on the idea of sinking a good chunk of her divorce settlement into a mortgage. The location, the northeast corner of Chatterley Heights's busy town square, couldn't be more perfect. She'd decided to open a cookie-cutter store downstairs, complete with its own kitchen, and she could live upstairs, all for one hefty monthly payment.

On this particular morning, she questioned the wisdom of her business and residential choices.

Olivia unlocked The Gingerbread House and stepped inside, bolting the door behind her. She could make out shapes in the darkness, but she knew better than to feel her way along without light. The store was a glorious cookie-cutter minefield—cookie cutters served as lamp and curtain pulls, themed cookie-cutter mobiles swung from the ceiling, and small tables holding elaborate displays dotted the room. Customers with aesthetic leanings felt free to rearrange tables on whim.

Olivia twisted the dimmer switch enough so she could cross to the kitchen without breaking several toes or her neck. Even in her crabby, sleep-interrupted state, she felt a ping of pleasure as dozens of metal cookie cutters caught the light and glistened like waves in the moonlight. For Olivia, each day began like her childhood Christmas mornings, when she would sneak downstairs before anyone else was up. She would plug in the tree lights and sit cross-legged in the dark, staring at the sparkles of color. If she swung her head back and forth fast enough, the lights would blur and appear to move, like multicolored shooting stars.

Then her younger brother Jason would bound downstairs, whooping and jabbering with excitement. He'd flip on all the lights and dive for his presents, ripping the shiny paper into shreds. She loved her baby brother, but he sure could destroy a moment of enchantment.

As she reached for the kitchen doorknob, Olivia took a deep breath to prepare herself for chaotic reality. At least the gospel music had stopped. Maybe Maddie was winding down, cleaning up the kitchen. Olivia turned the knob and opened the kitchen door. A blast of the Bee Gees singing "Stayin' Alive" knocked her a step backwards.

Olivia stepped inside to buttery warmth laced with nutmeg, which almost made up for the state of the kitchen. Maddie had a gift for exuberant baking, which always resulted in a huge mess, but this time she had achieved a personal best. Apparently, it had snowed in the kitchen. Flour dusted the surface of the large kitchen table, the counter, the floor. Globs of cookie dough stuck to the walls, the door, even the refrigerator.

Maddie's pretty round face showed smudges of flour wherever she had rubbed or swiped, including the tip of her nose. At least she'd thought to put an apron over her jeans and T-shirt. A magenta bandanna held back her springy red curls. Her curvy hips were swaying in time to the disco beat as she studied a color chart.

Olivia couldn't help but smile.

On the kitchen table, several dozen cut-out cookies lay cooling on racks. As always, they were baked to perfection and not one second beyond. At least a dozen soup-size plastic containers, plus a large mixing bowl filled with cream-colored icing, crowded the table. Maddie had her back to Olivia while she selected a small bottle from an impressive collection of similar bottles that lined the shelves next to the color chart. After executing a smooth disco spin around to the table, Maddie scooped some icing into one of the containers, then opened her bottle of food coloring. She existed only on Planet Maddie, alone with her colors, her tunes, and a gallon of royal icing.

Olivia saw only one easy way to get Maddie's attention. She pushed the stop button on the CD player. Maddie's hand froze over the bowl of icing. As her head snapped toward the CD player, a drop of royal blue coloring retreated back into its dropper.

Catching sight of Olivia, Maddie grinned. "Livie! Hey, sleepyhead."

"I don't suppose you know what time it is?"

"Not a clue. Is it time to open? Because I stowed some work clothes in the bathroom, so I can be changed in a jiffy." Maddie's eyes flicked to Olivia's attire. "You're in your jammies. Are you sick or—?"

"Or," Olivia said, "it's the middle of the night."

Maddie twisted her head to check the clock over the sink. "It's almost five o'clock."

"That's four twenty-four. In the morning. Your music woke me up at four. I was catching up on paperwork until midnight, so I had my heart set on at least three more hours of sleep. I *need* those three hours."

"Oh, Livie, I'm sorry. You'll get those three hours, I

promise. I'll open the store; you can sleep till noon if you want." Maddie reached toward a rack of cookies. "Only first let me show you what I'm making for our special spring event on Saturday. You'll *love* it, and you'll sleep so much better knowing how fabulously fun it will be. Please?"

"What the heck, I'm awake now." Olivia dragged a tall stool over to the table and crawled onto it. "I don't suppose you've made coffee?"

As Maddie shook her head, a red curl escaped its restraint and bounced on her cheek. She swept it behind her ear. "I've got extra icing, though. A good dose of sugar would perk you right up."

"Tell me your brilliant idea."

Maddie's face lit up. She pushed the rack of cookies toward Olivia and asked, "What do you think?"

"Flowers? For spring, right?"

"And?"

Olivia picked up a cookie. "This looks like a tulip, but I don't remember having a cutter quite like this in stock."

"And you would be correct," Maddie said. "I used our regular tulip cookie cutter, but then I worked the dough a bit to make it look more like a lily-flowering tulip. I did the same thing with all our flower shapes." She reached to a rack on the table and plucked up another cookie. "This is a daisy I'm turning into a sunflower. See?"

It still looked like a daisy to Olivia. "I'm sure I will once you've outlined the petals."

"Maybe you will and maybe you won't," Maddie said, with her signature mad-scientist smirk. "I'm decorating them with wild colors, and Saturday we'll ask customers to identify each flower. You guess right, you get the cookie. Whoever gets the most right wins a free lesson on making creative cutout cookies. We'll show customers how versatile cookie cutters can be, so when they buy a set of five ordinary shapes, they are really investing in endless possibilities."

Olivia bit a petal off her cookie and chewed, enjoying the sweet-butter feel of it melting in her mouth. Maddie was truly gifted when it came to anything cookie related.

When Olivia didn't answer immediately, Maddie's full lips began to droop. "You hate my idea."

Olivia swallowed quickly. "Girlfriend, your idea is nothing short of brilliant. Cleaning up after your fits of genius is a small price to pay. However, next time bring your iPod and plug it in your ear." She slid off her stool, taking the remains of the cookie with her. "And now I am going back to bed. I'll be down by nine."

Olivia was about to leave when she heard a knocking sound from the direction of a door that opened into the alley behind the store. She spun around. Maddie, her hand hovering over the bottles of food coloring, stared over her shoulder at Olivia. "Who on earth . . . ?" she whispered.

Another knock, louder this time. Olivia, who was facing the back door, saw the doorknob turn. The door rattled as someone tried to push it open. Olivia reached across the kitchen table toward the knife Maddie had been using to trim cookie edges. She curled her fingers around the handle, pulled it to her.

"Livie? Maddie? You kids okay in there?" It was a man's voice, authoritative, concerned, and familiar.

"Thank God," Maddie said. "It's Del."

Olivia realized how tense she'd been as her shoulders dropped about a foot. Del was Sheriff Delroy Jenkins. He was only in his late thirties, but he always referred to younger women as kids. Olivia suspected it was his way of keeping some professional distance. Which was fine with her—she'd felt the occasional spark between them, but she wasn't anywhere near ready for a new relationship. Her divorce was barely a year old.

Maddie unlocked the back door and flung it open. Sheriff Del stood in the dark alley, his hand on the butt of his service revolver. As he stepped closer to the doorway, his eyes darted around the kitchen.

"You scared the life out of us," Maddie said. She grabbed the shoulder of Del's uniform and pulled him inside.

The back door was small, and Del was one of the few men in town who didn't have to duck to go through it. However, he was still taller than Olivia's five foot seven. Which didn't matter, she reminded herself, because there was nothing whatsoever between them.

Sheriff Del locked and bolted the door behind him.

"What the heck are you doing out there?" Maddie demanded. "Are you on night shift or something, or is this a cop thing, wandering around alleys at—well, whatever time it is, it's still dark."

Del had an easygoing, unflappable manner, but to Olivia he looked shaken.

"You two sure you're okay in here?" Del asked, his eyes on the knife in Olivia's hand.

Olivia held the knife up, pointing toward the ceiling. "Everything's under control," she said. "The body's in the basement. Want to help bury it?"

Del relaxed enough to drop his hand from his gun handle. He grinned as his gaze flicked up and down Olivia's body. "You are looking lovely this morning, Ms. Greyson."

Olivia plunked the knife onto the table so she wouldn't throw it at him. Though she wasn't prone to blushing, she could feel her cheeks heat up. She'd forgotten what she was wearing when she'd been blasted out of bed. It wasn't pretty.

Olivia's ex-husband wasn't an evil guy, but he'd been a bit on the controlling side. Ryan was a surgeon, which eventually became more important to him than being an equal partner in their marriage. Over time, he'd begun laying down rules for Olivia to live by. Ryan despised dogs, said they were smelly and noisy and carried germs. He had also insisted that a surgeon's wife should always dress well, day and night. If even a neighbor saw Olivia wearing ratty clothes, it might trigger rumors that Ryan was a sloppy surgeon.

As soon as she moved to Chatterley Heights, Olivia set about breaking the rules. She'd adopted Spunky, a rescue Yorkie who liked to steal food off her plate. And she always wore her oldest, most dilapidated sweats to bed. The more holes, the better. It hadn't occurred to her that anyone besides Spunky or Maddie might ever spot her in them. So much for that hint of future romance. Probably for the best.

Del looked too tired to keep up the banter, so Olivia swallowed her scathing retort. "Has something happened?" she asked him. "Is that why you're out at this hour?"

Del hesitated, frowning. With a shrug, he said, "Everyone will know soon, anyway. I was on my way home from the Chamberlain house when I saw the lights on in here. It got me worrying. Not that there's anything for you to worry about, it looked like an accident, but I thought I'd check on you, to be on the safe side."

"Could you be a little less clear?" Olivia asked.

"Sorry," Del said with a faint smile. "We got a call around two a.m. from the Chamberlain housekeeper—you know Bertha, right? Anyway, Bertha said she'd found Clarisse unconscious. We got there right after the paramedics, but there was nothing anyone could do. She was dead."

Chapter Two

⊱⋆⊰

Olivia managed a whopping hour and thirty-seven minutes of sleep before the alarm woke her. After the events of the previous night, she knew the store would be busier than usual. Even Maddie's superhuman energy level might not be up to the demands of Chatterley Heights gossip.

After a shower, Olivia dressed in cords and a warm sweater to take Spunky on a quick walk. The morning air felt heavy and wet under slate clouds, so Spunky was more than happy to keep it short. He raced upstairs before Olivia could dry off his paws, leaped back onto her unmade bed, and burrowed his head under a blanket fold.

"Wish I could join you, kiddo," Olivia said. She left the bedroom door ajar so Spunky could get to food and water.

For the first time since The Gingerbread House opened, Olivia felt no quickening of energy and interest at the thought of going to work. Her slump had less to do with sleep deprivation than with her struggle to grasp the reality of Clarisse Chamberlain's death. In fact, Olivia had awakened that morning convinced that she'd dreamed the whole episode: the suspected intruder, Maddie's middle-of-the-night baking frenzy, and Del's bleak announcement.

She remembered feeling that same confusion when her father died, which told her how tightly woven into her life Clarisse had become. During the last few years of her marriage to Ryan, Olivia's identity had shifted so subtly from beloved partner to appendage that she hadn't been aware of it happening. One day they were working side by side to achieve a joint dream, and the next she was a mix of servant and arm candy. Looking back, the divorce was inevitable and necessary, but it had dealt yet another blow to Olivia's sense of competence.

It was Clarisse Chamberlain who'd yanked her upright, brushed the dirt off her derriere, and prodded her into a turnaround. Clarisse, a successful businesswoman for over forty years, had spotted Olivia's potential and encouraged her—okay, outright bullied her—into taking a chance on The Gingerbread House. She had become Olivia's ongoing mentor, most enthusiastic customer, and friend. Clarisse would tell her to go downstairs and attend to business.

Olivia decided not to change out of her cozy cords and sweater; she might end up napping in the kitchen during work breaks. On her way to the staircase, she stopped for a critical look in the bathroom mirror. She looked better than she had at four a.m., but there was room for improvement. A touch of makeup, a hint of blush, and her puffy eyelids were less obvious. Her short auburn hair was behaving for once, falling in loose curls around her face. A few men, Ryan included, had noticed her unusual gray eyes, which could look blue or green depending on the color of her outfit. Arm candy, however, she wasn't, and she had no wish to be.

Olivia drained her coffee cup and carried it with her downstairs. It was going to be that kind of day.

Maddie was opening the store as Olivia arrived. "Fresh coffee in the kitchen," she said, eyeing the empty cup.

Olivia followed the scent of brewing coffee. "Did you get any sleep?" she called over her shoulder.

"Nope, not really. Don't worry about me. My record is forty-eight hours without sleep. Always wanted to break that."

"Let me know when you need a nap."

"Will do."

In the kitchen, Olivia filled her cup, gathered a pile of orders, and sat down at her little work desk. She'd barely begun when the kitchen door opened and Maddie poked her head inside.

"I could use some backup out here," Maddie said.

"Sure thing." Olivia followed her into the store. "Did we announce a fire sale? There must be a dozen customers in here already."

"Thirteen, to be exact," Maddie said. "And I can see more arriving. I'm guessing they're curious to hear the latest about Clarisse's death."

"But why here?"

"Because," Maddie said, "you and Clarisse were close, that's why. If anybody has details, it'll be her sons or you. Edward and Hugh will stay out of sight. You don't have that option. You're not in Baltimore anymore. But fear not, I'm right behind you."

The moment Olivia appeared, customers flowed toward her like water through a sieve. She felt like a starlet who'd stopped in to ask for directions. However, unlike adoring fans, Chatterley Heights residents behaved with subtlety and restraint. Usually, anyway. She recognized every face, including several she'd never before seen inside The Gingerbread House.

For the next hour, customers vied for Olivia's attention. Most of them bought something, if only a spatula or one of the less expensive cookie cutters, for the chance to talk to her for a minute. She tried to quell the most shocking rumors—especially the one that Clarisse was murdered by a motorcycle gang during a home invasion. When word spread through the store that, as far as Olivia knew, Clarisse's death had been natural, the crowd began to shrink.

Olivia busied herself restocking shelves, while Maddie went straight for Lucas Ashford in the cookbook nook, which had once been a family dining room. A red plaid flannel shirt tucked into jeans draped Lucas's strong, lean body. He appeared to be testing the weight of a gray marble rolling pin as if he thought it might be useful at a demolition site. Maddie was nuts about him. Her descriptions of him always included words such as "yummy," but to Olivia, he was simply Lucas, the guy next door. When Maddie appeared at his side, he smiled down at her, and she touched his arm. A prick of sadness caught Olivia by surprise. She remembered those feelings.

"Sweetheart, how are you holding up?"

Olivia started at the sound of her mother's voice. "Mom. Sorry, I didn't see you."

"You didn't see me *down here*, you mean." It was an old family joke, but Ellie Greyson-Meyers laughed as if she'd just thought it up. At four foot eleven, Ellie was a good eight inches shorter than Olivia, who had inherited her height from her six-foot-two father.

"Maddie can handle the store for now," Ellie said. "Come talk to your mother." With a firm maternal arm, she pulled Olivia into the kitchen and closed the door. Ellie hoisted her small frame onto a stool. A child of the 1960s, now approaching sixty, Ellie still favored long, flowing skirts and peasant blouses. She'd long ago cut her waist-length hair, which now hung below her shoulders in loose gray waves.

"Oh my," Ellie said, eyeing the kitchen table. Maddie had managed to decorate about half of her flower cookies. "You and Maddie have outdone yourselves."

"All Maddie's doing," Olivia said. "She is the creative genius."

Ellie leaned forward and pointed to a cookie. "Is that a purple daffodil? If we were back in the commune, I'd wonder if Maddie's genius got a boost from—"

"Trust me, Mom, purple daffodils grow in Maddie's world."

"And what about your world, Livie? You look tired. I know how close you'd become to Clarisse; her death must be a blow. Now don't look at me like that, I'm not after gossip. It's just that . . ." Ellie gathered her hair and pulled it behind her neck, giving it a twist so it wouldn't fall forward. "When your father died, I grieved of course, but I also began to question myself. Should I have seen it coming? Should I have insisted he see a doctor sooner? Why didn't he tell me about his symptoms until it was too late?"

Olivia picked up a cookie that looked like a green and orange striped rose, snapped it in half, and handed one piece to Ellie.

"I honestly don't know how Clarisse died," Olivia said, "but . . ."

Ellie waited, nibbling the icing off an edge of her cookie half.

"Right up until three days ago," Olivia said, "I'd have sworn there was nothing wrong with Clarisse. She was as sharp and vibrant as ever. Then she came into the store Tuesday, and she seemed to be in a different world."

"Maybe she'd been given some bad news about her health," Ellie said.

The kitchen door opened, and Maddie poked her head in. "Hi, Ellie. Livie, could you come out and watch the store for half an hour, pretty please with buttercream frosting on top? Lucas wants to buy me a cup of coffee. Thank you, thank you!" She disappeared before Olivia could open her mouth.

"Are you sure you're all right? I was planning to go to Baltimore," Ellie said, "to take a seminar on natural healing, but I can skip that if you need me."

"I'm okay, Mom. I need to keep busy. You go ahead to your seminar and give me a call when you get back."

Ellie put her arms around Olivia and gave her a motherly squeeze. "I'll keep my cell on vibrate, so promise you'll call if you need to talk, okay?"

"Thanks, Mom. I promise."

"Take care of yourself, Livie. Don't beat yourself up about something you couldn't have prevented." She stood on tiptoes and pulled Olivia down by the shoulder to plant a kiss on her cheek.

Olivia followed her mother into the empty store, waved good-bye, and finished her restocking project. And thought about Clarisse. She wished their last time together hadn't been so odd and unsettling. Clarisse had seemed vague and scattered, at times unaware of Olivia's presence. Clarisse was a hardheaded businesswoman with laser-beam focus. She did not dither. But dither she did on that last visit to the store.

Olivia had the store to herself, so she sat on the high stool behind the sales counter and punched some numbers into her cell phone.

After three rings, Sheriff Del answered. "Livie, hello there. Sorry I disrupted your sleep this morning." Olivia heard some male guffaws in the background, then, "Hang on, I'm going outside." A minute later, Del said, "Sorry about that, I wasn't thinking."

"You're a bit short on sleep, too."

"No kidding. What's up?"

"I've been thinking about Clarisse. We had dinner together last Saturday, and she seemed fine. But when she came to the store on Tuesday, she was distant, distracted. She behaved oddly, though I wouldn't say she looked ill. I can't help but wonder. . . . Maybe something was wrong. I think I'd like to talk with you about it. Are you free for lunch?"

"Well, I don't know, will you be wearing that sweet little number you had on last night?"

"You get one pass for exhaustion, Del, then I start keeping score."

Del laughed. "Fair enough. Meet me at the café around one o'clock, and we'll talk."

Olivia hung up and slid her phone into her pants pocket. When she twisted the stool seat around, her breath caught in her throat. At the front of the store stood Sam Parnell, postal carrier, holding a bundle of mail. She hadn't heard him come in.

Chatterley Heights had three postal carriers, two part-timers and Sam, who'd been delivering mail for fifteen years. Every day, freezing or sweltering, he wore an official U.S. Postal Service uniform, complete with hat. He never left home without it.

"Anything interesting today?" Olivia had heard all the rumors about Sam. According to local gossip, he wasn't nicknamed "Snoopy" for nothing.

"Looks like a whole lot of bills," Sam said.

"Good to know. Thanks for bringing them in." She busied herself sorting through a stack of new receipts.

"Shame about Ms. Chamberlain." Sam's nasal whine reached across the room.

Olivia glanced up at him, which he took as an invitation. He flipped through her mail as he crossed the store. "I guess there's only so much stress a woman can take," he said as he handed the envelopes to Olivia.

"Stress?" she asked, then kicked herself. She knew how much Sam loved looking as if he knew more than everyone else, and she'd handed him an opportunity.

"A woman her age, I mean, with all those businesses going at once. And two grown sons wanting to take charge. I heard she was thinking of changing her will. Must have been tough on her. I mean, Hugh and Edward, hard to tell if either one will ever settle down and have kids to carry on the family name."

Olivia sorted through her mail without comment. She'd learned that whenever Sam was angling for information, he would string together several vague suggestions, hoping to see his listener react to one of them.

Sam cleared his throat. "One thing I know for sure," he said. "Having grandchildren, that was real important to Ms. Chamberlain. Real important."

It was probably another guess, but Sam's statement surprised Olivia. She remembered Clarisse mentioning the topic of grandchildren, but she hadn't given it any thought. Olivia said nothing, but she couldn't help meeting Sam's watery blue eyes. True or not, his comment was something to think about. Sam gave her a nod and sauntered toward the door, whistling.

* * *

Olivia rarely had time for lunch out, and even when she did, she avoided the Chatterley Café. At lunchtime, even on a weekday, customers sat on windowsills and crowded the doorway, waiting for a table.

Olivia slid onto the stool Del had saved for her at the counter. "You look awful," she said.

"It's good to see you, too, Livie." Del gave her a muted smile that only accentuated the puffiness around his eyes. His sandy hair, normally straight, was bunched and creased as if he'd wedged on his uniform hat right out of the shower.

Olivia scanned the café. It was a few minutes past one o'clock, but every table was occupied. No one appeared to be signing a credit card slip or donning a coat. "I was hoping for a lower decibel level," she said, leaning toward Del's ear.

The waitress sloshed two cups of coffee in front of Del, who slid one toward Olivia. "My treat," he said. "You can buy lunch."

"Thanks," Olivia said. "This makes an even half dozen cups since I got up this morning. I can feel my stomach lining dissolve."

Del nodded toward a table along the front window. "I think those two are about to leave," he said.

Olivia glanced at the couple, who appeared to be deep in conversation. "How do you know?"

"Because, Livie, I've been a cop for nearly fifteen years. I've learned how to read these kinds of situations."

Grinning, Olivia said, "This has something to do with donuts, doesn't it?"

"Oh ye of little faith." Del pointed to the same table, where the couple had stood up and were shrugging into their coats. Del grabbed his coffee cup and reached the table in seconds.

Both customers greeted him with smiles and motioned him to take their table. Del waved to Olivia to join him.

"Okay, how did you do that?" Olivia demanded as she opened a menu.

Looking pleased with himself, Del said, "I happen to know that those two eat here every day, and they tip heavily so the waitstaff will save this table for them. They keep a running tab, which they clear every two weeks on payday. Both of them work at the post office. If they clock in past one fifteen, their pay is docked."

"Impressive," Olivia said. "And I see you've even arranged for entertainment." She pointed out the window toward the sidewalk. A black Lab the size of a pony loped past, scattering passersby.

"The cavalry won't be far behind," Del said, shaking his head.

Within seconds, a tall young man with a frantic expression sprinted past the window. It was Deputy Cody Furlow, trying to dodge the folks his dog, Buddy, had nearly mowed down.

"Is Spunky still trying to run away, too?" Del asked.

"Not as often. I think he's feeling safer now."

"That's one plucky little guy," Del said. "Escaping from a puppy mill, living on the streets of Baltimore for weeks. It would make a terrific movie."

"Yeah, he's a great little con artist. It's part of his charm."

Once they'd ordered, Del rested his chin on his laced fingers and regarded Olivia with a concerned expression. "You wanted to talk about Clarisse?"

Olivia sipped her coffee, searching for the right words to describe Clarisse's behavior a few days earlier. It was the last time she'd ever see Clarisse, but she couldn't have known that, so she hadn't paid rapt attention to their conversation. Though it had struck her as off-kilter, she wasn't sure she could explain how or why. Del didn't prod her, for which she was grateful.

When their orders arrived, Del dug into his turkey club as Olivia said, "Clarisse Chamberlain was the sharpest, most determined woman I've ever met, and I admired her for that, even though sometimes I didn't agree with her. She always seemed to know what she wanted."

Del nodded encouragement while he chewed.

"But the last time I talked to her, she was like a different person."

"When was this exactly?" Del crunched the tip of a dill pickle.

"Tuesday afternoon. Tuesday is usually a slow retail day, so I was glad to see her and hoping for a chat. Her business insights were always so helpful to me. I offered her a cup of coffee, only she didn't seem to hear me."

"Livie, you know how distracted people can get, no matter how sharp they are. Hugh and Edward are both in their thirties, so Clarisse must have been nearing sixty. At her age, lots of folks are thinking about retiring to the golf course. Maybe she was tired, or maybe she wanted time to use all those cookie cutters instead of just collecting them."

"I wonder if you will feel that way when *you* are sixty," Olivia said. "Besides, Clarisse had no interest in cooking. She certainly wasn't longing to become a housewife."

"I didn't mean . . . Okay, help me understand. You said Clarisse wasn't acting like herself Tuesday afternoon. What did she say or do to leave you with that impression? Tell me everything you can remember."

Olivia munched on her salad, casting her mind back to that afternoon. Clarisse was wearing her long, wool winter coat, even though spring had touched the air that day. Olivia had glanced at Clarisse's face and sensed right away that something was wrong.

"Her lipstick was smudged," Olivia said, "badly smudged." Before Del could respond, she added, "And don't suggest she'd been eating an apple or making out. I never saw Clarisse without perfect makeup, even when I'd drop off a delivery at her home without calling ahead."

"Point taken," Del said. "What else struck you? Better yet, describe the whole scene to me, including any details that stuck with you. People tend to remember details that have meaning for them, even if they don't realize their significance at the time."

Fortified by food, Olivia placed herself back in time and described what she saw. "I noticed that Clarisse's face was sort of pinched, scrunched up—"

"Frowning? Angry?" Del leaned forward, elbows on the table.

"Not angry. More like she was thinking about a problem, something that worried her. When she saw me, she smiled. Not a big smile, and she didn't greet me by name, like she usually does. Did, I mean. It's so hard to believe—"

"I know."

Olivia exhaled a sigh. "She was carrying a large purse, the one she used when she had lots of errands or was delivering a package somewhere. I remember because she opened it, looked inside, then snapped it shut. Then she glanced around the store again, but she stood rooted in one place as if she couldn't remember why she'd come.

"I asked her, 'Is there something special you're looking for, Clarisse? We've gotten in several new spring collections since you were here last.' She didn't react, so I added that we'd received several vintage pieces from the 1970s

Hallmark Peanuts collection. She perked up and asked to see them, so we walked over to the curio cabinet."

Del interrupted, his voice muted. "Do you keep it locked? Just wondering."

"I always try to, although I'd let Clarisse sort through it. The average shoplifter wouldn't know the value of vintage cookie cutters—some can be worth hundreds of dollars— but serious collectors and antiques dealers do. At night, we lock the most valuable ones in the safe."

"Good," Del said. "Makes my job easier. Go on."

"When I got out the Peanuts cookie cutters, Clarisse picked up one with Snoopy dancing. She held it for several seconds while she stared off into space. Finally, she said something like, 'So gleeful,' softly, almost to herself. Then she said to me, 'I'll take this one.' As I walked over to the sales counter, she called to me, 'I'm going to look around a bit.' I looked over my shoulder, but she'd already turned her back on me.

"I said to her, 'Of course, take your time,' but she didn't answer. I felt a bit . . . well, rejected. Clarisse had never acted so distant, not with me."

Olivia picked at the remains of her salad. "I know it doesn't sound like much, but in the last few months, Clarisse had been treating me almost like a daughter, taking me out to dinner, offering unwelcome advice. . . ."

Del chuckled. "Sounds about right."

"The next thing she did during her visit on Tuesday was out of character," Olivia said. "She asked me for some of our cookie recipes."

"You said she didn't bake," Del said, sounding interested.

"I must have looked surprised, because she added that they were for Bertha. Even that didn't make a lot of sense. When Clarisse wanted decorated cookies for a gathering, she always hired us to provide them. Anyway, I said, sure, I'd go make copies of them."

"Anything else you can remember?"

"That's about it. When I returned with the recipes, Clarisse had put another cookie cutter on the counter—a flower shape, I think. I wrapped it up, then walked over to her, and . . . You know, I thought I'd imagined this, but after Sam's comment, I'm not so sure."

Olivia pushed her plate aside, so she could lean on her elbows. Rubbing her temples with her fingers, she said, "Clarisse was standing in front of a collection of cookie cutters meant for baby showers—you know, baby booties, rattles, a rocking horse, that sort of thing. She was holding a baby carriage shape. I touched her lightly on the sleeve of her coat, and her head jerked up as if I'd startled her home from another world. She looked right at me. I'd swear she had tears in her eyes. But she recovered so quickly I thought I'd imagined it. Then today, Sam insisted that grandchildren were very important to Clarisse—except she'd never mentioned it to me."

Del said, "Sounds like a safe, generic observation, the kind Sam often uses to elicit information. What mother doesn't want grandchildren? However, what you saw might be helpful."

Del was silent for a few moments. A wrinkle between his eyebrows told Olivia that he'd taken her seriously and was giving her observations some thought.

"You're actually pretty good at this," he said. "You have no idea how hard it is to get coherent details out of witnesses. I understand now why you've felt concerned. I might be able to put your mind at rest, at least partially." Del leaned across the table and lowered his voice. "I'm going to tell you some information we've gathered since

Clarisse was found. It hasn't been very long, and we don't yet have the autopsy and other test results, so this will be sketchy. Only here's the thing, Livie, don't tell anyone else, not even Maddie. Especially not Maddie. There are enough rumors out there already."

"Of course I won't," Olivia said.

"It's not that I don't trust you, or even that this information will turn out to be important, but . . . well, we simply don't know what we're looking at here."

"Del, are you saying that—"

"Keep your voice down."

Olivia leaned closer and whispered, "Are you saying that there's something suspicious about Clarisse's death?"

"No, I'm not saying that at all. I'm pretty sure it was an accident, only . . . Look, I'll tell you what I can, then you'll understand why it's important to keep this to yourself."

Del glanced around the half-empty café and seemed satisfied. "Okay. It looks right now like Clarisse drank a full bottle of red wine the night she died. Bertha said Clarisse asked her to open the bottle and bring it to her study. She also said Clarisse normally drank no more than one glass of wine, and only with dinner. Clarisse had trouble sleeping, Bertha said, and she had a prescription for strong sleeping pills. Since she had trouble swallowing pills, she always crushed the sleeping pills and added them to liquid, usually water or orange juice. Bertha said she'd seemed troubled lately. The evening of her death, she had barely touched her dinner."

"Which means," Olivia said, "she was drinking wine and taking pills on an empty stomach."

"Exactly. Bertha got up at about three a.m. to answer the shout of nature, as she put it, and saw the lights on downstairs. She found Clarisse on her study floor. She was lying facedown, halfway between her desk and the study door, as if she'd realized she was in trouble and had tried to get help."

Olivia stared out the café window. The sky had been darkening all morning; rain would arrive before long. "So what you're saying is that Clarisse was so disturbed, she didn't realize or care that she was doing something really stupid?" Olivia's mind flashed again to her many conversations with Clarisse. "I don't know, though. . . . Clarisse could be stubborn, but she wasn't ever stupid."

Del shrugged. "We'll see what the autopsy reveals. Right now I'm concerned about a third alternative, given what you and everyone else have told us about Clarisse's state of mind. I want it kept quiet until we've had a chance to eliminate the possibility." Del checked his watch. "I need to get back to the station. What you've recounted only supports what everyone else has said, that Clarisse was more distracted than anyone had ever seen her. We have to explore the possibility that Clarisse herself might have decided to—"

"No!" A couple of heads swiveled in their direction, and Olivia lowered her voice. "I know what you are going to say, but Clarisse would never choose to end her own life. She could face anything. Whatever was bothering her, she would have found a solution or gritted her teeth and carried on."

Del reached over and touched Olivia's arm for a brief moment. For some reason, it only made her angrier.

"I hope you're right," Del said. "Look, I know how much you want answers, but please don't go out there on your own, asking questions that might fuel rumors. Clarisse had several life insurance policies, and we don't want big-city insurance investigators getting the wind up while we're still trying to figure out what happened."

Olivia nodded her assent to a promise she wasn't sure she could keep.

Chapter Three

After her unsettling lunch with Del, Olivia walked back to The Gingerbread House in a funk. She couldn't accept the idea that Clarisse had died from an accidental overdose of sleeping pills and alcohol. Clarisse had been a nurse, for heaven's sakes. And after her marriage, she and Martin had created a medical supply business that grew to be their largest, most successful venture. Clarisse had been far too knowledgeable to make such an ignorant and deadly error, no matter how preoccupied she was.

Olivia understood why Del didn't want her to broadcast her doubts about Clarisse's death. Naturally he'd want to protect his town from outside invaders who might take over his investigation. She doubted he'd prevail once the circumstances of Clarisse's death became known. Insurance investigators were paid to be suspicious. Besides, Clarisse's reputation reached beyond little Chatterley Heights, and her death would capture media attention.

Olivia hated the idea that Clarisse might have chosen to end her own life. As she approached The Gingerbread House, an unwelcome thought wormed into her mind: Clarisse would have known how to make her death look like an accident. But why? What could possibly have driven her to such a desperate act? And how could she, Clarisse's friend, not have understood the signs?

She would be asking questions, that much was certain. She wanted, needed to know what had been going on in Clarisse's life during those days before her death. This wasn't idle curiosity. Olivia was angry, and the person she was most mad at was herself. She kept replaying in her mind Clarisse's last time at The Gingerbread House. She should have paid more attention, prodded Clarisse to share her troubles. Maybe she could have helped. Instead, she'd reacted like a rejected child.

When she entered the store, Olivia was relieved to see Maddie working with a talkative customer. She went straight to the kitchen, grabbing a small pile of invoices on the way. Paperwork wasn't her favorite part of her job, but it might help clear her mind. She settled at her little desk and fired up her laptop. Ten minutes of communing with numbers and her mind had numbed completely. She could barely keep her eyes open. She closed the laptop to put it to sleep, and then she joined it.

A moment later, or so it felt, someone was shaking Olivia's shoulder. She recognized Maddie's voice saying, "Livie? Wake up. You need to take Tammy off my hands before I kill her."

"Kill?" Olivia couldn't seem to lift her head. "Maddie? Did you say someone killed Tammy?"

"No such luck." Maddie pulled Olivia's shoulders to make her sit up.

Olivia lifted her head and winced. "What happened to my neck?"

"Well," Maddie said, "I'd say it has something to do with sleeping for half an hour on your right cheek. Here, I can fix it." She wrapped one arm around Olivia's head and pushed down on her right shoulder with the other.

"Ow!" Olivia heard a crack. She expected her head to fall off as Maddie let go, but instead her neck was back to normal, more or less. "Hey, that worked!"

"Yeah, those three hours in chiropractic school really paid off. Listen, Livie, you have got to go out there and talk to Tammy. She insists on showing you something, and she won't leave me alone to help actual customers. I told her you ran off with a circus lion tamer last night, but she just rolled her eyes. You'll have to handle her. I liked her a lot better when she was mad at you, but unfortunately all appears to be forgiven."

Olivia dragged herself to the sink and splashed cold water on her face. As she blotted the water with a paper towel, it occurred to her that Maddie was crabby. Maddie was never crabby. "You need a nap, don't you?"

"I'm fine. Wanting to strangle Tammy Deacons is an everyday urge for me."

"Yes, but you are normally cheerful about it. You need a nap." Olivia dug her keys out of her pants pocket and handed them to Maddie. "Here, use the guest bed. Spunky will undoubtedly join you."

"Good," Maddie said, taking the keys. "Spunky never irritates me, unlike certain childhood friends of yours."

While Maddie escaped upstairs, Olivia greeted Tammy with a wave. Her friendship with Tammy went back to nursery school, six years before Maddie and her aunt moved to town. There had always been a rivalry between her two old friends, but Olivia made a point of ignoring it. Life was much easier that way.

"Oh, Livie, there you are. I have to show you what I bought. It's so gorgeous, and it fits me perfectly if I don't gain an ounce." Tammy held up a large paper bag with black and gold stripes and a gold rope handle, the signature colors of Lady Chatterley's Clothing Boutique for Elegant Ladies. Tammy opened the bag so Olivia could peek inside. Something small and flat lay at the bottom, wrapped in layers of tissue paper and sealed shut with a shiny paper medallion.

Tammy's heart-shaped face glowed with excitement, which Olivia would have tried to share if she could see through the tissue paper. She was also very confused. Maddie was right: for the last few weeks Tammy had shunned Olivia. She hadn't visited the store or returned phone calls, she cancelled a shopping trip to Baltimore they'd had planned for a month, she even snubbed Olivia in public. Olivia still had no idea why. In all their years of friendship, this had never happened before.

The strange turn their relationship had taken made Olivia want to reconnect with her other old friend Stacey who taught at Tammy's school. Maybe she would know why Tammy was being so fickle. Olivia suddenly remembered that Stacey had never been a big fan of the woman who now stood before her, bursting with excitement. In the interest of keeping the peace, Olivia decided to put that call to Stacey on hold. The joyful nature of Tammy's forgiveness was puzzling, given Olivia had no idea what she'd done wrong, but they'd been friends a long time and Olivia felt the least she could do was share in her friend's present glory.

"Did you buy a dress?" Olivia guessed.

"Only the most beautiful, most perfect dress in the

world. I have to try it on to give you the full effect. I'll use the bathroom through the kitchen. Back in a sec."

Olivia glanced at the clock. Almost four, only an hour left before closing. She began to tidy up the store, which had reached what her mother referred to as "that lived-in look." Numerous cookbooks lay open as if a committee had been planning a townwide bake-off. After rearranging them on their shelf in the cookbook nook, Olivia reconstructed a large display of cookie cutters representing every dog breed imaginable; apparently, a group of children had played with them, then abandoned them all over the store. She located her favorite, a Yorkshire terrier shape, standing triumphant guard over a stack of pot holders. At the base of the pot holder hill, a vanquished Great Dane lay on its side. Olivia rescued the two creatures, held them nose to nose, and said, "No more dog fights in the store, is that clear?" She smiled for the first time since Del had told her that Clarisse was dead.

As Olivia finished rearranging the dog cutters on their display table, the store's door opened, followed by a joyful yap and the clicking of nails on linoleum tile. Spunky's front paws left the floor as he strained against his leash toward his mistress. Maddie dropped the leash, and Spunky raced toward Olivia, skidding on the tile. Olivia caught him as he leaped toward her arms.

"We couldn't sleep," Maddie said. "Spunky has requested a walk. Be back in twenty. I'll close up, and then I want to finish decorating the cookies for tomorrow's event."

"I could help you," Olivia said.

"Nope, this one's mine. Only my brain can envision the magnificent possibilities of this project. Bakers and horticulturists will sing of my flower cookies for years to come."

"I doubt it not," Olivia said. "Thanks for taking over. I

could use a break." She put Spunky on the floor and gave him a gentle push. "Go to Maddie," she said. He trotted to Maddie, who gathered him up right as Olivia heard the click of the kitchen door opening behind her. And she remembered—Tammy wanted to model her new dress. Judging from her earlier giddiness, it was a sexy new dress.

Olivia spun around in time to see the kitchen door fling open. Tammy emerged twirling. Admittedly, the dress was amazing, a silky swirl of pale pink and white, with spaghetti straps and a low-cut bodice. Excellent for Tammy's pale coloring. She had invested in a push-up bra, which did wonders for her slight figure. As she pirouetted toward Olivia, the skirt flared out in a circle, providing a quick view of pale pink panties.

Olivia expressed silent thanks that Tammy had not opted for thong underwear.

This was un-Tammy-like behavior. Maybe she'd cracked under the strain of teaching first-graders. Or perhaps she had drunk her lunch. However, she was as steady on her feet as a ballerina, so she must be sober. She was so deliriously happy that she didn't remember she was in a place of business, where anyone might walk in at any moment.

Tammy stopped in front of Olivia, her green eyes sparkling. Olivia tried to send a warning look, but Tammy was oblivious.

"Isn't it glorious?" Tammy gushed. "I can't wait for Hugh to see me in it."

Olivia stared at her, speechless. Tammy must have known that Clarisse, Hugh's mother, was just found dead. But if she was upset about it, no one would be able to tell. Even Maddie seemed to have run short of witty comments. Only Spunky had no trouble expressing his opinion in the form of nonstop yapping, which broke Tammy's enchantment. Her cheeks, already flushed from exertion, reddened when she realized she had an audience.

"Nice dress," Maddie said, deadpan. "We're off," she said to Olivia. She was out the door so fast that Olivia knew she'd been on the verge of hysterical laughter.

Thanks to Maddie, Olivia had the rest of Friday afternoon and all evening to herself. She poked her head into her bedroom, where Spunky curled in a nest of tangled blankets. "Spunks," she said. "Ride in the country? You and me, what do you say?"

Spunky's ears poked up. He leaped off the bed and trotted past Olivia toward the kitchen, where his leash hung. Olivia poured a handful of kibbles into a plastic container, in case they stayed out past Spunky's dinnertime.

"Hey, take it easy," Olivia said as Spunky yanked on his leash so hard his little paws scraped against the floor tile. When she released the leash, he shot out of the kitchen. She snatched her jacket from the back of a kitchen chair and followed him.

Olivia retrieved her 1972 Valiant from the small detached garage behind The Gingerbread House. The car had been her father's before he and her mother married, and he'd never been able to give it up. Her brother had honed his mechanic's skills on the old green machine. When Olivia moved back to Chatterley Heights, Jason had offered it to her, so she wouldn't have to pay for a car, in addition to a house and a new business. He kept it in running order. Olivia loved that it reminded her of her father and was also roomy enough to cart around the paraphernalia she and Maddie needed for cookie events. So what if it coughed and sputtered now and then?

She cracked open the passenger-side window so Spunky could sniff the air, but not wide enough for him to squeeze through and hurl himself after a fox. Or worse yet, a skunk.

Olivia felt her mood lighten as she left Chatterley Heights and headed northwest toward the rolling hills of Howard County. After a chilly beginning, the afternoon had turned springlike. Olivia lowered her window and let the wind lift her hair. Interstate 70 would be in the throes of rush hour. With no destination in mind, Olivia chose winding side roads leading in a general westward direction. Eventually, she reached the eastern edge of Patuxent River State Park.

She stopped at a familiar parking area. Spunky leaped on her lap, attempting to use it as a springboard to dive through her open window. Olivia grabbed him with one arm and latched on his leash with the other. "Okay, we'll have a walk," she said. "A short one, it'll be dusk soon." At the last minute, she remembered to extract a plastic bag from the glove compartment, in case Spunky deposited a memento of his visit.

They walked a trail until Spunky stopped straining forward and began to drag behind. Olivia scooped him up and carried him back to the car, where he curled into a ball and fell asleep. The hike left Olivia in a better mood—not content, but at least more settled, capable of clear thought. She pulled her car back onto the road and began the drive back.

As they approached the outskirts of Chatterley Heights, Olivia realized she had unconsciously chosen a route that led to the Chamberlain house. She reached the entrance to the estate and, without a second thought, drove through the open gate. A long, narrow road, paved with fine gravel, led through woods to the house itself. Olivia had driven it often. For the length of the drive, she recalled that feeling of comfortable anticipation. Then she reached the house. She stopped in a small parking area facing the house and cut the engine. Spunky stirred without waking, and Olivia lifted him onto her lap. She had no idea why she'd come, but it felt right.

Clarisse had loved that house. It was a Georgian farmhouse, built in the 1700s and well into decline when Clarisse and Martin bought it soon after their marriage. Over the years, they had restored the house, taking care to preserve its original form. Olivia had shared numerous meals and conversations with Clarisse, often in front of the fire in her office—the room where Clarisse died.

The only feature the Chamberlains had added was a large front porch for hot summer evenings. A brick walk, leading to the porch steps, wound through a large, lush garden designed to attract birds and butterflies. As Olivia watched, the porch door opened, and a large woman looked out in her direction. Olivia felt a flush of embarrassed guilt, as if she'd been caught peeping—but no, it was Bertha, the Chamberlain housekeeper, and she had always been friendly. Olivia waved as Bertha lumbered down the front steps, letting the screen door slap shut behind her.

"I thought that might be your cranky old car out here," Bertha said, panting from the effort of walking.

"I didn't mean to intrude," Olivia said. "We were out for a drive and, I don't know. . . . We found ourselves here."

"Well, of course you did. It don't take a mind reader to figure that one out. Come on in. I've got some beef stew bubbling; we can eat and talk. And don't tell me you already ate—you're both too skinny, you and the pup. Probably live on salads, the two of you. Bring his highness with you. I've got a marrow bone he can gnaw on." Without waiting for a response, Bertha headed back to the house.

Once inside, Bertha led the way to the large kitchen, where the warm, mellow aroma of beef stew simmering in red wine filled the air. When ordered to do so, Olivia settled at a table built to accommodate a crew of farmhands. The marrow bone consumed Spunky's attention, while Bertha filled two huge bowls with steaming stew and delivered them to the table. "Eat," she said, "I'll be right there." She returned with a pan of cornbread and a bowl of fresh green beans steamed with butter.

Finally, she delivered a tall glass of cold milk and put it beside Olivia's plate. "You need this for your bones."

Olivia took an obedient sip from the glass. It was best to do as Bertha ordered. As family housekeeper for thirty-five years, she had helped raise Hugh and Edward. She was also the only human being who'd been able to bully Clarisse.

They ate in subdued silence for a time. Olivia had so many questions, but she wasn't ready to change the mood. In the end, it was Bertha who scraped back her chair and said, "It don't seem right, not making up a tray and bringing it to the study for Ms. Clarisse."

"I know," Olivia said.

Bertha frowned into her empty bowl. "There was something wrong yesterday. I knew it, I just knew it, but I left it be. I should have said something, made her tell me."

Olivia hesitated, then asked, "Had Clarisse been acting differently in any way—I mean, even before yesterday?" She held her breath, hoping Bertha wouldn't shut down.

Bertha's plump face, flushed from the warmth of the kitchen, puckered up as she thought. "It got worse day by day," she said. "Ever since she got that strange envelope on . . . when was it? Monday I think."

"Do you know what was in it?" Olivia asked.

Bertha shook her head, and a tendril of gray hair escaped

from the tight bun at the nape of her neck. "Sam handed me the mail at the door, and I delivered it straight to Ms. Clarisse. Before she opened it, she asked me to leave. Usually she opened all the mail with me there, so she could hand me the household bills and such like. Anyway, right after that she got quieter."

"What happened to that envelope? Do you know?"

Bertha looked at her with red-rimmed eyes. "I never saw it again. And mind you, I looked for it. I should have asked Ms. Clarisse directly, but I figured she wouldn't tell me anything. I knew it was bad news, had to be."

"Could Clarisse have been ill?" Olivia asked. "Maybe seriously ill?"

Bertha snorted. "That girl had the constitution of a workhorse. Why, she had her physical only last month. I drove her, so she could get her eyes checked at the same time. I was right there when her doctor told her she passed everything with flying colors. He said her blood pressure belonged in a textbook, it was so perfect."

"Did you mention the envelope to the police?"

Bertha shook her head firmly. "I didn't like the questions they were asking: Was Ms. Clarisse getting confused? Was she depressed? All that nonsense. Even if she did make a mistake with her sleeping pills, that doesn't mean she was senile."

"What about Hugh and Edward? Did you hear either of them say anything about Clarisse getting bad news or being worried about something?"

"Oh those boys," Bertha said in an indulgent tone. "They don't notice things."

"By the way," Olivia asked, "where are they?"

"They came home today because of what happened, then back to Baltimore for the end of some business conference they were at all week. We can't bury Ms. Clarisse until the police give her back to us, so the boys are keeping busy. They'll be home tomorrow." Bertha opened the refrigerator. "I made their favorite, blueberry pie. Had to use frozen blueberries, but it'll taste the same." She cut two slices, slid them onto plates, and brought them to the table.

Olivia was stuffed, but Bertha would be insulted if she turned down dessert. She got through half of it before saying, "Bertha, this is so delicious, but I'm too full to finish. Could I take the rest home for a bedtime snack?"

Bertha, who had finished her slice, put Olivia's leftovers in a plastic container and left it on the table. While she covered the pie plate with plastic wrap, she said, "There's something I didn't tell the police. It probably isn't anything, but . . . well, Ms. Clarisse did mention your name."

"My name? When?"

"A couple weeks back, it was. When she got that other envelope in the mail."

"Wait. Clarisse received a previous envelope?"

Bertha avoided Olivia's eyes. "I didn't think about it until now because the first envelope didn't make her so upset. Right after we went through the bills, she opened that envelope in front of me and pulled out a letter. She looked sort of startled as she read it and then put it right back in the envelope. I never saw that one again, either. Then a few days later, I passed her office and she was having one of her little talks with Mr. Martin." Bertha saw Olivia's confusion and added, "I wouldn't tell this to the police, but you are family, or near like it. When Ms. Clarisse was chewing on a problem, she'd discuss it with Mr. Martin's portrait—you know, the one that hangs over the fireplace in her office."

Olivia knew it well. Clarisse's husband had died years earlier of a massive heart attack at the age of fifty-seven.

The portrait showed a handsome man with a confident smile, an older version of Hugh, his elder son. Clarisse once told her that chain smoking killed her husband, and Olivia remembered noticing the ghostly swirl forever spiraling from the cigarette in Martin's painted right hand. Clarisse used to claim she could smell the memory of that smoke.

"That evening," Bertha said, "I was passing the office and heard her talking to Mr. Martin about her will. Oh, they used to argue so about whether Hugh or Edward should run the businesses, or who should run the biggest one, and so on. Mr. Martin wanted the boys to work together, which is what they've been doing. They disagree most of the time, but it didn't matter because Ms. Clarisse was in charge."

"And now she isn't," Olivia said.

"I heard her tell Mr. Martin she wanted to change her will and leave one of them in charge, but she hadn't decided which one. She knew Mr. Martin would pick Hugh, if he had to pick, but Clarisse thought Edward worked harder."

Olivia didn't know Hugh and Edward very well, since they spent most of their time running the family businesses. "I don't understand—do you think this has something to do with her death?"

With an impatient shake of her head, Bertha gathered up the dirty plates and shifted them to the kitchen counter. "I'm not sure what to think, only Ms. Clarisse was all of a sudden talking about grandchildren. I don't know why she didn't like Tammy; that girl would have brought some life to this house. If Ms. Clarisse wanted grandchildren soon, why did she make Hugh break up with Tammy?"

Yet only a few hours earlier, Tammy had shown off her new dress to Olivia, delirious with joy in anticipation of wearing it for Hugh Chamberlain. "And why did Clarisse mention me?"

Bertha looked at her with surprise. "Well, you know how much she loved you. I heard her say she wanted one of the boys to marry you. I heard her clear as day, talking to that picture. She said, 'I'd never trust Tammy Deacons to handle a situation like this, but Livie could do it. Now all I have to do is find her.' That's the only time I thought Ms. Clarisse might be going round the bend—I mean, she only had to go to The Gingerbread House to find you. Does that make any sense?"

"Not to me," Olivia said. "Not to me."

Chapter Four

❧

Olivia found herself muttering as she and Spunky finished a chilly and hurried Saturday morning walk. Normally she kept her thoughts confined within her own mind, so this was not a good sign. Could it be true that Clarisse had wanted Olivia to marry one of her two sons? In the abstract, this wasn't an unnatural desire on Clarisse's part. Knowing of Olivia's divorce, Clarisse might have avoided any reference to the notion, waiting for time to heal.

Spunky yapped sharply, and Olivia realized she'd stopped walking. "Sorry, Spunks, Mom's a bit distracted," she said. *Which isn't like me.* Maddie was the distractible one, the creative genius chasing after every sparkling idea that flashed across her brain. Olivia focused. She observed, gathered information, considered options, handled situations. She was good at reading people, which had served her well in her business ventures. With a chagrined jolt,

Olivia realized that, when it came to understanding Clarisse, these skills might have let her down.

What else had she misunderstood about Clarisse? Was it possible she'd missed the earlier signs that Clarisse was upset and distracted? Distracted enough to drink an entire bottle of wine and lose track of how many pills she'd taken?

A car honked three times with staccato insistence, and Olivia's feet nearly flew off the pavement.

"Hey, Sis. Thinking of crossing the street anytime this millennium?" Olivia's brother, Jason, poked his head through the open window of his pick-up truck and gave her The Look. Olivia had once tried to explain The Look to Maddie. Without the benefit of siblinghood, however, Maddie didn't get it.

Olivia had been standing at a crosswalk like a life-size sculpture, lost in doubt. Spunky must have grown concerned, because he'd sat quietly on the pavement, gazing up at her. Probably wondering if it was time to hit the road and find a more reliable human companion.

A van filled with squabbling children stopped behind the pickup truck. The driver, a thirtyish woman with clumps of blonde hair escaping from a ponytail, narrowed her eyes at Jason. With the speed and precision of a race car driver, Jason maneuvered his truck to the curb next to Olivia. The woman hit her accelerator with a force that sucked the children against the backs of their seats. Instinctively, Olivia gathered Spunky into her arms and held him tightly.

When Jason's curly brown head poked through the car window, Olivia leaned toward him and said, "Morning, Baby Brother. Late for work again?"

"Oh geez." Jason checked his dashboard clock, as Olivia knew he would. Jason had no sense of time. In a moment, he reappeared. "You got me," he said. "I'm twenty minutes early. So we're even?"

"For now."

"Listen, Livie, I heard about Clarisse. That's raw."

Olivia nodded. "Raw" was a good word for it. Sometimes Jason could show amazing empathy.

"Well, gotta roll. Later."

Or not.

Except for a wave of sadness when she arranged the vintage cookie cutters in their curio cabinet, Olivia pushed her grief and confusion well to the back of her thoughts. She needed to concentrate on all the last-minute preparations for the store's spring event. By eight forty-five, fifteen minutes before opening, Olivia pushed up a west-facing window and poked her head out. A perfect day for a spring cookie extravaganza. The sky had cleared to a cornflower blue, and rows of red tulips, planted the previous fall along the front walk, had opened their petals to the sun.

From her vantage point, Olivia had a side view of the Chatterley Café entrance. A line of customers, waiting for tables, snaked out the door and down the sidewalk in her direction. Even for a spring-scented Saturday, this was impressive. A slender young woman in a swinging skirt emerged from the café and appeared to be heading toward the store. Her brisk, graceful stride looked familiar. As she approached, Olivia recognized the sleek blonde hair and air of determination. Tammy Deacons was about to be her first customer. Olivia had a sinking feeling that a discussion of cookie cutters was not on Tammy's agenda.

Olivia started to shut the window, but she was too late. Tammy caught sight of her and began to wave as if she were marooned on an island and The Gingerbread House was the only plane in the sky. With a twinge of guilt, Olivia closed the window and detoured to the kitchen. "Tammy is heading this way," she warned Maddie, who was finishing up a display of her flower cutout cookies.

Maddie paused in the act of placing a magenta sunflower next to a forest green daisy with leaf green polka dots. "Thanks for the heads-up. I'll leave her to you. Besides, I have to change." When Maddie said she had to "change," it wasn't into a clean T-shirt and jeans. She had the ability to create a persona, to morph into an entirely different being. When the two of them went antiquing together, Olivia hunted down the scattered displays of used cookie cutters, while Maddie went straight for the vintage clothing. She might buy a nightgown, a 1950s shirtwaist dress, a few scarves, then set to work on them. When Maddie appeared in the resulting outfit, she'd transformed herself into a garden gnome or a teapot or some creature never seen before on this planet.

As Olivia returned to the sales area, she heard a firm knock on the front door. The store opened in ten minutes, and she had yet to clear a display space for Maddie's decorated flower cookies, add money to the cash register . . . *Get a grip, Livie.* Life on the planet wasn't likely to end if The Gingerbread House opened a few minutes late. Besides, if Tammy insisted on a chat, she could tag along while Olivia finished her preparations.

Knowing Tammy's impatience when she had something on her mind, Olivia called out, "Just a minute," as she headed across the crowded store. She flipped the lock, opened the door, and said, "Hi, Ta—." She found herself looking at broad shoulders encased in plaid flannel. She raised her eyes about six inches to Lucas Ashford's chiseled features.

"Lucas! I thought . . ."

"Sorry, Livie, I didn't mean to startle you, and I know you're about to open, so you're busy. I was wondering . . ." With his muscular arms and shy manner, Lucas reminded Olivia of a lumberjack, more comfortable in the forest with the deer and squirrels than with other humans. It always surprised her when he spoke in compound sentences.

"We have to open in about ten minutes," Olivia said, glancing around at the still unprepared store. "We could talk after that, once Maddie is on the floor to help." When she turned back to Lucas, Olivia realized his eyes were focused on the kitchen door.

Lucas uttered a confused "Uh," and, with obvious reluctance, returned his sea green gaze to Olivia's face. "Well, I was actually sort of wondering if Maddie had a minute before, you know . . . I mean, I know she's busy getting ready for your . . ."

Olivia suspected he was searching for a more specific term than "thing." She took pity on him. "Our spring event, yes, she is, but I'm sure she'd be glad to see you." An understatement by about twelve miles, but she decided not to give Lucas reason to be overconfident. Maddie could do that all by herself.

"You know," Olivia said, "Maddie hangs out in the kitchen, and you are always welcome to knock on the alley door."

"She didn't answer," Lucas said. His dark eyebrows slid together, giving his face a worried expression, as if he believed Maddie might be ignoring him on purpose. Really, the man hadn't the slightest insight into his effect on women. Best to keep him that way.

"She was probably getting into her costume," Olivia said. "I'll see if she's dressed." As she turned around, the kitchen door opened and out walked a vision. Of what, Olivia wasn't certain.

"Hey there, Lucas," Maddie said, sounding pleased and oh so casual. "So? Have I outdone myself or what?" She twirled once and sashayed toward them. Sunshine yellow leotards encased her body from modest neckline to yellow ballet slippers, showing off her generous curves. A short, vivid blue skirt barely preserved her modesty. Around her neck, she wore a necklace of blue silk ribbon woven through small, flower-shaped cookie cutters used as charms, which tinkled as they bumped together.

As Maddie glided through the numerous displays of cookie cutters and baking supplies, Olivia stole a peek at Lucas's face. His smile spread like flood icing until it nearly reached his ears. "So who am I?" Maddie asked, striking a regal pose.

"A moveable garden?" Olivia guessed. "A sun nymph? Queen of the universe?"

"Nice tries, Livie, but so pedestrian. I am, of course, the newest and most flamboyant of the earth goddesses, the bringer of cookie flowers to those who ask politely. Only I need a name."

"You'll think of one," Olivia said.

Maddie reached into a pale yellow hobo bag hanging over her shoulder. She brought out a blue daisy decorated with yellow and navy polka dots. "A cookie for your thoughts, young Lucas," she said.

"Um."

Maddie held the cookie closer to him. "And?"

"Well . . . You look great!"

"I was going for 'delicious' or perhaps 'luscious,' but 'great' will work." Maddie handed Lucas the cookie, which he accepted without taking his eyes off her.

"And my name shall be?" When Maddie tilted her head and gazed up at Lucas, the light caught green sparkles in her froth of red hair. "I was thinking of 'Glorious.' Is that too over-the-top?"

"I like it," Lucas said, and took a bite of his cookie.

Olivia made a mental note not to suffer a life-threatening emergency if Maddie and Lucas were the only ones available to call for help.

Meanwhile, the minutes were ticking away. "Why don't you two head for the kitchen," Olivia said. "I have to finish out here. Maddie, we'll open in seven minutes, okay? Are you ready?"

Maddie tore her attention from Lucas. "Naturally," she said, lifting her eyebrows at Olivia. "When have I not been ready in plenty of time?"

The nickname Last-Minute Maddie came to mind, but Olivia thought it best to leave it unsaid.

Maddie took Lucas by the hand and led him toward the kitchen. He reminded Olivia of a huge little boy being taken off to choose his first pony.

While she hurriedly counted bills into the cash register and checked the receipt, Olivia found herself wondering about Lucas Ashford. For such an attractive man, Lucas had left very little impression on her over the years. He was somewhat older, so they hadn't crossed paths much in high school. She remembered him as a quiet boy, good-looking even then, but not one to chase the girls. As far as she remembered, he hadn't participated in any sports, despite his height and strong build. She'd seen him working at his parents' hardware store more often than at school events.

If Lucas had ever been deeply involved with a woman, Olivia hadn't heard about it. Not that she'd been around all that much after high school. Her mother would be the one to ask. It was a conversation worth having, Olivia decided. For some reason, as yet unclear, she was feeling protective of Maddie. Well, she was her best friend, after all, but it was more than that. Maddie had been engaged, right out of high school, to her first boyfriend, and it hadn't turned out well. Olivia had spent the summer following graduation helping Maddie piece herself together again. To others, Maddie might seem open to whatever life had to offer, but she had a well-earned cautious streak. Until a few minutes ago, Olivia had assumed Maddie's ongoing crush on Lucas to be her way of staying in a safe zone, since he seemed unlikely to notice her flirting, let alone respond in kind.

Now, it seemed, the situation had changed. Olivia shifted to mother-hen mode, and protectiveness came with the package.

With one minute to spare, Olivia took a quick walk around the store to make sure all was in place. She was heading back toward the front when she heard a firm knock on the door. Expecting a customer with a fast watch, Olivia opened the door wide. And there stood Tammy, fist raised to knock again. She'd forgotten all about seeing Tammy march toward The Gingerbread House.

"Hi there," Olivia said. "Weren't you headed this way about twenty minutes ago? I could have sworn it was you."

"Of course it was," Tammy said. She pushed past Olivia and closed the front door behind her. "You can open a minute or two late, can't you? I can't stand the suspense, tell me what happened." At the look of puzzlement on Olivia's face, she added, "What happened with Lucas? As soon as I saw him knock on your door, I decided to wait. I can't believe my plans are going so well."

When Olivia still didn't respond—confusion had rendered her wordless—Tammy became petulant. "Come on,

Livie, I set this up for you; the least you can do is tell me how it went. I've set up a little afternoon party at my place for tomorrow, and Hugh will be there, too, and I invited Lucas. You didn't tell him no, did you? After all the trouble I went to?"

"Tammy, I honestly have no idea what you're talking about." As soon as the words left her mouth, that rock-in-the-stomach feeling hit her—the one she used to get when she remembered the correct answer right as the exam ended. Tammy was trying to get Lucas and her together, which was never going to happen. That was bad enough, but she was willing to bet that any second now—yep, there it was, the kitchen door opening. *Please let Lucas have left by the back door.*

"Livie, fun news," Maddie called across the store. "You and I are invited to a shindig at Tammy's house tomorrow afternoon, and Lucas asked me to be his date." Maddie's arm was looped through Lucas's elbow. They both grinned like teenagers posing for their prom picture.

Spotting Tammy, Maddie said, "Hey, Tam, thanks for the invite." For once, she sounded friendly to Tammy. As Olivia watched, Maddie's smile sagged and she drew Lucas back into the kitchen with her.

Olivia wanted to follow them.

Tammy's face had turned a shade that would be, if Olivia were to describe it in icing colors, terra cotta with perhaps a drop of electric purple. "I need *you* there tomorrow," Tammy said. "It's really important to me."

"Then I'll be there."

Tammy sniffled and pulled a folded tissue from the pocket of her skirt. "Good," she said, dabbing the tip of her nose. "Two o'clock and wear a dress. Oh, and bring along the leftover cookies."

* * *

Three hours into the spring event, The Gingerbread House was packed with customers, and Olivia caught herself scanning for Clarisse Chamberlain's tall, silver-haired figure. Clarisse had never missed an event at the store. If she were here, Olivia thought, she'd take one look at this crowd, hang her coat in the kitchen, and start working the floor as an unpaid clerk. She would dismiss Olivia's objections with a wave of her hand, saying, "It takes me back to my youth."

The crush of customers would ease soon with lunchtime approaching. The flower cookie contest was drawing to a close, and Maddie was about to announce the lucky recipient of a free cookie-decorating lesson. After that, most townsfolk would wander off to their various weekend activities. Most customers from farther away would disappear by midafternoon as well.

From the amount of cash in the register, Olivia figured the event was the most successful they'd hosted so far, but she hadn't enjoyed it much. She remembered that last summer vacation to Cape Cod, when she was fifteen. Every year her family had traveled to the same lakeside spot and stayed for two weeks. After each visit, they would leave a down payment for the same two weeks, at the same cottage, for the following summer. Six months before that last visit, Olivia's father had died of pancreatic cancer. He was diagnosed in mid-January and gone by the end of February. Right after the diagnosis, he'd made the family promise to go back to the cottage in Cape Cod, even if he wasn't around to go with them. They'd kept that promise, even gone swimming every day and eaten dinners at the same little seafood restaurant, but the comfortable joy of it had died with her father. They never went back.

Clarisse had been so much a part of The Gingerbread House's creation, even before Maddie became half the team. Clarisse had prodded, advised, and cheered every step of the way. Olivia didn't want to lose her love for The Gingerbread House the way she had for that lovely lake in Cape Cod. She knew she'd have to find out what really happened to Clarisse. Even if the truth came with a high price tag.

Meanwhile, Olivia badly needed a break, and Spunky would welcome a walk. He was willing to use puppy pads, but he hated being cooped up for long. With no customers claiming her attention, Olivia joined the small group surrounding Maddie as she announced the name of the customer who'd identified the most flower cookies. The contenders consisted of seven women and one man—Lucas Ashford.

"And the winner is . . ." Maddie made full use of her considerable theatric sensibility by pausing to meet the eyes of each contestant, stoking the delightful agony of anticipation.

Olivia had a bad feeling right before the winner's name emerged from Maddie's mouth. She wouldn't, would she?

"Our own Lucas Ashford."

She would.

After a moment of hesitation, the losers clapped politely, mostly because they knew and liked Lucas. However, they dispersed quickly, heads bending toward each other and shaking. The Heights Hardware might sell petunias and pansies in the spring, but Lucas didn't garden and everyone knew it. Moreover, Lucas had followed Maddie around all day, hanging on her every outrageous word. She and Maddie were due for a private discussion about insider trading.

A few moments later, Maddie joined Olivia at the cash register. Frizzy red tendrils had escaped from the confection of curls she'd created for her role, but otherwise Maddie looked as if she'd awakened from a refreshing nap. Olivia found this irritating.

"Wow," Maddie said. "Was that ever fun. We should have a contest for every event from now on."

"And will Lucas win them all?"

"Huh?"

"We'll talk," Olivia said. "But right now, can you watch the store while I walk Spunky and grab some lunch?"

"Sure, no problem. Lucas thought he'd get some sandwiches from the café and bring them back here. So take all the time you want. Take a nap, even. You look peaked. Lucas and I can manage, even if it gets busy again. After all, he grew up with a cash register under his fingers. Better yet, take the rest of the afternoon for yourself; Lucas and I can close up."

Olivia was certain she would grow to hate those three little words: Lucas and I.

Chapter Five

꧁꧂

Olivia had no intention of napping. Though it was past two p.m., and she had resisted Maddie's flower cookies—even those little violets, the ones with the peach colored icing and creamy orange dots—Olivia was too distracted to eat. She needed a walk.

Spunky greeted her with joy, barely standing still long enough for her to snap on his leash. If he'd been a bigger dog, she'd have gone down the stairs head first. She'd changed into her tennis shoes, so they ran through the grass in the town square until Spunky's little legs finally tired out. Olivia carried him into the Victorian-era bandshell that marked the center of the square.

They settled on one of the benches that formed a semicircle around a small dance floor, which hadn't been used for decades. Spunky presented his ears for scratching, then curled into a ball on her lap and fell asleep. Clouds had rolled in since morning, shrouding the dance floor in shadow. A burst of wind raised swirls of dust, as if dancing couples glided in time to a waltz. For a moment, Olivia was a young teenager on a hot summer day, reading a Regency romance in the cool shelter of the band shell's curved ceiling. Before her father died and her marriage ended, before Clarisse . . .

Spunky stirred and whimpered in his sleep. "At least I've got you," Olivia said, smoothing his long fur. "As long as you don't take to the road again."

A plan, that's what she needed. A strategy. The thought gave Olivia a comforting sense of purpose. Her business plan for The Gingerbread House had provided the same feeling—that she was forging a path to her vision. Without it, she'd felt mired in anxiety and confusion about where to go next.

So, a plan it is. As soon as she thought the words, all the hurdles in her way began to arrange themselves into a list of problems requesting solutions. She could almost see, waiting in the wings, a growing crowd of ideas vying for attention. Olivia knew from experience that most of those ideas would turn out to be useless, but the right ones would appear.

Olivia extracted her cell phone from her jacket pocket and punched in her mother's home number. She wasn't surprised to hear her mother's chipper voice say, "Hi, this is Ellie. I'm out protesting at the moment, so leave a message. If I haven't been arrested, I'll get right back to you."

"It's me," Olivia said. "Maddie's minding the store, so I wondered if you had time for coffee or a late lunch this afternoon. I'll try your cell, too, unless the cops have confiscated it again."

At the sound of Olivia's voice, Spunky's head popped up, and he jumped off her lap. Hoping for another walk, he

yapped and strained at his leash. Olivia pressed the button
to lengthen the leash and managed to punch her mother's
cell number before her puppy tried to leap off the edge of
the bandstand in pursuit of a squirrel.

Again, she left a message, crankier than the first. Didn't
her mother ever stay home, like a normal person? Olivia
checked her watch; it was two thirty, so okay, she still had
plenty of time to get started on her quest for information,
but—

The opening notes of "Night Fever" announced a call
on her cell. Maddie had been messing with her ring tone
again.

Olivia managed, "Hi," before her breathless mother said,
"Livie, just finished my kung fu lesson, love to meet for
lunch, meet me at Pete's and order me a spinach salad if you
get there first. I'll order scallops for you, if I get there first.
Give me ten minutes for a quick shower. I know you have a
plan to discuss. I can hear it in your voice. Peace out."

"What do you mean, you can hear it in my voice?"
Olivia demanded of a dead connection.

"Exactly what did you mean, you could hear it in my
voice?" Olivia had arrived breathless at Pete's Diner,
having delivered a tired Spunky back home. Her mother
had already commandeered a table by the window and was
sipping a cup of coffee.

Ellie Greyson-Meyer tried to look innocent, but Olivia
saw the corners of her mother's eyes crinkle in silent laughter as their food arrived. Olivia slid her mother's plate out
of reach. "No food until you explain."

"Oh all right," Ellie said. "Even when you were tiny,
I could always tell when you were hatching a plan. I

remember when you were learning to walk, you'd pull yourself up a table leg with this big triumphant grin on your pudgy little face. Then you'd let go and plop down on your behind. You did that over and over."

"Tell me you didn't stand around and laugh at me."

"Now, now," Ellie said. "I tried to help, but you wouldn't let me. You were so determined to do it yourself. Finally, I watched you sit on the floor for a bit, frowning and apparently thinking deep thoughts. Then you faced down that table leg, pulled yourself right up, and walked two steps sideways, holding onto the edge of the tabletop. When your father got home, I told him we had spawned a brilliant little problem solver." Smiling with motherly pride, Ellie snared one of Olivia's scallops and popped it into her mouth.

"And after the two steps, what happened?" Olivia said, moving her plate out of snaring distance.

"You couldn't figure out how to slide your hands along the tabletop without letting go, so you fell down. That's when I laughed, and you burst into tears. But you kept on figuring things out. Once you'd learned to talk, I could tell by the tone in your voice when you were about to implement one of your action plans. Which brings us to the reason for this impromptu lunch, not that I don't treasure every fleeting moment you can spare for me." Ellie dipped a forkful of bacon and spinach into her side bowl of dressing.

"I need to catch up on Chatterley Heights happenings for the last dozen years or so," Olivia said. "At least for the period I lived in Baltimore."

A mouthful of salad prevented Ellie from speaking, but her forehead puckered in puzzlement.

"And yes, I guess you could call this a plan. Don't try to talk me out of it, okay?"

"It would be pointless," Ellie said, having swallowed.

"Does this have anything to do with what happened to Clarisse Chamberlain? Because you knew her better than I did. Our circles rarely intersected, and even when they did, we usually had little to say to each other. What do you need to know?"

Olivia skewered a scallop and let the butter sauce drip back to the plate, breathing in the pungent aroma of garlic and lemon. On second thought, she sloshed the scallop through the sauce and ate it, butter and all. Some experiences were worth a clogged artery or two.

"I can't accept the way Clarisse died," Olivia said. "At least not without understanding what led up to it. All I know is she was upset when I saw her on Tuesday, and then suddenly, two and half days later, she has her accident. If it was an accident."

"You think it might have been suicide?"

"Not that, either. Sheriff Del wants to call it an accident, but try as I might, I cannot imagine Clarisse Chamberlain so distracted that she wouldn't notice she was taking too many sleeping pills and drinking a whole bottle of wine. It's even more absurd to think she would purposely take her own life. But maybe I didn't know her as well as I thought. And I know very little about Hugh and Edward, only what Clarisse said about them."

"You know," Ellie said, "your stepfather might be able to fill you in on Clarisse's history, at least as it pertains to business. He knew Martin Chamberlain well. They often got together to talk shop, right up until Martin's death. He and Clarisse worked so closely together. It's too bad their sons didn't inherit the cooperation gene. Anyway, Allan might know if Clarisse was having business problems."

"If she was having serious business problems, surely I'd have gotten some hint about it. Apparently she was in perfect health. If I'm as good at planning as you say, why do I feel so confused?"

Ellie pushed aside her empty plate and settled her elbows on the table. "I can think of several reasons, starting with shock and guilt. Now don't roll your eyes at me. I'm still your mother; I occasionally have useful insights about my own progeny. You were quite fond of Clarisse. She seemed strong and vigorous, and you didn't see her death coming. You're in shock, you can't understand how this could have happened, and you are upset with yourself because you should have seen the signs. Tell me I'm wrong."

"I'd love to, but I'd be lying."

"Okay, then. So good to know I haven't lost my touch."

Olivia signaled the waitress to their table and ordered a double chocolate brownie for dessert. "The biggest one you've got." she said. "With chocolate frosting."

"Just more coffee for me," Ellie said. Once the waitress had left, she added, "Livie dear, I didn't mean to drive you to triple chocolate." She sounded contrite, though the corners of her mouth twitched.

"Mom, you're good but not *that* good. It's this whole situation. Sometimes I need endorphins, the gooey kind."

"Understood. After your father died, I ate my way through a chocolate cake every four days."

By the time her brownie arrived, Olivia had serious misgivings, but they didn't stop her from digging in. With a second forkful of chocolate almost to her lips, she paused and asked, "Do you know Bertha, the Chamberlain's housekeeper?"

"Of course, we're in a knitting group together. Why?"

"She told me the strangest story. She said she'd heard Clarisse say that she wanted one of her sons to marry me. I barely know them."

"Perhaps I'm biased," Ellie said, "but I don't find that strange at all. She was fond of you, respected you, so it's only natural she would hope to have you as a daughter-in-law."

"But according to Bertha, she also heard Clarisse say something about feeling she could trust me to handle some unspecified situation, but she could never trust Tammy to do so."

"Ah," Ellie said. "That is interesting. It brings to mind . . ." She began to stir her coffee in an absentminded way while her eyes wandered around the restaurant.

"Mother, are you aware that you aren't speaking actual words?"

"Hmm?" Ellie dropped her spoon and it clattered against the side of her cup. "Oh, sorry, I was connecting several bits of information in my head. Tammy Deacons has been in love with Hugh Chamberlain for years, everyone knows that, but Clarisse was dead set against the union. The odd thing is that she didn't always feel that way. When Tammy and Hugh first started dating—oh, it must have been about ten years ago, while you were still in college. Anyway, Bertha told me back then that Clarisse was glad Hugh was ready to settle down."

"I've known Tammy since kindergarten," Olivia said. "She can be a handful at times, but I can't believe she'd do anything outrageous enough to alienate Clarisse. I know Clarisse wanted grandchildren, and Tammy desperately wants children, dozens of them. She teaches first grade; what could be better training?"

Ellie frowned. "If I'd taught first grade, I might have thought twice about having my own kids."

"Thanks so much."

With a good-natured laugh, Ellie said, "I suspect Clarisse's change of heart had more to do with the Jasmine situation." She scooted her chair closer to the table and lowered her voice. "It didn't turn out well."

"Who the heck is Jasmine?"

"Oh my dear, you have been spending too much time working and not enough engaged in one of the guilty pleasures of small-town living—gossip." Ellie's eyes glittered. "You know, there's often a grain of truth in gossip, if you know how to ferret it out."

While Olivia nibbled on her brownie, Ellie began. "It started seven or eight years ago. This impossibly beautiful young woman named Jasmine Dubois appeared in town and was hired as a waitress right here at Pete's Diner. She had jet black hair that hung down her back in those soft natural curls that other women pay good money for."

"All except you," Olivia said. She snatched a loose, gray ringlet that had escaped from the fuchsia scrunchy holding back her mother's hair.

"You'd have curls, too, if only you'd let your hair grow out a bit. And would it kill you to wear a dress once in a—"

"Could we stay on topic, Mom?"

"I'm only saying . . . Oh all right, Jasmine. She was stunning and graceful, and the male population of Chatterley Heights swooned at her feet for about a week, until it became clear that she wasn't easy and she was smarter than all of them put together. One day I was here having a late lunch—after my Pilates class, I think it was—anyway, a man came in and sat at the counter. Some guy traveling through, I didn't recognize him, but it was clear right away that he wasn't entirely sober. Well, he took one look at Jasmine and whistled. Jasmine got this tight look, like her teeth were clenched, but she politely asked for his order."

"Let me guess," Olivia said. "He ordered Jasmine."

"Exactly, and he did not use his indoor voice. Aren't you

going to finish that brownie?" Ellie asked, her hand hovering within plucking distance.

Olivia shoved the plate across the table. "I'm aching to know how Jasmine handled this jerk, so feel free to talk with your mouth full."

"Triple chocolate must be savored." Ellie closed her eyes in ecstasy. Olivia was beginning to wonder if the story would ever reconnect with Clarisse and her changed attitude toward Tammy, but she had to admire her mother's sense of dramatic timing.

Licking a crumb off her index finger, Ellie said, "I had a good view of Jasmine's face. She looked straight at the guy, slowly arched one black eyebrow— she had these intense eyes, nearly black, and even I felt a chill go down my spine. But the idiot didn't get it. I couldn't see his face, but he sat up straighter, like he thought he'd scored. He reached around to his back pants pocket and pulled out a key on a plastic ring, like they still use at the old Nightshade Motel south of town. Why they don't switch to key cards, I'll never know, except the owners are so old I'm pretty sure they died years ago and came back as zombies—"

Olivia edged back her sweater sleeve and examined her watch.

"You're just like your father," Ellie said. "Anyway, the guy plunked the key on the counter in front of Jasmine. He said, loud enough for the whole diner to hear, 'I'll get the whiskey, you bring your tasty self.' Well, Jasmine leaned toward him a bit, let him see a hint of cleavage while she picked up the key. She took his empty cup over to that big, old urn they use for the coffee. She put down his cup and lifted off the top of the urn, like she was checking to see if it was empty. I can still see the steam swirling into the air as Jasmine held the lid in one hand and dropped that hotel key right into the urn. I saw coffee splash up, so I knew it was full. Then she gave the guy the sweetest smile and said, "Oops."

"Wow. Did she lose her job?"

"As you can imagine, that wretched man made quite a fuss, which brought out the cook and Pete—Pete was still alive back then. They were both big fellows. Pete had been a prizefighter, you know. The customer sputtered about how he'd done nothing, nothing at all, and Jasmine threw his motel key in the urn for no reason. The cook exchanged a glance with Pete, then turned around and went back to the kitchen. Pete was quiet for a bit. Finally, he said to Jasmine, 'Guess you'd better make fresh coffee.' He crossed those muscular arms and stared at the guy."

"That was it?"

"That guy didn't say another word. He backed away from the counter, tripped over a chair, and left." Ellie captured the last morsel of Olivia's brownie and downed it.

Their waitress, a tired woman who looked to be in her seventies, appeared at their table and retrieved the empty dessert plate. Without asking, she filled their coffee cups. "You girls want another brownie?" Her eyes strayed to a crumb on Ellie's chin. "Maybe two?"

"No, thank you, Ida," Ellie said. "Olivia is watching her figure."

Ida's gaze shifted to Olivia, looked her up and down, and shrugged.

After Ida shuffled off to the kitchen, Olivia said, "I gather you two know each other."

"My goodness, yes," Ellie said. "Ida used to babysit me when I was little."

"I don't remember her."

"Her husband had a stroke in his forties. She took care

of him for decades afterwards until he finally died a few years ago. Right after the funeral, she rented out her house, collected his life insurance, and went on cruises until her money ran out. That's when she came home and went to work. She's in my Wild Widows group."

"Your *what*?"

"Yes, there really is such a group, and I am one of the founding members."

"But you married again."

"I'm still a widow, I know what it's like, and you never forget the friends who stand by you when you are no longer part of a couple. Our mission is to demonstrate that life goes on and can even be great again, whether or not we remarry." Ellie reached across the table and patted Olivia's hand. "Divorced women could do with a group like ours."

"Mother . . ."

"I'm only saying, it's a fun group. We asked Clarisse to join several times, but she always refused. Politely, of course. Which brings us back to Clarisse and Jasmine." Ellie pushed aside her half-drunk coffee and reached for her macramé bag. "You thought I'd gone off on a hopeless tangent, didn't you? Unfortunately, my timing was off, so I'll have to talk fast. My papermaking class starts in fifteen minutes. Jasmine was, as you can now see, an extraordinary young woman. She was secretive about her origins, but she had gifts and great charm, when she chose to use them. Clarisse thought she had promise and was delighted when both her sons became friends with her. Rumor has it she dated Hugh Chamberlain, at least for a while. By all accounts, Clarisse was thrilled. So much so, in fact, that when Jasmine began to date Lucas Ashford, Clarisse quashed the relationship. She told Lucas that Jasmine was out of his league and off limits."

"I can't believe—"

"Believe it," Ellie said quietly. "Clarisse could be remarkably single-minded when it came to her family. When she decided Jasmine should marry Hugh, Tammy Deacons was, as they say, toast, and she never regained Clarisse's approval. Even though I suspect Hugh genuinely loves her now. Jasmine and Hugh were off-again, on-again for a long time, until Jasmine packed up and left town. No one knew why. Maybe she simply felt it was time to move on.

"Anyway, gotta run, sweetie. The store is still closed on Mondays, right? Then here's an idea: come to the house about eleven on Monday for brunch. I'll cook all your favorites, and you can talk to Allan about Clarisse and the boys. He still has a fair amount of contact with Hugh and Edward, and he's quite good at observing people. For a man, that is."

Ellie slid off her chair, which was, like all furniture, too big for her tiny frame. She gave Olivia a quick kiss on the cheek and turned to leave. After a couple steps, she stopped with her back to Olivia. She tilted her head to the side, as if she'd thought of something.

"Mom?"

Ellie pivoted around. "It's nothing really," she said. "I remembered a question I've been meaning to ask you. Are Maddie and Lucas seeing each other? If it's still hush-hush, you don't have to tell me, but I noticed a few looks between them the other day, when I was in the store, and I've been hearing rumors that Maddie . . . well, that she fixed the cookie contest this morning so Lucas would win a private baking lesson with her. So I wondered. . . ."

"The answers are: yes, they are seeing each other, and no, it isn't a secret, since they practically shouted it through the entire event this morning. And yes, I'm pretty sure Maddie fixed the contest. We will have a serious chat about that before the next event. Do please spread the word that it will never, ever happen again."

"Of course, Livie dear, don't give it another thought. Most folks seem to have found it more amusing than irritating. This time, anyway." Ellie's normally sunny features gathered into a small frown. "Lucas and Maddie," she said, almost to herself. "That is interesting. I wonder. . . ."

"What, Mom, what do you wonder?" Remembering her own concerns about the relationship, Olivia felt a ping of anxiety.

At that moment, the call of a wood thrush announced four o'clock from the restaurant's Audubon clock. "Now I really will be late," Ellie said. She raced for the door on her small but well-exercised legs.

"Mom, wait, what did you mean about the relationship being 'interesting'? What kind of interesting?"

"Don't fuss, Livie," Ellie called over her shoulder. "We'll talk Monday morning." The door snapped shut behind her.

Chapter Six

◁──◦✦◦──▷

When her cell phone rang, Olivia let it go to voice mail. She was running through what her mother had told her about Jasmine. The mysterious woman certainly had an effect on the Chamberlain family. And what about Lucas? Was he in love with Jasmine, too, and did he hate Clarisse for keeping them apart? Olivia needed to know more for Clarisse's sake and for Maddie's. One thing she was sure of, the upcoming lunch at Tammy's was going to be interesting.

She was stretched out on her living room sofa with Spunky nestled on her stomach and the Animal Planet channel on mute. At eight o'clock on a Saturday evening, it was the best she could find, and Spunky seemed intrigued by a show about a golden retriever being taught to fetch a beer for his owner. Olivia believed such education should be encouraged.

The phone went silent for about twenty seconds, then

began ringing again. She'd left it, along with her unopened mail, on a small table in the hallway, midway between the front door and the living room entrance. She let it go to voice mail a second time. Almost at once, it began ringing for the third time.

Olivia felt a twinge of apprehension. Maybe something had happened to her mother . . . or Jason or Allan. Maddie might be stranded somewhere, trying to reach her. She moved Spunky to the sofa and trotted toward the insistent sound. In her haste to answer before the call went to voice mail, she didn't check her caller ID.

"Hello?"

There was a pause at the other end. Then a tentative, "Livie? I'm at the front door, but the doorbell doesn't seem to work, and you never gave me your new phone number."

"*Ryan?* What are you doing here? I mean, it's eight o'clock on a Saturday night, why aren't you in Baltimore?" What she meant was, why wasn't her ex-husband out with the soon-to-be new Mrs. Dr. Ryan Nathaniel Jeffries? She'd heard at once from friends when, four months after their divorce, Ryan became engaged to a wealthy Baltimore socialite. Not that she cared, but given how hard he'd begged her to stay, he had certainly recovered in record time.

"Can't I stop by when I'm passing through?" Ryan's tone was a familiar blend of cajoling authoritarianism.

"It's late, Ryan. I'm tired."

"I remember when we used to sit up until two or three, watching old movies."

"You sat up. I conked out on the sofa." Olivia didn't like her own tone, either. She sounded harsh, resentful, which was, she knew, a reaction to the sadness she still felt. She also knew that Ryan would not give up easily.

So Olivia decided to tell a small fib. "You really should

have called ahead, Ryan. I have plans for this evening."
Falling asleep on the sofa with the TV on could be called
a plan, couldn't it?

"I thought you were tired. Do you have a big date or
something?" He chuckled smugly, as if he'd just said the
most preposterous thing in the world.

Olivia's sadness evaporated in an instant. She knew
what he was doing. If he could get her to feel defensive,
to begin justifying herself, she might weaken enough to
let him in. However, now she knew better. Maybe she saw
through him more easily now—or he needed something
from her. Perhaps he was the desperate one. Otherwise,
why show up on her doorstep? She felt a twinge of curiosity
but not enough to allow him into her home.

"That's why I'm resting up right now, for my big date.
Nice of you to drop by, Ryan," she said. "Next time, give
me some warning, at least a week." With relief, she clicked
the little red telephone icon on her cell. She opened the
small drawer of the hallway table and slid the phone under
a pair of gloves. For good measure, she dropped her mail
on top of the gloves and slammed the drawer shut.

When she returned to the sofa, Spunky was so entranced
by the Animal Planet show that his greeting consisted
of half a tail wag. "What a good little student you are,"
Olivia said as she snuggled up next to him. On the screen,
a charming little puggle pranced up to a group of young
women stretched out on beach towels. When one of the
women knelt to pet him, he stretched his neck over her bent
back, caught the string tie of her bikini top in his teeth, and
pulled. The young woman screamed and grabbed her top
in time to keep it from falling off.

Olivia switched to the cooking channel. Four pastry chefs
were constructing four different gingerbread houses for

Halloween. A repeat, but a classic, and preferable to watching a cute pup learn to humiliate young women in public.

As one of the pastry chefs struggled to salvage a gingerbread house damaged in transit, the phone in Olivia's kitchen began to ring. She'd never bothered to hook up an answering machine to her home phone, so the blasted thing kept on ringing, finally ending at fifteen. Ryan must have found her number using his iPhone Internet connection.

Olivia's temper leaped to code scarlet. She went rigid and counted the silent seconds through grinding teeth. Spunky sensed her mood and whimpered. Fifteen seconds passed, then twenty, twenty-five. Olivia considered relaxing. At thirty-five seconds, the phone rang.

With a primal growl, Spunky leaped off the sofa and began to yap. Olivia knew she had to answer the phone or listen to her pet go noisily insane. She marched into the kitchen, followed by a frantic dog, and placed her hand on the wall-phone handset. For two full rings, she inhaled deeply to calm herself. She told herself that Ryan would love it if he knew how much he'd upset her. That helped.

Olivia lifted the handset and answered with a clipped, cold, "Yes?"

The next few seconds felt like a repetition of Ryan's earlier call, only this time she could hear a quick intake of breath, even with Spunky yapping. She reached down to stroke his ears to quiet him.

"Livie?" A moment passed. "Livie, is everything all right?"

"Oh geez, Del." Olivia groaned and sank cross-legged onto the kitchen floor. Spunky leaped onto her lap and whimpered.

"Livie, answer yes or no. Are you in danger? Is someone there with you?"

"Del, I didn't expect—"

"Yes or no."

Olivia sucked in a lungful of air, then answered, "No and no, unless you count poor little Spunky. He's had a bad night. Me, too."

"Somehow I guessed," Del said. "Want to talk about it? I come bearing pizza. Actually, I got the pizza from the café and was heading home when I saw a man leave something on your doorstep. Thought I'd investigate. It's a huge bouquet of flowers in a glass vase. Must have cost a bundle. I don't see a card. Any idea who it's from?"

"Oh, I most certainly do."

"Sounds like you have a story to tell. So how about it? Triple-meat pizza and a sympathetic ear?"

Olivia glanced at her bare knees sticking out of torn jeans, her grubby tennis shoes with no laces, and knew they didn't matter, not to Del. If Ryan had caught her dressed so casually, he'd see it as a game point, something he could use to dent her self-assurance. He didn't quite realize what he was doing, of course. Probably never would. Del might tease her, but that's all it would be.

"I'll come right down and let you in," she said. "I had triple chocolate for lunch, so the day is a cholesterol disaster anyway. Might as well go for triple meat. I'm assuming one of them is sausage?"

"Of course."

"Excellent. Oh, and I'd be grateful if you'd chuck the flowers in my garbage can, vase and all. Preferably before I get there."

"Really? I could save the vase for you."

"Only if you want to watch me smash it."

* * *

"So, this ex-husband of yours seems to have a gift for pushing your buttons." Del helped himself to a third serving of the salad Olivia had thrown together to create the illusion of healthy eating. She'd opened a bottle of cabernet sauvignon as well, for the same reason.

"You could say that. The sad part is he's really not such a bad guy. It's more that he's . . ." What *was* going on with her ex-husband? He had worked so hard and done well in medical school, won a surgical residency at Johns Hopkins, but she'd always felt his equal. It was only after he'd become a thoracic surgeon with a growing reputation that he'd begun to treat her as if she weren't quite good enough for him.

"Are you thinking 'controlling'?" Del offered. "Domineering, maybe? Needs to get over himself?"

Olivia laughed out loud. It felt good. "No, but thanks. I guess I'd describe Ryan as driven. More and more with each passing year." Two pizza slices remained in the box, and Olivia picked up the smaller one. A thinning string of mozzarella stretched behind it like the fading tail of a shooting star. "When his hard work started to pay off, it didn't seem to help him relax. He worked harder than ever, worried more, demanded more—money, respect, obedience from underlings. He got what he wanted, but it seemed to make him into an unhappy person."

"I can understand that," Del said.

The understated tone of his voice caught Olivia's attention. He didn't smile or meet her eyes. She wanted to ask about his marriage, which had ended in divorce many years earlier. After all, hadn't they discussed her ex-husband? But she hesitated, not certain how to ask the question without sounding intrusive.

Instead, she refilled his wineglass and said, "The

last piece of pizza is yours. Shall I give it a jolt in the microwave?"

"Are you kidding? I eat it straight out of the fridge."

While Del had his mouth full of pizza, Olivia asked, "Have you learned anything new about Clarisse's death? I still can't believe she'd be careless, no matter what was bothering her. She was so strong willed and determined."

Del took a sip of wine. "This sure isn't my cheap Chianti." He took another sip.

"Well, it isn't Chianti, but it is cheap."

Del put down his glass and leaned back in his chair, hands clasped behind his neck. "I'd have to say that I share your confusion, based on my knowing Clarisse. She went through some mighty tough times and survived better than anyone I've ever known. She was one smart lady. The forensics we've gotten so far haven't helped much. The autopsy revealed nothing remarkable. She'd been in good health, no sign of incipient disease. A little arthritis in her knees, but the medical examiner doubts she'd even have felt the effects of it yet."

"Clarisse was very active," Olivia said. "We used to take long walks together around her property and through the woods beyond. I was half her age and an inch taller, but I had to struggle to keep up with her. She never seemed to be short of breath."

"There was no indication of dementia, either," Del said. "It's clear from the autopsy results that she died from an overdose of sleeping pills and alcohol. Her sons and house-keeper confirmed that Clarisse seemed disturbed about something prior to her death, but she kept the reason to herself."

Olivia slowly twirled her half-full wineglass by its stem and watched the contents slosh up the side like tiny red waves. "I can't tell you how many times I had dinner at Clarisse's home, with Bertha watching over us. Clarisse would usually have a glass of red wine. It took the entire meal for her to finish it, and sometimes she didn't. She showed much more enthusiasm for her after-dinner espresso."

"Which Bertha confirmed," Del said. "But remember that the night of her death Clarisse had asked Bertha to bring an entire bottle of red wine, uncorked, to her study. Then she closed the study door and kept it closed until Bertha went upstairs to bed at ten. All of which was, according to Bertha, uncharacteristic. So something was up."

A sliver of an idea poked at Olivia's mind, and she struggled to make it whole. She had seen enough to agree that something was bothering Clarisse and that her behavior had been uncharacteristic. Yet even those closest to her seemed unable to give a reason. Or were unwilling to do so. Either Clarisse was trying to think through and solve a problem by herself, or someone was holding back information.

"What was Clarisse's alcohol level?" Olivia asked. "Can you find out that kind of thing after . . .?"

"Up to a point, but not very accurately," Del said. "Are you sure you want to talk about this?"

"Very sure."

"Well then, the ME found she'd consumed some alcohol, but there wasn't a whole bottle's worth in her system. If she drank the wine over a long period, some of it would have metabolized."

Shaking her head, Olivia said, "I cannot imagine Clarisse guzzling down an entire bottle of wine under any circumstances. I doubt she'd have been conscious to even take the pills."

"Well, there were high levels of a sleeping pill,

eszopicione, in her system," Del said. "Also, the same drug was found in the wine dregs, both in the empty bottle and her glass. And only Clarisse's fingerprints found on both. Bertha confirmed that Clarisse had trouble swallowing pills, so she always ground them up and dissolved them in liquid."

Olivia closed the lid on the empty pizza box, scrunched it in half, and tried to stuff it in her kitchen wastebasket. It wouldn't fit. With a hard push, she crammed it farther down.

"I'm sorry, Livie," Del said. "Clarisse Chamberlain was a remarkable woman, but we all make mistakes. Sometimes a mistake is fatal."

Olivia stared at her overstuffed wastebasket, wishing she could be satisfied with never knowing.

"Here, let me take that," Del said, nodding toward the wastebasket. "I'll empty it on my way out and leave it outside the alley door." He put on his uniform jacket and hat. "Anyway, I'm relieved there's no clear evidence of suicide. Got a call today from an insurance investigator, and I told him as much. That won't stop him from coming here to investigate for himself. Clarisse had a pretty hefty life insurance policy, which wouldn't pay off in the case of suicide. But it'll be tough to make a case for suicide with no note and no health or business problems." Del lifted the full wastebasket. "Anyway, I hope so."

With Spunky under her arm, Olivia led the way downstairs to the front door. Her hand on the doorknob, she asked, "Do her sons inherit everything?"

"I shouldn't be telling you all this, but nothing stays a secret around here for more than a minute or two. I'd swear the police station is bugged." Del grimaced and shook his head. "So the answer to your question is yes, the bulk of her estate goes to Hugh and Edward equally. She left Bertha a tidy sum, too, and made some bequests to her favorite charities." He gave Olivia a quick smile. "Including the Yorkie rescue group you got Spunky from."

At the sound of his name, Spunky squirmed in Olivia's arm, his paws reaching toward Del. "He's probably trying to grab the pizza box," Olivia said. "Or planning his next escape." She held the door open for Del and breathed in the cool, damp air, scented with lilacs.

As Del stepped through the entryway, he paused and said, "One more thing."

The porch light brought out gold flecks in Del's brown eyes. Olivia felt a rush of awareness.

"In case that brain of yours starts wondering if Clarisse was somehow murdered, both her sons have alibis. They were attending a conference in Baltimore."

Chapter Seven

❦

Olivia possessed three dresses, none of which had she worn for almost a year. Early in their marriage, Ryan had always complimented her when she wore a dress. Over time, his response had changed. He began to ignore her in a dress and criticize her appearance if she wore anything else. After their divorce, she had given away most of her dresses, keeping only the three she actually liked.

When Tammy first commanded her to appear, wearing a dress, at a Sunday afternoon gathering, soirée, tea party, whatever, Olivia's first instinct was to roll her eyes and vow to wear jeans. But that was before she had a plan.

The previous evening, Del had assured her that Clarisse wasn't murdered. He'd made sense at the time, but the more she thought about, the less convinced she felt. Murder could be made to look like an accident or suicide. And murder as the cause of death made more sense, or at least it did to Olivia. Clarisse had amassed an enviable fortune. Her extraordinary success in business hadn't been luck. She was capable of what some might call ruthlessness in her decisions to close businesses that didn't perform to her expectations, and she had acquired failing businesses as cheaply as possible. She was never cruel, only practical and single-minded. Olivia had loved and admired Clarisse without ever wanting to be exactly like her.

Even if Hugh and Edward had airtight alibis, surely there were others who were resentful, who felt they had suffered at Clarisse's hands. Lucas Ashford, for instance—though she wouldn't mention that to Maddie without scads of proof. And, not to doubt Del's police work, but what about Hugh and Edward? How thoroughly had he checked their alibis?

Olivia was willing to bet that Del had considered, then dismissed, the possibility of murder. He loved Chatterley Heights; the last thing he'd want was a sensational murder investigation involving a highly respected family, espe-cially one with businesses that provided jobs for the town's citizens. Times had been tough recently.

Without clear evidence of foul play, Del would resist digging any deeper. However, he took his job seriously. He might listen if Olivia gave him a reason to do so. She wouldn't talk about her suspicions to Del until she had something to back them up.

Really, did Maddie have to choose this moment to fall in love and virtually disappear, right when she was needed? Maddie would listen, and no matter what Del thought, Maddie could keep secrets when she wanted to. Well, she'd be with Lucas at Tammy's event, and Olivia intended to rip her from his arms and wrestle some help out of her.

If Tammy was throwing a shindig, Hugh Chamberlain would also be there, no matter how recent his bereavement. It was that simple. Tammy might seem flighty to some people, but Olivia knew her well. Inside the ruffles and the first-grade-teacher persona, the woman had a spine of tempered steel. Tammy knew what she wanted, and she wanted Hugh. So Hugh would be in attendance. Possibly Edward, too. And Olivia wanted very much to talk to both brothers.

Her plan required the right costume. Put in those terms, Olivia was more than happy to wear a dress.

There might be one snag, though. All three of her dresses were fitted at the waist. For the past eleven months, Olivia had been sampling, testing, and downright gobbling the sugary delicacies she and Maddie created for their store events. Every now and then her jeans felt a bit snug. Luckily, jeans were forgiving, especially if she washed them in cold water and let them air dry. Which was environmentally responsible, and naturally Olivia was a friend to the environment.

On the other hand, for the past few months she had been walking or running her dog several times a day. If there was any justice in the world, that ought to count for something.

Olivia selected her favorite, a teal cocktail dress with a flouncy skirt. A matching scarf wrapped around the waistband. Her mother had made the dress for her when she'd first moved back to Chatterley Heights, in a blatant attempt to encourage her to wear something besides pants.

"Might as well get it over with." Olivia slipped into the dress. It fit perfectly, even when she breathed. Spunky, who had been watching sleepily from the bed, lifted his head and yipped. Olivia reached over to scratch his ears. "The next time I complain about taking you out for a walk at six a.m., you may remind me of this moment."

Since she could dress in ten minutes and Tammy's get-together was two hours off, Olivia changed back into her jeans and made another pot of coffee. She settled at her kitchen table to brainstorm questions. Instantly, she missed Maddie. She reached for the kitchen phone, then decided to call from her cell, so she could pace around.

Fifteen minutes later, Olivia had looked in all the obvious pockets without finding her cell phone. She tried calling her cell number from the kitchen phone. If the phone rang, she couldn't hear it. Maybe it was out of juice. Spunky, awakened by Olivia's frustrated search, trotted into the kitchen and circled her feet, making pathetic little yipping sounds as if he were too weak from hunger to bark properly.

As Olivia opened the treat drawer, she remembered. Ryan's persistent calls the previous night had upset her, which upset Spunky, which led her to bury her cell in a drawer. She tore down the hallway toward her front door, followed by a dog who kept leaping at the hand holding his treat.

There it was, under Saturday's unread mail, right where she'd stuffed it. Spunky was nipping her ankle to get her attention, so she dropped his treat on the rug as she lifted out her cell phone. Maddie didn't answer after three rings. Olivia left a brief but insistent message for her to call back before two o'clock, when they were to arrive at Tammy's house.

Olivia flipped her phone shut and slipped it into the pocket of her jeans. She rescued her mail and settled on her sofa to sort through it. Spunky snuggled up next to her. Bills, invoices addressed to The Gingerbread House, junk mail . . . the last envelope puzzled her. The postmark said

Baltimore, but there was no return address. Her own name and address were printed in block letters in blue-black ink by an unsteady hand, as if the writer had been in a hurry or perhaps upset.

Blue-black ink. Olivia had watched Clarisse write notes in blue-black ink, usually when they were discussing business ideas. Her handwriting had always been firm and distinct, showing an old-world flourish. Olivia ripped open the envelope and removed one sheet of white linen stationery. Clarisse's full name and address were printed at the top. The date in the upper-right corner said Thursday, April 23. The last day of Clarisse Chamberlain's life.

Olivia read the brief note and called Maddie's cell. Once again, she was sent to voice mail. After Maddie's recorded message ordered her to "Talk now," Olivia said, "Madeline Briggs. This is Olivia Greyson. It is Sunday, twelve forty-seven p.m. I need you at the store right away." She texted the same message.

When Olivia and Maddie, at age eleven, first vowed eternal best-friend-hood, they had designed a set of secret codes. They'd used the system through high school for notes they slipped each other between classes. If they used their full names in a message, it signaled urgency and a need for secrecy. Of course, in high school, an emergency usually meant a broken zipper or boyfriend trouble. Olivia hadn't thought about those codes for a decade, but she remembered them all. Maddie would get the point.

Taking Clarisse's letter, Olivia went downstairs, unlocked the store, and locked herself inside. Maddie always carried her own keys. Olivia turned on the lights and settled cross-legged in front of the antiques cabinet to reread Clarisse's letter:

Dearest Livie,

Since I haven't heard from you, I can only assume that something must have interfered with your routine. I know how careful you are. However, I know that soon you will find my odd message to you and will worry unduly. You were the only one I felt I could trust to be impartial and to keep confidential anything I might tell you, but I should not have burdened you. I do apologize for letting myself get into such a state. At any rate, I have recently received further information. I am hoping to resolve this matter soon.

So, my dear Livie, when you do come across my little packet, please return it to me unopened. If you have already opened it, I know I can trust you to keep the contents to yourself. Please don't worry on my account. If you have any concerns, we can chat at your Saturday event. By then, I am determined that this issue will be concluded and all will be well.

With great affection,
Clarisse

All will be well. Clarisse—clearheaded, meticulous, supremely competent, and so very wrong. Dead wrong.

Olivia thought back to Tuesday afternoon. When they'd stopped at the cabinet to look at some vintage cookie cutters, Clarisse had asked for some cookie recipes. What if Clarisse had made such an odd request simply to get the room to herself for a few minutes? She'd known that Olivia normally tidied the store and emptied the antiques cabinet, including the bottom drawer, every day at closing time, while Maddie straightened the kitchen and reconciled the day's earnings with receipts.

However, Olivia was human. On Monday they'd received a large shipment of wonderful antiques, which had completely filled their safe. So Olivia had decided to risk leaving the cabinet filled and locked until Saturday's event, when she hoped the extra customers would work down their inventory. After everything that happened, Olivia had simply forgotten to empty the drawer.

A small, ornate key fit both the glass doors and the drawer at the bottom. As Olivia unlocked the doors, she heard rapid scratching at the front door. It wasn't the sound of Maddie's key in the lock, unless Lucas had plied her with liquor at lunch. Maddie wasn't much of a drinker, so a couple of mimosas might affect her aim.

The scratching became more frantic, this time accompanied by a distinct whine. Spunky. The little sneak had learned how to escape as Olivia left her apartment. If she was at all preoccupied, she wouldn't notice him hiding in a dark corner of the landing.

"If you're so smart, you can let yourself in." Olivia's voice sounded unusually loud and must have carried beyond the door, because Spunky stopped scratching and barked.

"Oh all right," Olivia called, "don't pout, I'll come get you." She pocketed the cabinet key and headed for the front door. "You'd better not be using the hall carpet as a pee pad," she said. As she reached toward the knob, the door opened.

Maddie stood in the entryway, holding a squirming Yorkie. "Not to worry," she said. "I went before I left the house." She thrust Spunky into Olivia's arms.

"So, Olivia Greyson, what's the big emergency?" Maddie, already dressed for Tammy's get-together, wore an emerald green, curve-hugging sweater dress. A tiny silver earring in the shape of a tulip cookie cutter dangled from each ear. Her springy hair was freshly washed and wind-blown, a look only she could pull off.

"Did I catch you in the shower?" Olivia asked.

"You sent me an SOS to discuss my bathing habits? Come on, Livie, what's up? We've only got half an hour before we have to be at Tammy's, and Lucas made it crystal clear that he did not want to arrive unaccompanied by his date."

"Understood." Olivia handed her Clarisse's letter. "Here, read this while I start emptying the drawer." Kneeling on the floor, she lifted out cookie cutters one by one and secured them inside a padded basket.

"Odd letter," Maddie said. "You knew Clarisse way better than I did, but this doesn't sound like her. Too dithery. Are you sure she didn't have a drinking problem?"

"Quite sure." Olivia stowed the letter in the basket of antiques. "I suspect the packet she left for me is in this drawer."

Maddie hitched up her dress and knelt beside Olivia. "I see something." She removed a red-handled Scottish terrier cutter made of tinplate steel during World War II. "Looks like the corner of an envelope."

Olivia pushed aside a few remaining cutters and lifted a business-letter-size envelope out of the drawer. It was unsealed and addressed simply to "Olivia Greyson," in Clarisse's handwriting. Olivia reached inside and with-drew a folded piece of wide-ruled lined paper, the kind a schoolchild might use. She unfolded the paper and held it so Maddie could see.

"The light in here is terrible," Maddie said, leaning in closer. "What does it say?"

Squinting, Olivia said, "The pencil mark is faint, as if the writer wasn't bearing down hard enough. Let's go over to the register. There's a flashlight in the drawer.

Maddie checked her watch and groaned. "I have exactly six minutes to rescue Lucas from Tornado Tammy, so let's step on it."

"You go on ahead. I can be late. I can fill you in later."

"Not a chance." Maddie had the powerful legs of a hyperactive dancer, and she used them to shoot to her feet. By the time Olivia reached the sales counter, Maddie had found the flashlight and turned it on. Its bright light revealed no salutation. The letter itself was short, only a few lines, which read

You have a grandchild, and you need to step up and do what is right. It will be out of my control soon, so you need to act fast. Call me as soon as you get this.

Faith

A phone number followed the signature.

"Wow," Maddie said.

"Wow, indeed." Olivia whipped out her cell and dialed the number. A few moments later, she closed her phone.

"Well?"

"This number is no longer in service."

Chapter Eight

❧

"Livie! I was afraid you'd forgotten, and after I invited a date for you, too. It's lucky he'll be late." Tammy grabbed Olivia's elbow and pulled her into the tiny foyer. "You can hang your coat on a hook with the others, and—oh, you *did* wear a dress."

"As I recall," Olivia said, "I was ordered to do so."

"Yes, but you usually ignore me and do whatever you want." A hint of amusement softened Tammy's comment.

Olivia followed Tammy into the living room, where a subdued group of five sat and sipped coffee. Fine bone china cups clicked on their saucers as Olivia entered the room.

"Everyone, this is Olivia Greyson. You all know her, don't you?" Tammy directed her question to a young couple huddled together on a deep plush sofa.

"I'm not sure I . . ." The young woman's voice trailed off into a whisper. She was so petite that her feet lifted off the floor as she retreated toward the sofa's high back.

"Oh, of course," Tammy said with a light laugh. "We'd graduated by the time you two started at Heights High. Olivia, this is Dottie and Timmy, my neighbors. They've been married for six months." Tammy announced this information as if Dottie and Timmy were her family and she couldn't be more pleased. "Olivia owns that sweet little cookie-cutter shop on the town square."

"Along with Maddie Briggs," Olivia added, darting a glance at Maddie, whose expression reminded her of a carved stone bust.

Dottie's face lit up. "Of course, I love that store. I didn't recognize you at first. All dressed up, I mean."

Tammy made a faint chortling sound in her throat that Olivia hoped no one else could hear.

As Tammy fussed through her hostess duties, allowing no guests to get anything for themselves, Olivia sat in a wingback chair and observed the group. Lucas Ashford, wearing a gray suit that strained across his broad shoulders, occupied a stuffed armchair. His dark eyes skittered around the room as if he were searching for the exits. Maddie perched on one arm of the chair, leaning into him.

Hugh Chamberlain was the only remaining guest. Olivia had seen Hugh on many occasions during her visits to the Chamberlain home, but they'd exchanged no more than a few sentences. Whenever she looked at him, she thought of the portrait of his father that hung in Clarisse's study. Hugh had his father's easy charm and good looks, with a well-proportioned body that always looked good in a suit. Olivia remembered that he had played basketball in high school. He'd looked the part and seemed to enjoy himself, but his playing was mediocre. Yet most of the girls had treated him like a successful jock and longed to stand beside him as homecoming queen.

Hugh caught Olivia watching him and smiled. She noticed that his light blue eyes lacked the dark intensity that shone from the deep blue ones in Martin's portrait. Hugh looked tired. Hardly surprising, given what he'd been through the last few days. Olivia wanted to offer him her condolences, but it just didn't seem like the right moment. She found it curious that he'd allowed himself to be talked into a gathering so soon after his mother's death. Perhaps her mom was right that he did love Tammy.

A flash of green in the corner of her vision alerted Olivia that Maddie was trying to get her attention from across the room. Maddie raised her cup and waved it in a circle. Puzzled, Olivia glanced at her own cup, which was white with a thin filigree design in silver. She gazed around the room and noticed white linen cloths covering the coffee table and two side tables. A white vase of white tulips decorated the bureau under the living room window.

When Maddie casually wriggled her own bare ring finger, then nodded her head toward Tammy, Olivia started to catch on. She squirmed in her chair to get a better look at Tammy, specifically at her left hand. Yep, there it was—a diamond ring. No wonder Tammy wanted her guests to stay put. There was to be an announcement.

Olivia glanced again at Maddie, who rolled her eyes. With the slightest tilt of her head, Olivia indicated that Maddie should follow her. When Tammy leaned toward Dottie to answer a question, Olivia slipped into the nearby hallway, which she knew, from previous visits, led through the study, Tammy's bedroom, and ultimately to the bathroom.

Tammy's small study was neat, as always. Even when she was in the throes of lesson planning for her first-grade classes, Tammy kept her materials organized in stacked plastic trays. Her bookcase had four shelves, one for children's books and three for romance novels. On the corner of the desk, Olivia noticed a stack of women's magazines, their edges even. The top magazine advertised a special section on "Your Perfect Wedding."

Sometimes Olivia wondered why she and Tammy had remained friends. They were so different. Her thoughts drifted to her other childhood friend Stacey, and she made a quick mental note to give her a call. Those childhood bonds were tough to break, but she knew that having friends, even ones who didn't like each other, made her life richer.

Tammy's bedroom repeated the theme in the study, minus the children's books and plus a stuffed bear collection. Olivia noticed a new adornment for the Victorian-style walnut dresser—a framed photo of Tammy and Hugh on a rocky shore, possibly in Maine, where Tammy's family used to vacation. Tammy stood on tiptoe, her face tilted upwards toward Hugh, who held her upper arms as he kissed the tip of her nose. From Tammy's hairdo, Olivia guessed the photo was recent.

Olivia slipped into the bathroom. She left the light out and the door ajar, so she could watch for Maddie. She heard footsteps approach, and her heart began to canter. When Maddie walked through the bedroom door, Olivia was so relieved she laughed.

"Isn't this a kick?" Maddie closed them into the bathroom. "I think Tammy is bursting to announce her engagement, so we should keep this short. Did you notice that photo in the bedroom? Tacky."

"I think it's touching," Olivia said. "Reassuring, too. I was afraid Hugh didn't return her feelings. My mom told me about Jasmine."

"Jasmine," Maddie said. "I haven't heard that name in a while." She settled on the edge of the tub, and Olivia joined her. "I liked that woman. She had moxie. Everybody thought she and Hugh would get married, but I wasn't surprised when she up and left. She was so independent, plus I always suspected she had a 'past,' you know? She never talked much about herself."

"Maddie, you don't suppose . . . I mean, what if she disappeared because she was pregnant?" On her way to the party, Olivia had been feverishly mulling over the letter from Clarisse and the note she left with the cookie cutters. She was growing more certain that both items had to somehow tie into the information her mother had given her.

A sliver of curl worked loose from Maddie's casual hairdo and bounced on her nose. Her eyes crossed as she blew it away from her face. "I suppose Jasmine might have gotten pregnant, but if it was Hugh's, they would have gotten married. Clarisse adored Jasmine, so she'd have been floating on clouds if she found out a grandchild was on the way. You knew Clarisse. Do you think she'd have been bent out of shape by the whole premarital, out-of-wedlock thing?"

"I doubt it." Clarisse had flouted numerous conventions during her life, and Olivia remembered her emphatic disdain for double standards when it came to acceptable male and female behavior. She had been ahead of her time in that regard.

"Well, there you are. If Jasmine was pregnant, she'd probably be here today, and Clarisse would have been swimming in grandbabies."

Olivia felt a moment of sorrow as she thought about what might have been. Clarisse had deserved to grow old surrounded by grandchildren. "What if it wasn't Hugh's baby? And what about Jasmine's 'past'? Her independent streak?" Olivia asked. "Maybe Jasmine didn't want to have a sea of babies."

Maddie's eyebrows wrinkled together in thought. "I guess she might have left to have the baby and put it up for adoption."

"If Jasmine had wanted to end the pregnancy, Clarisse would never have forgiven her. So either way, she'd have left if she didn't want a baby and Hugh did."

"Makes sense," Maddie said. "So that means—"

"Shh." Olivia put a finger to her lips and held her other hand over Maddie's mouth. She dropped her hand when Maddie nodded to indicate she understood.

Olivia had heard the click of a door. A second click told Olivia that the door had closed. Her worst fear was that someone had entered the room, heard their last few words, and was now lurking in the bedroom waiting to hear more.

Maddie put her mouth close to Olivia's ear and breathed, "We are so busted."

They had locked the bathroom door behind them but hadn't turned on the light, since the night-light was sufficient. Olivia watched the doorknob, willing it not to turn. When she'd held her breath long enough to see spots in front of her eyes, she began to feel safer. That is, until she heard whispering from the other side of the door. The whispers became voices, and the voices became Tammy and Hugh arguing. Olivia glanced at Maddie, who grinned.

"Sweetie, we've come this far, we can't move back time." Tammy sounded cajoling, with a hint of first-grade teacher in her voice.

"I think we should slow down, wait a bit," Hugh said. His rich baritone usually commanded attention, but his voice sounded flat, tired. "It's all too much right now. It wouldn't look right."

"I don't care what it looks like. People can think whatever they want. This is our life, and we've come too far to turn back now, you know that. Your mother would never have let us have a life together. We had no other choice. Now you have your businesses, and we have each other. You do want that, don't you?"

"Of course I do."

Maddie wrinkled her nose at the sound of kissing, while Olivia's mind began to churn. If she weren't wearing a dress, she'd have her little notebook and pen in her pocket and could write down, in exact words, Hugh and Tammy's exchange. What had Tammy meant when she said they'd had no other choice? Olivia didn't know Hugh very well, but Tammy? Could she commit murder to marry Hugh? Maybe.

Tammy said, "Let's go back to our guests. I don't want them to wander off before we make our announcement."

A couple of seconds after they heard the bedroom door close, Olivia and Maddie cracked open the bathroom door and peeked out. Once they were sure it was safe, they escaped through the study and into the hallway. It occurred to Olivia that Tammy would arrive in the living room before they could, and she'd realize they were gone. She might wonder where they'd been while she and Hugh were talking.

Olivia gripped Maddie's arm and led her into the empty kitchen, where they leaned against the counter as if they'd been having a casual conversation. A moment later, the door to the outside opened, and Edward Chamberlain entered, along with the acrid smell of cigarette smoke. He froze momentarily when he saw Olivia and Maddie.

"Tammy won't let me smoke inside," Edward said.

Olivia had encountered Edward only sporadically over the past year, and each time she had been intrigued by his apparent lack of concern for the social graces. He'd never been rude to her, only abrupt. Perhaps his curt manner stemmed from preoccupation with important business matters.

"Edward," Olivia said, "I am so sorry about your mother. She was my dear friend, but I can only imagine what her loss means to you and Hugh."

Edward's right hand lifted to the left breast pocket of his suit coat, which bulged in the shape of a cigarette packet. He did not reach inside. Staring out the kitchen window, he said, "Thank you."

Tammy appeared at the entrance to the kitchen, cheeks flushed. "There you are," she said.

At the sound of her voice, Edward's head tilted toward her. Olivia thought she saw tears glisten in his vivid blue eyes.

"I've been looking all over for you three. I was afraid you'd left," Tammy said with genuine distress in her voice. "Come on back to the living room. Please? Hugh and I have an announcement to make." She clutched Olivia's wrist and hooked her arm through Edward's. With a forlorn glance at his cigarette pocket, he allowed himself to be dragged along.

"Talk about an anticlimax," Maddie muttered to Olivia after a bubbling Tammy had announced her engagement to Hugh. Everyone exclaimed over her ring, even though they'd all seen it as Tammy served coffee, offered cookies supplied by The Gingerbread House, and provided refills.

Another new guest had arrived during Olivia and Maddie's absence—Sheriff Del. He had dressed for the occasion in a dark blue suit and light blue shirt. *Not bad.* When Edward entered the room, Del went over to talk to him, and she noticed Edward's hand touch his cigarette pocket again. She wondered who was supposed to be her date, Del or Edward.

Once the glad nuptial tidings had been delivered, Del moved his folding chair next to Olivia's.

"You look nice," Del said. "As always."

"You're wearing a tie."

"Nothing much gets past you."

Del Jenkins had a way of throwing Olivia off-kilter and darned if she didn't enjoy it. When he smiled at her, she found herself smiling back. "I guess that was my way of saying you look nice, too."

"Thanks, I thought it might be." His smile faded as he leaned toward her and whispered, "Did you know about this engagement? I thought those two were on the outs."

"You keep up with Chatterley Heights gossip?" Olivia asked with genuine surprise.

"I try. It helps me anticipate problems." Del frowned at the floor. "I've learned a lot about the Chamberlain family in the last few days. The general consensus was that Clarisse was opposed to Hugh marrying Tammy. It seems she was very vocal about it during the last few days of her life. It's odd, though, no one was really sure why." Del narrowed his eyes at Olivia. "So I was thinking, outside of her family, you probably knew the most about what went on in Clarisse's mind."

Olivia hesitated. If she told Del what she and Maddie had overheard and what Clarisse had left for her in the store, it might convince him to delve more deeply into Clarisse's death. On the other hand, Tammy and Hugh hadn't admitted any wrongdoing. What if there was an innocent explanation for their conversation? Olivia needed time to think.

"I wish I could help," Olivia said. "I have no idea why Clarisse disapproved of Tammy."

Maddie appeared, holding Lucas's hand. "We're out of here," she said to Olivia. "Hey, Del, nice duds."

"Right back at you, Maddie." With a quick movement, Del pushed aside his shirt cuff and checked his watch. "I need to get back to the station. Cody gave up part of his Sunday so I could come to this gathering."

So why exactly *did you come?* Olivia thought but didn't say.

"How about I walk you home, Livie?" Del stood and reached a hand toward her. "After all, I believe I am supposed to be your date."

Chapter Nine

"You grab the cookies from the freezer," Maddie said. "I'll get out the mixer and start throwing together some royal icing. Ah, there's nothing like decorating cookies to fire up the synapses."

"The entire freezer is stuffed with undecorated cookies," Olivia said.

"Get out the package of round ones. We can do anything we like with those." Maddie whistled "Stars and Stripes Forever" while she yanked confectioners' sugar and meringue powder off shelves and clattered through the measuring spoons. Pausing in the middle of the piccolo part, she said, "Note to shopping-list maker: we're out of lemon extract. I'm using orange, unless you have serious reservations."

"Orange is good." Olivia unpacked the frozen cookies and placed them on racks to thaw. The stand mixer whirred, a sound that always gave her a warm, cozy feeling. She and her mother, whose energy and enthusiasm rivaled Maddie's, had made dozens of holiday cookies together every year until Olivia left for college. The sharp sweetness of the orange extract, the sheen of royal icing, even the flour and confectioners' sugar that dusted the table around the mixer—all of it brought back those safe, protected years of childhood, before marriage and divorce, before the suspicious death of a friend.

"I'm having brunch at my mom and stepdad's house tomorrow," Olivia said. "I was planning to ask Allan about Clarisse, but now I'm thinking he might have some insights about Hugh."

"Such as?" Maddie was racing to divide the icing into lidded bowls so it wouldn't dry out.

"Such as, how skilled a businessman is Hugh? Clarisse said once that each of her sons inherited part of Martin's genius, but not all of it."

"Clarisse was no slouch when it came to business," Maddie said. "Bring over the food color gels, would you? You can start coloring, if you want."

Olivia brought over some small bottles and arranged them in a spectrum of color next to the covered containers of icing. She selected her favorite, teal. She added one drop to a portion of icing and stirred, watching the blue-green color swirl and spread through the light buff icing.

"I wonder how well Clarisse understood her sons," Olivia said.

Maddie collected a pile of pastry bags and a box of metal tips. "Where's this leading?"

Olivia added one more drop of teal and stirred. "It occurred to me that we need to know about Clarisse's will, and if she was planning to change it. I know that Martin's will gave Clarisse control over all their businesses, with instructions that she equally involve both sons in running them. She had pulled back a bit in the past year to give Hugh and Edward more experience."

"Clarisse was planning to retire? Hard to believe." Maddie was already coloring her second container of icing a gentle peach, a dramatic contrast to the color she chose first, a rich burgundy.

Olivia tightened the lid on her teal icing. "I doubt she was thinking about retirement. I think she was testing them. That's why I'm wondering about her will. What if she was planning to give one of her sons control over all the Chamberlain businesses, or at least the bigger ones?" She opened another icing container and added a drop of purple. "That would be a great motive for murder."

"Lucas went to school with Hugh, and Edward is only two years younger. I could ask him what he thinks of them. I know he's quiet, but he's very observant."

"Have I said he wasn't?"

With an irritated sigh, Maddie said, "No, not you. Tammy made some comment to me about my being 'so vibrant,' like I was going to overwhelm poor, shy Lucas."

"It might actually have been a compliment," Olivia said. "In most circles, vibrant is considered a good thing."

"Not in Tammy's circle of one."

"All righty, then." Olivia twisted the lid back on her final contribution to the icing choices and started filling pastry bags.

"You can start piping if you want," Maddie said. "I'll make the flood icing."

The whirring of the mixer discouraged conversation for a time. When it stopped, Maddie said, "You know what I'd like to know? I'd like to know why Clarisse disliked Tammy so much. I mean, aside from the obvious. I have to admit, she and Hugh are a good fit. He doesn't appear to have a spine, and Tammy has at least two of them. If I'd been Clarisse, I'd have been relieved Hugh had found someone so strong willed. She'll push him to succeed, you wait and see."

"I hadn't thought of that," Olivia said. "Mom told me Clarisse did approve of Tammy before Jasmine came along. You'd think Clarisse would have been disappointed in Jasmine when she up and left. Tammy was the loyal one."

Olivia finished piping the outline of a Yorkshire terrier on a round cookie. She put the bowl of brown icing back with the others and pulled up a chair to rest her back. "If Clarisse's death was a suicide, which I still don't accept, what might have led her to it?"

"Which was more important to her?" Maddie asked. "Her sons or her family businesses?"

Olivia wanted to say that of course Clarisse's sons were her top priority, but could she? Clarisse had said little to her about Hugh and Edward. She'd often talked about her husband with admiration, even when she was recalling how he drove her crazy at times. But Hugh and Edward? Olivia wondered if Clarisse had loved her sons unreservedly, or if, ultimately, they had disappointed her.

"A Sunday evening well spent," Olivia said. "I'm so glad we didn't open a health food store."

"Here, here," Maddie said, holding aloft her empty wineglass.

After decorating and boxing up all but a few of the cookies, they had retired to Olivia's upstairs apartment for debriefing. They both slouched on the sofa, their bare feet resting on the coffee table, having consumed a plate of turkey sandwiches and several cookies. Spunky cuddled between them.

Olivia retrieved the merlot bottle from between her feet and refilled both their glasses. She lifted the cookie plate, now mostly crumbs. "Only one cookie left, and it's Spunky. Shall we share him?"

At the sound of his name, Spunky's head popped up.

"Sorry, kiddo," Olivia said. "Cookies are not good for your tiny digestive system. I don't intend to stay up all night nursing you." As she snapped the cookie in half, one chunk broke off and fell on the sofa. Spunky grabbed it with his teeth and swallowed before Olivia could stop him.

"I blame the wine for slowing our reflexes," Maddie said. "And speaking of cookies, what should we do with the remaining three dozen? I suppose we could put them out at the store on Tuesday, though we did go a little crazy with the color combinations. Customers might suspect we'd been drinking."

"How about taking them to the food bank? I could drop them off on my way to brunch tomorrow. Polly was telling me—Polly Franz took over running the food bank—anyway, she's been seeing more and more families that need food. I bet some parents would love to bring home some decorated cookies for their kids. "

"You, Livie Greyson, are a sensitive and thoughtful person," Maddie said, "who stocks excellent wine for her friends."

"And there's plenty more where this came from." Olivia emptied the remaining inch of wine into Maddie's glass. "I'm not so sure about the 'sensitive and thoughtful' part, though. My recent record hasn't been impressive. I did nothing to help Clarisse, and I had no idea what was going on with Tammy, friend of my childhood."

"Not true," said Maddie. "Go open another bottle of wine, and I will explain."

When Olivia returned with the wine, Spunky was on Maddie's lap, watching a lion stalk an antelope on the animal channel.

"I know it's the natural cycle of life and all that," Olivia said, "but I really can't handle these shows."

Maddie clicked off the television. "Precisely my point: you are sensitive. Although that was a bit wimpy. Anyway, remember what you told me when Bobby broke off his engagement with me, way back after we graduated from high school?"

"My memory only goes back about a month."

"Okay then, as you might not recall, we'd planned a September wedding. Bobby went to DC for a summer job. I stayed here, worked as a waitress at the café, and planned the wedding. Bobby came back in August, announced he'd changed his mind about the wedding, turned right around, and moved to DC."

"I do remember he'd met someone else," Olivia said. "Only I don't see how this—"

"Because, my impatient friend, we didn't find out the truth until months later. Meanwhile, Bobby blamed me for the breakup. He said I was selfish and immature and not smart enough for him. Ha!" Maddie swept the fur back from over Spunky's eyes. "What do you think, Spunks? Selfish and immature, okay maybe, but not smart enough? Please."

"I'm not touching that one," Olivia said.

"Anyway, after we found out he'd married some other girl, I kept right on blaming myself. You said to me, and I remember the exact words, 'You can't control another person's agenda. You can only be clear about your own.'"

"And my point was?"

With a soft laugh, Maddie said, "I don't know, something about staying on your own side of the court and letting your opponents do the fumbling."

"I would never have used a sports metaphor, and I'm not even sure that one makes sense."

"I'm just saying, it meant something to me. I realized Bobby was the immature one. He couldn't take responsibility for his behavior, so he blamed it all on me. It helped me move on to become the brilliant, successful businesswoman you see before you."

Olivia felt relaxed and warmed from the inside by the wine, but her bare feet were chilled. She pulled an afghan off the back of the sofa and draped it over her legs. Spunky raised his head a notch. The blanket lured him over to his mistress's lap, where he curled into a ball.

"Traitor," Maddie said. She stretched a corner of the afghan over her own feet. "Livie, you observe more about people than you realize. You knew something was bothering Clarisse, but she didn't invite your help, so you let her handle it. As for Tammy, you sensed a certain, shall we say, ongoing drama in her love life, and you kept your distance, as any sane person would do. Instead, you so wisely chose me as your best friend and business partner." She raised her glass to Olivia.

"I'd drink to that," Olivia said. "But if I do, I'll never make it off this couch."

"Lightweight," Maddie said. "What time is it, anyway?"

"Exactly ten o'clock," Olivia said, checking her cell. As if on cue, the phone in Olivia's kitchen rang. "Who would . . .?" After the second ring, Olivia slid Spunky onto the sofa and hoisted to her feet. "That better not be Ryan."

"I thought your number was unlisted and unpublished," Maddie said.

"That would only slow Ryan down for a minute or two. He used to spend hours surfing the Internet. He could find my home number if he wanted to."

Maddie crossed to the front window, which offered a view of the front stoop. "No one out front," she said. "I could take care of him for you."

"I really don't want his head lopped off," Olivia said.

"You never let me have any fun."

"My ex-husband, my problem."

Olivia heard a male voice when she answered the phone, but it didn't belong to Ryan. "Ms. Greyson, my name is Aloysius Smythe. I am a longtime personal friend of Clarisse Chamberlain and also her attorney."

"Oh?" Olivia held her hand over the receiver and whispered, "Clarisse's attorney," to Maddie.

"I do apologize for calling so late on a Sunday evening. I only now returned to my office, and, as you will see, time is of the essence. I am calling in my capacity as executor of Clarisse's will. As you may or may not know, in her most recent will, Clarisse included a bequest for you, Ms. Greyson."

"I had no idea," Olivia said. "I'm speechless."

The attorney chuckled, then cleared his throat. "The reason I am calling so late is to invite you to dinner tomorrow, Monday evening, at the Chamberlain home, following the reading of the will. It was Clarisse's desire that you be included as family, so I do hope you are able to attend both events."

"I can, as it happens, but I'm just very surprised. However, if Clarisse wanted me to be present . . ."

"She did, Ms. Greyson. And so do I. Seven o'clock, then," he said. "Casual dress."

Olivia replaced the receiver and turned to Maddie, who was bouncing on her toes with excitement. "Well," Olivia said, "it seems that many of our questions about how Clarisse divided her estate will be answered within twenty-four hours."

Chapter Ten

At six a.m Monday morning, heavy, cold dew bent the grass in the Chatterley Heights town square. The iron gray dawn threatened a drenching soon, so Olivia had decided to sneak in a walk with Spunky. Through a break in the clouds, the rising sun spotlighted a black speck moving across the south end of the square, near Pete's Diner. Spunky began to bark with all the intensity his tiny body could produce.

"Spunky, that's enough," Olivia said. "Reasonable people are still trying to sleep." Olivia herself had awakened before five, with questions tumbling over each other in her mind. Sensing her restlessness, Spunky had insisted on exercise.

"Don't make me come down there," she said to Spunky. The threat failed. She gave up and watched as the black speck passed the band shell. It was fast approaching the statue of the town's founding father, Frederick P. Chatterley, immortalized in the act of mounting his horse. When the creature reached the marble foot on which F. P. Chatterley had balanced for over two hundred years, it lifted its leg.

Olivia laughed out loud, while Spunky skittered about and whimpered with eagerness to see his pal, Buddy, the aforementioned black speck. A taller figure was following Buddy at a run. That would be Deputy Sheriff Cody Furlow. When Spunky pulled hard on his leash and yipped, the Lab changed course and loped directly at them.

Cody cupped his hands around his mouth and shouted, "Don't move." At least, that's what Olivia thought she'd heard. It made sense, in a way. If she and Spunky ran, Buddy would shift into chase mode. Anyway, Buddy traveled like a locomotive at full throttle, so the escape option was moot. Olivia stood her ground as the Lab drew closer. Spunky backed up a step but wagged his tail, which Olivia took as a good sign. It was. Buddy slowed down to a trot, then stooped down to exchange sniffs with Spunky.

"Morning, Ms. Greyson." Deputy Cody sucked in air and shook his head. "Whew. Nothing like an early run. Hey, Spunks," he said, squatting down to scratch Spunky's ears. When he stood up, Olivia had to arch her neck to look up at him. He had to be at least six foot three. She was willing to bet he didn't weigh much more than she did. Despite being in his midtwenties, Cody always reminded Olivia of a teenage boy whose weight hadn't caught up with his sudden growth spurt.

Cody's smile faded as he said, "I'm real sorry about Ms. Chamberlain. Del says you were friends." His eyes, nearly the same warm brown as Buddy's, shifted to his feet.

"It's still hard to take in. Cody, do you mind if I ask you a question? About Clarisse's death, I mean?"

"I guess, but the sheriff knows more about it than I do."

"But you were with Del when . . . ?"

Cody nodded. "I was on duty when the call came through, so I called Del right away, like I'm supposed to. I picked him up on the way."

"I keep wondering. . . . Del said Clarisse was on the floor, as if she'd tried to go for help. Was that your impression, too?"

"Well, I'd never contradict Del, he's got a lot more experience than me, but since you ask, I wasn't so sure. I mean, yeah, she looked like she'd fallen on her way to the door, but her arms were lying straight beside her. Del doesn't think it means anything. Only I thought that, you know, she'd have tried to break her fall or something."

"Might she have been unconscious before she landed?"

"That's what Del thinks, because she'd drunk all that wine, and with the pills. Which makes sense, of course."

"Was the wine bottle on her desk?"

"That's another thing," Cody said. "It was right beside her, with a little wine spilled out onto the rug. Didn't seem right to me." He had lost all hint of reserve by this time, and his words came in a rush. "See, the bottle was almost empty, so why would she take it with her? And if she drank a whole bottle of wine with all those pills, how could she even stand up?"

A sudden flush spread across Cody's cheeks, as if he'd realized he shouldn't be sharing his own speculations with a mere citizen. "Del said it wasn't enough to go on and not to speculate. He said to wait for the evidence."

"I see what you mean," Olivia said. "I suppose we might never know for sure. But your observations are very insightful."

The deputy's tense shoulders relaxed. "I keep trying to learn more. I want to be a police detective. That's my dream, I guess you'd call it. Detectives pay attention to little things, so that's what I do. And the more I looked at those photos, I more I thought—"

"Wait, there were photos?" Olivia had blurted out the question without thinking, but to her surprise Cody did not seem flustered. If anything, he looked irritated. "I don't mean to intrude," she added quickly. "All I know is what I read in mysteries." She willed herself not to react to Cody's derisive snort. "I suppose the sheriff ordered photos of the scene to be on the safe side? In case there was any question about it being something other than an accident?"

"Del didn't order any photos," Cody said. "He said not to bother, it was clearly an accident. I took those photos on my own."

Two thoughts occurred to Olivia: Cody was irritated with Del, not with her, and she'd need to be careful how she approached Del for any more information. Could Del have a hidden agenda, some reason all his own for wanting Clarisse's death to look like an accident? Olivia had a hard time believing that, but what if . . . ?

"See, I'm taking this online crime scene investigation course," Cody said. "So I went ahead and took photos anyway, for practice. It's what you're supposed to do whenever there's a sudden death that might be foul play. Del is smart, but really, how many murders have we had in Chatterley Heights? I heard about one back in the 1800s, a jealous husband or something like that, and maybe a couple others, but not since I was born."

"Something tells me I'm not in Baltimore anymore," Olivia said.

"Huh?"

"Never mind," she said. "I think it was a good idea to take photos. I have trouble believing that Clarisse is gone.

Would you be willing to let me see your photos? It might help." Her reason sounded flimsy to Olivia, but it was the best she could come up with on short notice.

"Are you sure?" Cody asked. "Won't it upset you to see her so . . . I mean . . ."

"Her death is what upsets me. Maybe seeing the photos will help me accept and understand it better."

"Well, if you think they'll help. I used my digital camera, so I could download the photos and email them to you, if that's okay."

"That would be fine." Olivia found an old receipt and a pen in her jacket pocket. "Here's my email address. Thanks so much, Cody. And maybe we shouldn't mention this to anyone?"

"Especially Del," Cody said, pocketing the paper. "I'm pretty sure he'd kill me if he found out."

Olivia took the stairs two at a time up to her apartment, with Spunky struggling to keep up. Before taking off her jacket, she woke up the laptop at her bedroom desk and checked her email. For once, Spunky wasn't interested. He jumped onto Olivia's bed and collapsed into a ball of boneless dog flesh.

Aside from a plea from her mother that she pick up a dozen eggs on her way to brunch, Olivia had no new mail. Not surprising, since only about seven minutes had elapsed since she'd left Deputy Cody in the town square. Under ordinary circumstances, Olivia considered herself a patient person. These were not ordinary circumstances. Clarisse's death had never made sense to her, neither as accident nor as suicide. With Cody's photos, she might find another possibility. She wasn't eager to discover signs that Clarisse had been murdered, but if she was murdered, Olivia would never be content until she'd found the truth.

Staring at her email inbox would only frustrate her, so Olivia decided to spend some time downstairs in The Gingerbread House. Spunky didn't so much as flicker an eyelid when she slapped her laptop shut. Olivia figured he'd be out for several hours thanks to all that exercise, but she added food to his bowl and gave him fresh water. When he did wake up, he'd be one hungry pup. On her way out, she picked up her laptop.

Olivia's mind churned nonstop as she unlocked the store and turned the lights on low. Several of the display tables needed reorganizing, a job she always enjoyed, but first she had to wrap up the cookies she and Maddie had decorated the previous evening. The Food Shelf opened at nine a.m. weekdays, so Olivia could drop off the cookies and run some errands before arriving at her mom and stepdad's house for brunch.

A second switch outside the kitchen allowed her to turn off the store lights, but Olivia decided to leave them on dim. She hoped Maddie might see them and stop in, so the two of them could look over Cody's photos when they arrived.

Olivia switched on the kitchen light and realized she had some cleanup to finish. She and Maddie had washed the baking equipment, then left it in the sink strainer to dry. Leaving her laptop on the kitchen desk, Olivia finished putting everything back in its assigned storage spot, scrubbed out the sink, and cast a critical eye around the kitchen. Not bad—except for the large worktable, which showed sprinklings of flour and numerous bits of cookie dough, evidence of how absorbed they'd been in their brainstorming about Clarisse's death.

For once, Olivia didn't care about the state of the kitchen. She knew she wouldn't be able to refocus until she'd checked her email again. As she threw her used dishtowel in the laundry bag, she heard something through the kitchen door. She couldn't remember locking the store's front door behind her. Maybe a customer had wandered in, thinking the store was open.

Maddie. Of course, it had to be Maddie. Granted, she wasn't usually so quiet, but she had packed away a fair quantity of merlot the previous night. Several glasses more than Olivia, and she wasn't feeling all that perky herself. Maddie was lucky she still lived at her Aunt Sadie's house, so she could walk home.

Olivia yanked open the kitchen door and said, "Hi there—" Someone was indeed standing at the sales counter, leafing through a pile of opened mail Olivia had left for later attention, but it wasn't Maddie or a customer. It was Sam Parnell, decked out in his mail carrier uniform and holding a small clutch of envelopes in his left hand. From the expression on his face, he hadn't heard her movements in the kitchen.

"*What* are you doing? That is private mail, and you of all people . . ." Olivia was so angry the words got stuck in her throat.

Even in the dim light, Olivia could see the fiery flush that covered Sam's face. The paper in his hand fluttered to the counter. "I wasn't . . . I mean . . ." Sam Parnell's voice wasn't deep to begin with, but now it had slipped into high tenor. He cleared his throat and said in a more controlled tone, "Your door was unlocked, the inside door to the store, I mean. It's always locked on Mondays. I usually come in the front door and slip your Monday mail through the mail slot." He twisted around and pointed to the slot in the middle of the store's door. As if she might not have been aware of its existence.

Olivia mentally prepared to slice him in half with a few well-chosen words. She had to admit some satisfaction as she watched Sam's bony face take on the look of a rat that had found itself cut off from all available methods of escape. And then a thought poked through her righteous rage—Sam loved gossip. He might be useful.

Olivia stepped into the store and flipped the light on fully. "Let's start over," she said. "I was about to make a pot of coffee. How about joining me? I've been back in town all these months, and we haven't had any chance to chat." That one minor role in a high school melodrama had been time well spent.

Sam had the dazed look of someone dropped into an alternate universe. "Well, uh . . ." He waved his hand at the mail sack hanging over his left shoulder.

Olivia decided to misinterpret. "That thing must weigh a ton. Why don't we go into the kitchen; you can leave it on the table while we have coffee." She gave him a delighted smile. "Isn't this the most perfect timing? I mean, I'm almost never in the store on Monday mornings, and here you are, ahead of schedule. You usually don't reach here until about ten, and it's . . ." Olivia pushed up the sleeve of her sweater to check her watch. "It's not even eight o'clock." She opened the kitchen door and waved him inside.

"Okay, sure, thanks," Sam mumbled. He slid the mail sack off his shoulder as he shuffled into the kitchen.

Only minutes earlier, Olivia would have laid odds that Sam Parnell would never willingly enter her kitchen for a chat, let alone thank her for inviting him. However, she had watched Sam's expression transform while she delivered her spiel. The sharp edges of his face seemed to soften, and his small, pale eyes assumed a puppylike quality. At a certain point, Olivia had stopped acting. However, empathy aside, she fully intended to learn what she could from Snoopy Parnell.

A few minutes later, Olivia had the Mr. Coffee fired up and dripping. "I think I can produce a cookie or three," she said, glancing over at Sam. He'd pulled his chair right up to the edge of the kitchen table, where he sat like a schoolboy with his hands on the tabletop, fingers interlaced.

When the coffee was ready, Olivia filled two mugs. "Do you take milk or sugar?"

"Black," Sam said. "None of that muck for me."

"Here you go," Olivia said, setting a steaming mug in front of him. She placed a plate holding six decorated cookies within his reach. She added milk and sugar, lots of both, to her own mug. "I go for the muck, myself," she said lightly.

Sam made no comment.

"I have to admit," she said, as she pulled up a kitchen chair opposite Sam, "I envy you your job. I mean, you get to be outside all day, plenty of exercise, lots of contact with people. You must have seen and heard everything by now." Olivia sipped her coffee, watching Sam over the edge of her cup.

Sam's shrug conveyed agreement rather than modesty. "Folks have no idea how much we see and hear. We're sort of invisible to most people, like a doorman or a waiter or something." An edge of resentment had crept into his voice. "Hardly anyone knows they're supposed to tip me at Christmas."

Olivia clucked her sympathetic disapproval and silently vowed to tip anyone who ever delivered anything to her. "I guess I've been one of those people," she said. "I hope you will accept these cookies as a late Christmas gift?"

To Olivia's relief, Sam gave her a broad grin and select-ed a second cookie. She noticed his teeth were crooked, especially his two upper-front teeth, which virtually over-lapped. Had he grown up too poor for braces? She couldn't remember.

"Ms. Chamberlain, now," Sam said, his mouth still full of emulsified cookie. "Mind you, I'm real sorry about what happened to her and not to speak ill or anything, but she wouldn't so much as look me in the eye, let alone offer me a cookie." A chunk of his cookie broke off and dropped to the tabletop. Sam picked it up and ate it. "Bertha, though, she sometimes invites me in for warm stew on cold days."

"Let me warm up that coffee for you," Olivia said. Sam relaxed against the back of his chair and allowed himself to be served.

After refilling cups, Olivia slid onto her chair and leaned toward Sam. "I imagine the police were eager to pick your brains after Clarisse died. I mean, you'd be in the best posi-tion to know all sorts of things, like whether she'd received any mail that might have upset her? I think there was some speculation about whether her businesses were suffering in this economy, so maybe she was getting overdue bill notices or letters from collection agencies." A blatant lie, but at least it was a place to start. "Clarisse could have hidden those things from Bertha or her family, but not from you." Olivia held her breath, hoping she hadn't gone overboard.

Sam responded with a short, angry "Ha." Resentment puckered his face and seemed to taint the sweet orange air in the kitchen. "You'd think so, wouldn't you." It wasn't a question. "That Sheriff Jenkins, he looks right through me like I'm nothing but smoke. He was like that in high school, too. Thought he knew all there was to know and nothing else was important."

Olivia hadn't realized that Del and Sam were the same age. Sam looked ten years older, perhaps from being outdoors so much. His skin looked dry and rough, deeply wrinkled around his eyes. It must not have occurred to him to wear sunglasses. Olivia had no recollection of ever seeing him smile or laugh with delight. His mouth seemed to have frozen somewhere between a frown and a sneer.

"High school kids can be thoughtless," she said.

"Yeah, well, seems to me most folks never change. Nobody listened to me then, and nobody listens to me now."

"Which is foolish of them," Olivia said. "Especially when a death is involved."

Sam drained his coffee cup and twisted in his seat as if to stand. She was losing him, and he'd shared nothing about Clarisse's mail. Well, she wasn't about to let that happen.

Olivia scraped back her chair and grabbed Sam's empty cup. "Let me get that for you," she said. "You do enough walking about; you don't need to fetch your own coffee."

Sam sat down. While Olivia drained Mr. Coffee's contents into Sam's cup, she sneaked a glance at his profile. He looked relaxed and smug. Maybe she still had a chance to coax some information from him.

"Here you go," Olivia said, setting the cup near Sam's hand. "You better have these, too." She slid the last of the cookies onto his plate. "I've downed too many already. I don't get the exercise you do, and I'm afraid it's beginning to show."

"Not an ounce of fat on my body," Sam said.

Olivia watched him devour the sky blue, tulip-shaped smiley face. "I've been thinking a lot about Clarisse Chamberlain," she said. "She and I were friends, you know. I worry that something was bothering her, and I didn't see it."

"You know, a couple days before she died," Sam said,

"I had a very interesting visit with Ms. Chamberlain. *Very* interesting. The sheriff doesn't know about it. He couldn't be bothered to ask. See, we got this next-day priority package that required a signature from Ms. Chamberlain, and one of the new guys put it aside and forgot about it." He dunked a pink and red basketball in his coffee and sucked the soggy part into his mouth before it disintegrated into the cup. A clump of wet crumbs lodged in his graying beard.

Olivia's patience was approaching the end of its life span. Yet she waited in silence as Sam dunked and slurped his way through the cookie.

"I knew it was real important, see, because the envelope was legal-size with an embossed return address. I figured it was maybe from a lawyer. So I volunteered to deliver it myself after work."

"That went above and beyond the call of duty," Olivia said. "Very professional of you."

"Now the really interesting part," Sam said, "which Sheriff Del would know if he'd asked me, is what happened when I handed that envelope to Ms. Chamberlain, which I did personally. I didn't just leave it in her box."

"That was wise of you," Olivia said.

"Well, what's really interesting is, Ms. Chamberlain opened that envelope right in front of me. I guess she didn't notice I was still there because she stood on that fancy porch of hers and ripped that envelope open and pulled out some papers. And you know what happened then?"

Olivia shook her head.

Sam paused for a gulp of coffee. "Well," he said, "she made this little sound, like a cry or something, and she put her hand over her mouth."

"Did you see what was on those papers? A name or a

title, anything at all?" Olivia knew at once that she'd taken a wrong turn.

"I am not a snoop. I know that's what people around here call me."

"Oh no, Sam, I only meant that . . . Well, if it had been me handing Clarisse that envelope, I'd be worried about her. I'd want to help. You must have felt the same way."

"Of course I did," Sam said. "That's exactly how I felt. As it happens, she got so upset, she lost her hold on those papers and one fell out of her hand. She didn't even notice, just collapsed on the porch swing. It was windy and the paper blew off the porch. Naturally, I rescued it for her. She didn't even thank me." He scowled at the memory.

"Anyway," Sam continued, "I couldn't help but see what it said on that paper, could I? Ms. Chamberlain didn't even miss it, so why should I hurry to give it back? Not that it said all that much. Something about hoping the enclosed information would be helpful to her and that she should let them know if she wanted them to keep looking for the child's location."

So there *was* a child.

"Ms. Chamberlain looked like she was about to pass out."

"Did you see who signed the letter?"

Sam perked up at the question. "Yeah, it was a private detective agency in Baltimore somewhere."

"Do you remember the agency's name or address?" She'd sounded too eager; she could tell from Sam's smug expression.

With an exaggerated shrug, Sam said, "I guess I did, but it must have slipped my mind." He scraped back his chair and slung his mail sack over his shoulder. "That name and address might come back to me in a day or two. Thanks for the cookies." Then he left, whistling.

Olivia felt so drained, she needed a cookie herself. At least she was now fairly sure that Clarisse had discovered she had a grandchild. Sam might be bluffing about seeing the private detective's signature, but she'd have to continue their little game to find out.

Chapter Eleven

◌⟡◌

The Chatterley Heights Food Shelf was located in the southern part of town, an area where successive waves of immigrants had settled. Rows of brick apartment buildings alternated with small Cape Cods and 1940s saltboxes. Delivering her cookies would require a short detour from Olivia's route to her mother and stepfather's house, but she hadn't allowed herself much time. She had rushed to encase each decorated cookie in plastic wrap, so Polly could hand them out individually, after which she'd had to wash a container that would hold all three dozen. She'd nestled the container inside a large Gingerbread House bag, the only one with a flat bottom. Meanwhile, she thought about the quickest yet most casual way to elicit the information she hoped Polly, heart and soul of the Food Shelf, might be able to provide.

Polly was alone when Olivia arrived. "How thoughtful of you and Maddie," Polly said when she saw the container stuffed with cookies. "I tell you, I was run off my feet all morning, what with all these layoffs. I swear, folks are coming from farther and farther away. They must be looking for work is all I can think, so they pack up the family in the car, if they still have a car, or maybe—"

"That's what I've heard," Olivia said. She felt guilty for interrupting, but it was well known that Polly didn't need to breathe as often as mere mortals. "Maddie and I did get a bit carried away. You know, Clarisse Chamberlain was a dear friend, and whenever I'm upset, I bake." She hoped she hadn't sounded too rehearsed, which, of course, she'd been doing ever since she'd come up with the idea halfway through wrapping the cookies.

"Oh, my dear, of course, I understand completely," Polly said, grasping Olivia's hands in her own. "Ms. Chamberlain was a true lady. Why, do you know, every single month without fail she'd walk over here to drop off a donation, always a generous check, which can be so useful when there are gaps in my inventory or for items people don't normally think to donate, like soap and, between you and me, toilet paper or those more intimate—"

"It was like Clarisse to think of that," Olivia cut in. She forced herself to pause a beat before adding, "Of course, you'd know that. Weren't you in high school with Edward?"

In fact, an online search had revealed that Polly and Edward had graduated the same year and served together on the yearbook committee.

While online, Olivia had also noticed an email from Deputy Cody, which she'd left unopened. Despite her earlier impatience, she realized she would need calm, quiet, and probably Maddie's company to face seeing Clarisse's lifeless body.

"I've never really gotten to know Edward," Olivia said.

"Clarisse always said he took after his father, even though he looked more like her."

"Parents can be so blind about their children, can't they? I see that every day here." Polly gazed into the distance. For once, she wasn't voicing her every thought, which made Olivia want to shake her.

"So are you saying that Edward was . . ."

Polly said, "Oh that Edward, my goodness. He wasn't the least bit like his father, I'd say. Edward—he insisted we all call him that, you know, not Ed or Eddie, only Edward. Anyway, we all—the yearbook committee, that is—we used to meet at his house all the time. He was proud of his family position, not that he didn't deserve to be, but he did like to show off that lovely home. He was so intense about everything." Polly snickered, then covered her mouth in embarrassment. "I shouldn't tell you this, but Edward and another boy almost came to blows one time because Edward insisted we place several pictures of his house in the yearbook."

"From all I've heard," Olivia said, "Martin Chamberlain was quite intense, too. Maybe that's what Clarisse meant?"

Polly placed an index finger on her upper lip, as if she were thinking hard about Olivia's suggestion. "Well, you know, Mr. Chamberlain sure looked intense, pacing around all the time and always, always smoking those cigarettes. But it was a different kind of intense, more like he had so much energy he couldn't sit still. With Edward, it was more that he couldn't let go once he'd decided something. Much as I loved Ms. Chamberlain, she was more like that. Once she made up her mind, she never changed it."

Olivia wanted to press for more information, but voices announced the arrival of visitors to the Food Shelf. Polly glanced at the family and reached into Olivia's package for three decorated cookies.

"Thank you so much, Olivia, and thank Maddie, too," Polly said.

She shifted into her role and greeted the family of five, who looked tired. The young woman, who held a toddler in her arms, gave Polly a brief smile, then glanced sidelong at the man. The toddler leaned away from his mother and reached for a cookie with both hands. Olivia slipped away before Polly could introduce her as the treat provider.

Olivia stood outside her mother and stepfather's front door, trying to quiet her mind, which roiled with questions. Was Clarisse's grandchild a girl or a boy? Was Hugh the father? Was Jasmine Dubois the mother? Where were Jasmine and the child? Were they even alive?

How much, Olivia wondered, could she trust Sam's account? He had a reputation for inflating a kernel of knowledge until it popped, especially when he perceived a rapt audience.

Olivia shook her head to clear it, but another idea intruded. What if Clarisse had been searching for Jasmine? From the conversation Olivia and Maddie overheard, Clarisse was determined to keep Hugh from marrying Tammy Deacons. Maybe she hoped Jasmine's reappearance would break Tammy's hold on her son? Something Polly had said flashed across her mind—that once Clarisse made up her mind, she never changed it. But she did change her mind about Tammy. Why?

And then there was Edward, who sounded more ambitious than she'd realized. Had Clarisse decided to change her will and leave the leadership of the Chamberlain businesses to one or the other son? Had she been overconfident enough to tell them—and then unyielding when the one left out objected?

Red gingham curtains covered a small window in the Greyson-Meyer front door. When the curtains twitched, Olivia pasted on a smile and pressed the doorbell. Temple bells rang as the door opened.

"Livie dear, I was beginning to wonder if you'd forgotten our brunch today, which would be so unlike you." Ellie had twisted her hair into a loose braid intertwined with a gold ribbon. She wore pantaloons of gold silk with red threads woven throughout. Over her red silk tunic, she'd thrown a stunning shawl made of a shimmery metallic yarn.

"Mom, you look amazing." Olivia gave her a quick hug. "I suppose you made this . . ."

"Ensemble?" Ellie said with her tinkling laugh. "Only the shawl. I saw the rest online and couldn't resist. Come along now, time's a-wasting." She wrapped her arm around Olivia's waist and guided her toward the kitchen. "The clothes discussion can wait. Allan is making his special pancakes."

Olivia caught the rich, smoky smell of bacon frying and the cakey aroma of pancakes as they arrived. On the stove, a jar of Vermont maple syrup warmed in a pan of steaming water. Olivia wished she could simply relax, laugh and eat with her family, and stuff all her thoughts and feelings about Clarisse's death into a drawer.

"Jason might stop by later," Ellie said. "He has a late lunch break."

Olivia didn't get many chances to see her younger brother, but his presence might be a hindrance. She figured Jason was too young to know the Chamberlain family well. He'd probably get bored, and boredom made Jason

testy. He wasn't known for his patience. She'd better find
out what she could from her mom and Allan as quickly as
possible.

"Livie, welcome," Allan boomed as Olivia entered the
kitchen. "How about a hug for the cook?" He gave her a
firm, one-armed squeeze while he flipped a pancake with
his free hand.

Allan Meyers wasn't more than a few inches taller than
Olivia, and he tended toward hefty, though she had to
admit he was solid muscle.

It had taken Olivia some time to accept Allan's appearance in her mother's life. She had been fifteen when her
father died, old enough to be in the throes of teenage angst,
rebellious yet in need of her father. Right when she needed a
stable place to struggle toward adulthood, she found herself
at her father's funeral. For years afterwards, he'd retained
an almost mythical perfection in her mind. He'd been tall
and thin. She remembered him as someone who listened
with his full attention, who watched with gentle curiosity as
life swirled around him. He had loved to grow vegetables
and write poetry, and he had achieved unexpected success
as the author of a book on ornithology. The book's popularity was due in large part to her father's insightful observations of bird behavior. And his photos—he'd had a gift for
capturing heartwarming moments and hilarious antics in
the bird world, from the vivid red cardinal feeding a sunflower seed kernel to his chosen mate to a nuthatch hanging
upside down from the bottom of a bird feeder.

Next to Olivia's memories of her father, which she now
admitted were romanticized, Allan Myers had seemed
rough-edged and loud. She'd tried to accept him early on
because she could see how happy he made her mother, but
she didn't get it. Once she had grown up, and especially

after experiencing the realities of marriage, Olivia began to perceive and appreciate Allan's better qualities. Like her father, Allan was thoughtful and kind. He simply displayed these qualities at a higher decibel level.

"Come and get it while it's hot," Allan said. With a flourish, he flipped a pancake into the air and held a plate underneath, shifting it quickly to catch the pancake. The first two slapped on target, but the third hit the edge of a plate and broke in half. "Two out of three," Allan said. "I'm ahead so far."

Olivia hovered between amusement and anxiety as she watched the performance. She was relieved when most of the pancakes had made it to plates and they could sit down to eat. She had missed breakfast, resisted sneaking a cookie from her Food Shelf package, and the sweet smell of maple syrup made her want to stuff an entire pancake in her mouth.

Half a stack of pancakes and two slices of bacon later, Olivia felt much better.

"Are you eating regular meals, Livie dear?" Ellie asked. Her expression was gently bemused. "Should I be sending over hot casseroles?"

Olivia looked at their plates and realized she'd already gobbled twice as much as her mother and stepfather. "Now you mention it, I have been missing meals lately. I've been so busy with the store. And I do have a lot on my mind."

Ellie passed the bacon, pancakes, and syrup in her direction. "How can we help?"

"Your mother tells me you'd like to pick my brilliant business brain about the Chamberlain clan," Allan said. He leaned across the table and filled Olivia's coffee cup to the brim. "She said you're having trouble believing Clarisse's death was an accident. I'd have to say, it's the last thing I would have expected, especially the way it happened."

Allan leaned his beefy arms on the table and frowned at the coffeepot. "Over the years, I've worked on deals with Clarisse, haggled over prices—you remember when she bought my printing business a few years back? I'd expanded right before a downturn in the economy. Clarisse offered to buy, and I was getting bored with printing, anyway, so I was ready to sell. But I owed a lot to the banks. Clarisse could have put on the screws, but she didn't. Mind you, she insisted on a good deal, and she got it. She was tough and fair. And smart. Too smart to mix a bottle of sleeping pills into a full wine bottle and drink the whole thing."

"Not even if she were very upset about something?" Ellie asked.

"Nope," Allan said with a firm shake of his head. "Clarisse had a heart, but she was no delicate flower. She'd tough it out, whatever it was."

"I think the sheriff is afraid Clarisse might have killed herself," Olivia said.

Allan slapped the table with his hand, and the plates rattled. "Absolutely not. I've known Clarisse for twenty years. There's nothing that woman couldn't face down. She adored Martin, they were two peas in a pod, but when he dropped dead right in front of her, did she fall apart? Nope, not even for a day. She had plenty of reason to, no one would have thought less of her, but no sirree, not Clarisse Chamberlain. She called 911, gave him CPR. And after the funeral, she went right back to work. Don't get me wrong, she grieved in her own way, but she never felt sorry for herself or turned to drink or anything like that. She stood on her own two feet and kept on walking."

Allan picked up the last piece of bacon on his plate, folded it in half, and devoured it in one bite. "Now," he said, wiping the grease off his fingers with his napkin, "how else can I help? Can I sell you a used car?"

Ellie began clearing the table.

Allan grinned at his wife's back. "I've been told more than once that I sound like a used-car huckster on TV. No one has meant it as a compliment. Ellie hates hearing it. Not me, though. I don't mind one bit if people see me that way. It makes them underestimate me."

Olivia remembered thinking used-car salesman when she'd first met Allan. And she had, indeed, underestimated him.

"You see, Livie," Allan said, "when folks underestimate you, they tend to let down their guard. And when they let down their guard, you can get a good look at their strengths and their weaknesses."

"Was Clarisse ever fooled?"

"Nope, not when it came to business. Martin, neither."

"And when it came to her family?"

"Parents see their kids through a filter," he said. "For better or for worse."

"What is your take on the Chamberlain brothers?"

"Edward and Hugh?" Allan threw back his head and laughed. "Opposites. Hugh has the charm without the drive. Edward, he's got the drive without the charm. Put 'em in a blender, you'd have a damn fine businessman."

Ellie passed by close enough for Allan to reach around her waist and pull her to him. Ellie's cheeks pinked up. Olivia tried to hide the fact that she still felt a vague discomfort at witnessing the affection between her mother and Allan. Maybe by the time she turned forty, the feeling would disappear, but she wasn't holding her breath.

"Frankly," Allan said, "I think it would have been better

for Edward and Hugh if they'd gone off on their own, developed their own style. Martin, though, he wanted a family dynasty, and Clarisse, well, I suspect she wanted her sons nearby."

"Jason should be here soon," Ellie said. "We decimated the pancakes. I'd better start more bacon cooking." Ellie squeezed Allan's hand, removed it from her waist, and headed toward the stove.

"Oops, sorry I forgot the eggs, Mom. Jason will be hungry."

"Jason won't starve. He can have bacon and toast sandwiches."

"One last question, Allan," Olivia said. "Only this one is about Lucas Ashford."

Ellie and Allan exchanged a quick glance. "Are you concerned for Maddie?" Ellie asked as she put bacon into a frying pan. "They must be getting serious."

"No, it's not about Lucas and Maddie, although if there's anything I should know, I order you to tell me instantly."

With her light laugh, Ellie said, "If I ever find out that Lucas is an ax murderer, I'll be sure to let you know. As far as I've observed, he is a perfectly nice man, if a bit quiet for my taste."

"Maddie can supply the noise," Olivia said. "I was wondering, though. . . . Allan, maybe you know, is the hardware store doing all right?"

"As far as I know," Allan said. "There's no swelling demand for hammers and nails, but Heights Hardware seems to float along modestly. Why? Have you heard something?" His tone was casual, but Olivia sensed the businessman in him leap to attention.

"No, not in so many words." Olivia wished she hadn't brought up the topic.

Allan shrugged, but Ellie turned sideways so she could

see the table and keep an eye on the spitting bacon at the same time. "I can answer that one, Livie. The hardware may be doing fine, but the Ashford family went through a rough patch."

"I'll be in my office, paying bills," Allan said. "Give me a holler when Jason gets here."

"Allan gets bored by too much talk about other families' troubles," Ellie said, without a hint of criticism. "Anyway, about the Ashfords, all this happened while you were busy in Baltimore, no reason you'd have heard about it. Although, I suppose a better mother would have emailed you regularly with all the Chatterley Heights news."

"Thank you for not being a better mother."

"You're welcome, dear." Ellie paused to move several strips of bacon from the pan to a length of paper towel she'd placed on the kitchen counter. She added raw strips to the pan, each landing with a sizzle.

"It all started about four years ago," Ellie said. "Lucas's father was diagnosed with colon cancer. He had surgery and chemo, and it looked hopeful, but the shock of his illness was too much for Lucas's mother. She had a stroke, a bad one."

"Poor Lucas," Olivia said.

"Poor Lucas, indeed. He was trying to care for both parents and keep the hardware store running. His dad needed to be transported back and forth for the chemo, and then he'd be sick from it. His mom was . . . well, you probably remember her."

"Do I," Olivia said. "She terrified me when I was a kid. I'd wait outside the hardware store when Dad took me on errands with him."

"Yes, well, the stroke seemed to make her even more of a tyrant. All of us tried to help out by staying with her while Lucas carted his father to and from treatments. But nobody lasted very long. I have to admit, Shirley tried my patience."

Olivia began to scrape the dirty plates and arrange them in the dishwasher. "As I remember, not only did Shirley have a demanding personality, but she must have weighed at least two hundred and fifty pounds. If you were trying to help her to bed, she could have squashed you."

"Illness did whittle her down considerably," Ellie said. "Though she still possessed nearly two hundred of those pounds."

"And you a wraithlike ninety-nine pounds," Olivia said.

"Sadly, with the arrival of middle age, I've packed it on. I'm up to one hundred and four. Three digits."

Olivia snickered. "I wonder how you can show yourself in public."

"Loose clothing helps." Ellie had finished frying the bacon and was pouring the grease into a Maxwell House coffee tin. From the rust, Olivia assumed it was the same tin her mother had used since she and Jason were kids. The thought comforted her.

"As to your question," Ellie said, "Lucas had to hire caregivers almost around the clock, so he could keep the hardware store going. From what I heard, he had to mortgage the house, which they'd paid off years earlier, and also take out a hefty loan, using his business as collateral. Both his parents passed on shortly before you came back home, but the loan remains to haunt poor Lucas. That's why I was surprised to hear he and Maddie are spending so much time together—for years he's done nothing but work."

"Is his loan with the bank here in town?" Olivia asked.

"Not a bank, dear. The loan came from Clarisse Chamberlain."

* * *

"Hey, where is everybody?" Jason's voice came from the living room.

"Does he always walk in without knocking?" Olivia asked.

"Look who I found loitering outside our front door," Allan boomed. He appeared in the kitchen a moment later, Jason following behind.

"Hi, Olive Oyl." Jason gave Olivia a light tap on the shoulder and raked his fingers up the back of her head, causing unruly curls to poke out from her carefully smoothed hair.

"Hey!" Olivia grabbed Jason's hand before he could strike again. Looking at his long, oil-stained fingers, she said, "Here's a suggestion: why don't you scrub your hands instead of cleaning them in my hair?"

"I could scrub this stain for hours and it wouldn't come out."

Jason had spoken with pride, and Olivia swallowed her next retort. She knew what that job at the garage meant to him. He'd stuck with it for two years already, and he was earning a reputation for quality work. After quitting college and a string of other jobs, he needed to feel good about this one. However, he also needed to stop messing with her hair—and calling her Olive Oyl, a nickname given her as a young teen, after a dramatic growth spurt left her with long, skinny legs.

"This looks great, Mom," Jason said. He piled several strips of bacon on a piece of buttered toast, folded it in half, and finished it off in three bites. "I smell pancakes and maple syrup," he said.

"All gone," Ellie said. "There's plenty more toast and bacon."

Jason's forlorn expression reminded Olivia of Spunky when he hoped she'd forgotten that he'd already had his dinner.

Ellie sighed. "No, I can't make more," she said. "No more pancake mix, no eggs, no time to get any before you go back to work." She pushed the bacon and toast closer.

Jason accepted defeat and rolled another half sandwich. "S'okay," he said between bites. "The boss has been ordering pizzas every afternoon, 'cause we all get so hungry we start to slow down."

"I'm surprised you haven't gotten fat," Olivia said.

"I'm surprised you're not in jail," Jason said just before forcing another half a sandwich into his mouth. He closed his eyes in ecstasy while he chewed, which left him unaware of the reason for the sudden silence. Only when he opened his eyes and reached for the last of the food did he notice the confused stares from his nearest and dearest. "Wassup? Do I have a piece of bacon up my nose?"

Ellie frowned at him, a rare occurrence. "That was an unusual statement you made about your sister," she said.

"What? About her being in jail?" Jason looked from his mother to his stepfather and finally to Olivia. "You really haven't heard, have you?"

"Heard what?" Allan's tone was clipped, no-nonsense.

Jason wiped his mouth with his napkin and scraped back his chair. "We found out soon after it happened because a customer came in to get his car right after watching the ambulance arrive. Sam Parnell was rushed to the hospital, unconscious. I guess he finally got too snoopy for his own good and somebody tried to kill him."

Olivia was first to break the stunned silence. "How do they know it was a murder attempt?" she asked. "And even if it was, what could it possibly have to do with me?"

Jason started to laugh, but the dangerous look on Olivia's face sobered him quickly. "I don't have the inside scoop or anything, only what's going around town."

"Which is?"

"Well . . . Look, Livie, don't kill the messenger, okay? What's going around is, Sam was eating a cookie when he collapsed, and he didn't choke or have a heart attack or anything. He had a bag from your store, and there were still cookie crumbs and icing bits inside."

"That doesn't mean the cookies were ours. What do we sell in our store, for heaven's sakes? Cookie cutters, that's what. There are scads of people who've bought them from us and could have made that cookie."

Jason said, "What about the bag?"

Ellie said, "Jason, I have a stack of bags from The Gingerbread House." At a look from her husband, she said, "What? I like them."

"I gave Sam a few cookies this morning but none 'to go' in one of our bags. Who found him?" Olivia asked.

"Ida, that ancient waitress at Pete's Diner. I guess she's off on Mondays. Anyway, she opened her front door and reached around to empty her mailbox and there was Sam, out cold on her porch. She called an ambulance."

"None of which means that—"

"Sis, all I'm saying is, it doesn't look good."

Chapter Twelve

"What the heck is going on in this town?" Olivia paced around The Gingerbread House kitchen, moving objects from one place to another for no apparent reason.

"Don't ask me." Maddie sounded exasperated. "I'm as confused as you are, not to mention irate. It seems as though somebody went to a lot of trouble to make us look like bad guys. At least Sheriff Del hasn't arrested us."

"He hasn't eliminated us as suspects—or me anyway. I don't think he believed I didn't know about Sam being diabetic. He sure packed away the cookies this morning."

"You don't get out much," Maddie said. "Sam is funny about the diabetes. He's so proud of being fit, I think he sees diabetes as something he shouldn't have. It's hard to believe he'd blow off his insulin after eating so many cookies, though."

"If something was wrong with his insulin, I guess it'll show up when they test his supply," Olivia said. "Meanwhile, we need to get organized." She removed a container of confectioners' sugar from a cupboard and put it on a shelf.

"That's the third time you've moved that sugar," Maddie said. "That isn't the type of organization we need right now. Stop moving, you're making me nervous."

"Right. You're the one who can't sit still, I'm the calm one. And if I ever find out that someone tried to set us up, I will calmly break their nose."

"Good, that'll leave a few appendages for me."

They had returned twenty minutes earlier from the Chatterley Heights Police Station, where Sheriff Del had questioned them without any of his normal friendly teasing. He had confirmed Sam's condition as serious and being treated as a diabetic coma. He hadn't regained consciousness. The cookie crumbs, Del had said, were undergoing analysis, along with Sam's stomach contents. Otherwise, all Olivia and Maddie had received was a warning to stay quiet and in town.

"I've known Delroy Jenkins since I was ten years old," Maddie said. "As long as I've known you. He treated us like suspects!"

"That's what sheriffs do. It's pretty much their job. Although he didn't have to be so officious about it."

"You sort of like him, don't you, Livie?"

"Yeah. I hate when that happens."

They looked at each other and burst into laughter, with a tinge of hysteria. Minutes later, when they'd quieted down, Olivia said, "I feel better. Let's get to work."

"What can we do?"

"We can put our heads together. The attack on Sam, if it was an attack, must be connected with Clarisse's death." Olivia fetched her laptop computer from the kitchen desk and settled at the table. "I'm setting up a file to record everything we know about Clarisse's death and everything we need to find out," she said, her hands flying across the keys. "Give me a password only you and I will know."

"Teal42," Maddie said.

"Good," Olivia said. "Now we need suspects and alibis. Edward and Hugh, of course. Presumably they will inherit almost everything, and I happen to know that Clarisse was worth at least a million dollars."

Maddie whistled. "She told you that?"

"She wanted to show me what was possible. She and Martin started from nothing, made careful decisions, invested, saved. . . . They took calculated risks and admitted when it was time to cut their losses. Clarisse was trying to teach me." Olivia felt herself slip into grief and yanked herself back to the present. "Hugh and Edward supposedly have alibis for the night of their mother's death. Do they hold up? And what about the attack on Sam today?" She set up a table with suspect names down the left side.

"This is awfully linear," Maddie said. "It hurts my brain, but here goes. Didn't Del say Hugh and Edward were at a conference when Clarisse died?"

"In Baltimore. But he didn't say whether he talked to them in person or left a message. We can probably check that. It shouldn't be too hard to figure out what conference they attended."

Olivia typed "Alibi" at the top of the first column in her table. "Martin and Clarisse used to visit all their businesses every Monday, and I know Hugh and Edward have carried on that tradition."

"Do they travel alone or together?"

"Alone. Either of them could have slipped in a stop at Sam's house. Everyone knows he arranges his route so he can stop at home for lunch."

"What about Bertha?" Maddie asked. "Does she inherit

anything from Clarisse? Although I'd hate to think that anyone who bakes such luscious pies could be a murderer."

"Would you rather everyone believe that two women who make luscious cookies might be poisoners?"

"Point taken," Maddie said. "We include everyone."

Typing as she spoke, Olivia said, "Clarisse told me that Bertha was well provided for. I'm not sure it would be enough to kill over, especially since Bertha already had a secure situation." Her fingers paused over the keyboard.

"May I suggest Tammy Deacons as our next suspect?" Maddie asked. "From what we overheard, she and Hugh did *something* they don't want anyone to know about— something that involved Clarisse. We need to find out where Tammy was the night Clarisse died."

Olivia added a row for Tammy Deacons.

"Tammy had lots of cookies at her house," Maddie said, "left over from her engagement shindig. Although, if she was teaching that day, I suppose she wouldn't have been home to hand Snoopy Sam a bag of cookies when he delivered her mail."

"Don't sound so disappointed. I'm sure we can find out if she was at school today . . ."

"I'll bet you a dozen cookies Tammy doesn't have an alibi for either time period." Maddie's cell phone sang a muddy phrase of Gregorian chant. "That'll be Lucas," she said, reaching into the pocket of her jeans. "He's calling about when we'll meet for dinner. He's taking me to Pete's for scallops night."

While Maddie paced the kitchen and spoke to Lucas, Olivia shook her shoulders to loosen them. Hunching over a computer had begun to leave its mark on her once-flexible limbs. She had one more suspect to list, and she wasn't looking forward to it.

"Okay, it's scallops at six," Maddie said as she snapped her cell shut. "What time is your will-reading dinner at the Chamberlain mansion?"

"Sherry and will reading at six-thirty, dinner at seven."

"Sherry? La-de-da. Sounds like the setting for a British murder mystery. Wish I could pose as a serving wench and watch the show."

Maddie rinsed out her coffee cup and reached for her jacket. "Gotta roll if I want a shower before dinner."

"Maddie," Olivia said, "there's one more person we ought to discuss."

"Really? Who?" Maddie's eager curiosity made Olivia's stomach clench.

"Well, my mom and Allan were talking. . . . There's no easy way to say this, so . . . Maddie, did you know that Lucas borrowed money from Clarisse, using the hardware store as collateral?"

Maddie's sunny expression clouded over. "Of course I knew. Lucas told me early on. He's very honest. Anyway, he's been paying it off gradually, and the store is doing okay in spite of the economy."

Olivia closed the lid of her laptop to put it to sleep— and to ease the tension. "I wondered, did Clarisse pressure Lucas at all? Did she offer to forgive the loan in exchange for Heights Hardware?"

Maddie threw the kitchen towel on the counter and folded her arms. Olivia could almost feel sparks shooting from her friend's eyes.

Olivia took several deep breaths, then a couple more. Part of her wanted to leave Lucas out of it, for Maddie's sake. On the other hand, she couldn't stop imagining Clarisse's last moments. "I can't let this go, Maddie. I have to know what happened."

"Okay. I get it." Maddie kept her arms crossed and leaned against the kitchen counter.

"Couldn't we talk about it, friend to friend?"

The silence lightened maybe an iota.

"Sleuth to sleuth?" Olivia asked.

Maddie didn't uncross her arms, but her shoulders lowered a bit.

"Over cookies and milk?" Olivia opened the refrigerator door and removed a half gallon of milk. "I wonder if Del seriously suspects us."

Maddie lifted two glasses and two plates from the cupboard. "Our alibis aren't so great. We alibi each other for part of the night Clarisse died, and those cookies Sam ate were undeniably ours. By the way, I did stash away a few for emergencies." She pulled down a tin from on top of the refrigerator. "If either of us refuses to eat these, it won't look good."

They settled at the table. Olivia waited through one red and yellow striped beach ball cookie and half a glass of milk before saying, as gently as she could, "I do need to know about Lucas, you know."

"I know." Maddie selected a second cookie, decorated with looping strings of white pearls. She set it on her plate and ran her index finger across the hardened dots of icing. "The truth is, Clarisse was pressuring Lucas to sell the hardware store to her. She said something about wanting to see what Hugh could do with it on his own. She only wanted the business to test Hugh. It was tearing Lucas apart. The way things are going, he'll be paying off that loan for the rest of his life, assuming he lives to be one hundred. And yes, once Clarisse was gone, the pressure was off. Hugh doesn't want the hardware; he said so. So Lucas has been a lot happier, and we avoid talking about money. We haven't finished our first flush of romance yet."

Maddie bit a half circle out of her cookie. She put the remainder back on her plate and pushed it away. "To be honest, I think that's why Lucas and I finally got together. I've been crazy about him for years, as you well know. He is so easy to be with, and he accepts me with all my weirdness. He says I make him laugh." She smiled at the tabletop. "But with his mom and dad and all that debt, plus the fear he'd have to give up the family business . . . So yes, he's relieved the pressure to sell is gone, but he still has the loan to pay off, so it's not like killing Clarisse would have gotten him very far. Unless you think he has plans to knock off Hugh and Edward, too."

"I'll admit that hadn't occurred to me," Olivia said. She didn't add that Lucas would stay on the suspects list, for now.

Olivia glanced at her watch. "I have to be at the Chamberlain home in two hours. Can you stay a bit longer? There's something I have to do, and I need company." She explained to Maddie about the photos Deputy Cody took the night Clarisse died.

"No kidding," Maddie said. "You bet I'll stay. I showered this morning. Fire up that computer."

Olivia awakened her sleeping laptop and called up her email. Maddie scooted her chair closer. "Here goes." Olivia had seven unread emails, six of them from other businesses. She opened the seventh, Deputy Cody's, which said only, "Here they are. Please don't mention this to Sheriff Del."

"Rest easy, Cody," Olivia mumbled. She clicked on the first email attachment, and a photo appeared. No matter how much she'd tried to prepare herself, Olivia wasn't ready to see Clarisse Chamberlain's body lying facedown on her office carpet. She forced herself to study the details.

"Somehow it looks different than it does on those

television cop shows," Maddie said. "Sadder. What was it Cody said about her arms?"

"See how her arms are straight back along her body? Cody thinks that if she'd been conscious, she'd have tried to break her fall, so her arms might be under her. Maybe even above her head."

Olivia opened the second photo, which Cody had taken from farther away. Now they could see a wine bottle on the carpet next to Clarisse's shoulder. The bottle lay on its side, its pouring end pointing toward the office door, a corner of which showed in the photo. A small area of darkness appeared near the top of the bottle, as if a bit of wine had dribbled out. Olivia zoomed in, which made the area fuzzy, but it did look like a wine stain.

"Del said that Clarisse had drunk a whole bottle. At some point, she must have crushed her sleeping pills into it." Olivia had a sudden, strong need to move. She bolted out of her chair and began to pace around the kitchen. "I thought at the time that Clarisse couldn't have stayed conscious through an entire bottle of wine laced with sleeping pills. She wasn't used to drinking more than a glass or so. Seeing these photos, I'm more sure than ever that her death wasn't an accident, and it wasn't suicide."

"Explain it to me," Maddie said.

"Okay, even if Clarisse did something as uncharacteristic as crush a handful of sleeping pills into a bottle of wine, she would never have made it through the bottle, not even a third of the way, without passing out."

"What if she chugged the wine on purpose?" Maddie said. "You know, like those kids when they turn twenty-one."

Olivia waved her hand impatiently. "She didn't have enough alcohol in her system. Clarisse once told me that one of her pills dissolved in water was enough to knock her out in ten minutes. Clarisse was a planner. If she'd really wanted to kill herself, she would have dissolved the pills in maybe one glass of wine, so she could get it down quickly. She wouldn't have stuffed any of them in the bottle and then tried to drink it all before passing out. Clarisse would never have been that inefficient."

"Unless, maybe, she didn't mean to actually kill herself? You know, like a cry for help?"

"Clarisse Chamberlain did not cry for help," Olivia said. "Not ever. No, the real question is, why did she ask Bertha to open a full bottle of wine for her. I have to wonder if she was expecting a visitor."

"Of course," Maddie said, "and that person killed her, then set it up to look like an accident."

"Click on the next photo," Olivia said. Too agitated to sit, she stood behind her chair and leaned on the back.

The photo was taken from farther back and showed half of Clarisse's cluttered desk. Her substantial leather chair faced away from the desk, as if she had realized she was in trouble, picked up the wine bottle, turned her chair on its wheels. . . . From the position of Clarisse's body, it looked as though she had made it about halfway to the door.

"Maddie, think a moment—under what circumstances would Clarisse have picked up the wine bottle and taken it with her?"

It was Maddie's turn to roam around the kitchen, mumbling and running her fingers through her already tousled hair. Finally, she hoisted herself up on the edge of the worktable facing the computer. Olivia swung a leg over the seat of her chair and sat backwards, arms folded over the back.

"If Clarisse was determined to commit suicide," Maddie said, "the only reason I can think of would be to make her death look like an accident—you know, so her heirs could still get the life insurance. Maybe she hoped it would look like she wanted Bertha to know right away that she'd accidentally overdosed herself."

Olivia shook her head. "Too convoluted. And not really necessary. She could have stayed at the desk or stretched out on the love seat by the fire, as if she'd gotten sleepy. Her death would look accidental, especially without a suicide note. Also, remember she was in perfect health and had no financial problems."

"Okay, let's eliminate the suicide idea altogether," Maddie said. "If she did accidentally poison herself, she might take the bottle for the same reason—to get help as quickly as possible."

"She was sitting at her desk," Olivia said. "Why not pick up the phone? She could dial Bertha's room upstairs with one number. Help would come much quicker."

"I'm tired of being the straight man," Maddie said. "It's a waste of my histrionic talents. Answer your own question, and I'll shoot you down."

Olivia turned back to the photo. "I can't say if Clarisse was sitting or standing when she lost consciousness, but I don't think she got to that spot on her own. I think she was dragged. I also think that bottle was placed beside her by the person or persons who positioned her body, maybe, as you suggested, to make it look like Clarisse suddenly realized she was in trouble and went for help."

Maddie slid off her perch on the table and joined Olivia at the computer. After a long stare at the screen, she said, "I think you might be right. Why didn't Sheriff Del notice what you did? He's a smart guy. You don't think he's hiding something, do you?"

"I'm irked at him," Olivia said with a light laugh, "but

not enough to see him as part of a townwide conspiracy. I suspect Del is hoping all this will go away. The Chamberlain family is a big employer in Chatterley Heights and beyond. A murder investigation would mean Hugh, Edward, even Bertha would be questioned, hounded by the press, maybe arrested. Their pasts would become common knowledge. Even if they are all cleared, there'd likely be some lingering doubt about their innocence."

"If that happened to me," Maddie said, "I know what I'd do. I'd sell my business, take the money, and move far, far away."

"Me, too," Olivia said. "I decided to start a business here partly because I knew the town had a solid financial base. Let's be honest, would a store specializing in cookie cutters survive for long in a declining town with nothing else going for it?"

"Far be it from me to wimp out to save our livelihood," Maddie said, "but maybe we should tell Del about what we've come up with and consider letting him handle the investigation?"

Olivia fixed her with a glare that would have leveled a nursing grizzly bear.

"Only a suggestion," Maddie said with unaccustomed meekness.

Olivia leaned toward the screen. "What's all that clutter on Clarisse's desk?" She tried to zoom in on the desk, but the image was too fuzzy. While she tried some adjustments, Olivia said, "Clarisse was neat to the point of obsession. She told me once that it drove her crazy to misplace something, so she had a place for everything, and everything went back in its place, no exceptions." She gave the zoom key one last frustrated poke. "Darn, this isn't going to work. There's one more photo; let's try that."

When the image sprang to life, both women stared at it in puzzlement. Finally, Maddie said, "Cookie cutters. Not what I expected."

"Me, neither. I was hoping for clues, like family records or maybe notes for a new will. Although I suppose her killer would have taken those with him."

"Or *her*," Maddie said. "Tammy is in the running, as far as I'm concerned."

"Clarisse showed me her cookie-cutter collection many times. It is quite extensive, not to mention valuable. She'd acquired dozens of wonderful antiques even before our store opened. Do you know, Clarisse had an almost complete collection of vintage Hallmark cookie cutters." Olivia swallowed hard and said, "I asked her who she had to kill to get them. She laughed."

Maddie squinted at the photo. "I can't tell what I'm looking at. Did Hugh and Edward know much about her collection?"

"Not really," Olivia said. "Clarisse said the boys were never interested enough to listen. This photo does convince me of one thing, though I can't prove it. Clarisse loved to relax with her cutters. I think they gave her a warm, cozy feeling. It's one of the reasons we became friends—our emotional connection with cookie cutters and the good memories they produced. If Clarisse was looking at her collection when she died, she might have been troubled, but she wasn't contemplating suicide. She was comforting herself."

Chapter Thirteen

❦

By the time Olivia and Maddie tore themselves away from Deputy Cody's crime scene photos, it was almost six o'clock. The reading of Clarisse's will was scheduled for six thirty. Olivia rushed through her shower and grabbed the first clean clothes she came to in her closet—black wool pants and a pale gray angora sweater. Applying a loose interpretation to the posted speed limit, she managed to arrive at the Chamberlain home by six thirty-five, only five minutes late.

Bertha answered the doorbell. "There you are, Ms. Olivia," she said, taking Olivia's coat. She opened the hall closet door and began to search for a free hanger.

Olivia felt a twinge of guilt when Bertha, who was neither young nor slim, began to wheeze. "That's an old coat," Olivia said. "You can throw it anywhere."

Without wavering from her goal, Bertha reached one arm behind her and flipped her hand dismissively. A second later, she said, "Aha," and pulled out a free hanger. "It's been a long time since we had any guests but you in the house. Not since Mr. Martin passed on. God rest his soul, Mr. Martin did love his dinner parties."

Olivia lightly touched Bertha's forearm. "Are you feeling all right?"

"Now, don't you fret about me," Bertha said. "My asthma is flaring up a bit, that's all, although the only thing that ever caused me a problem is cats, which I never go near. Come along now, everyone is here but the lawyer. All gathered in the parlor, like in a play. There's you and me, Hugh, Edward, and Ms. Tammy, looking very pretty. I never understood what made Ms. Clarisse take against her so sudden."

The Chamberlain house was old enough to have a front parlor, where the family would once have received visitors. To Olivia, the room felt stern, with its dark-stained mahogany furniture. The only light piece in the room was a gray marble side table, which held a round silver tray filled with canapés. It was the perfect setting for the reading of a last will and testament.

Olivia and Clarisse had chosen cozier settings for their visits, such as the front porch in warm weather and Clarisse's office, in front of the fireplace, during the damp cold of winter. Olivia wished for a welcoming fire now, but sherry would have to do. However, she was going through hers faster than a person with an empty stomach ought to, and she wanted to keep her mind clear. She sidled over to the canapés. The smoked salmon ones looked tempting, as did the mushrooms with cream sauce. Olivia took one of each, then added a second mushroom canapé to her plate. After all, the cream sauce might help soak up the sherry.

As she nibbled, Olivia looked over the little group. Edward Chamberlain sat alone in a wingback chair, leafing through a magazine, his untouched glass of sherry on a small table next to him. Smoke floated up from the cigarette in his right hand. Olivia was struck by how much he resembled his mother, yet how different he seemed from her. Like Clarisse, he was blond, with a red sheen to his hair that showed up in sunlight or, as here, under bright incandescent light. Normally, she wouldn't gaze so directly at someone, but Edward seemed oblivious. Even the sudden tinkle of Tammy's laughter didn't cause so much as an unconscious flicker of his eyelids.

Tammy chattered happily to Hugh and Bertha. She wore yet another new dress that Olivia remembered seeing recently on a window mannequin at Lady Chatterley's. It was a figure-hugging sheath that showed off Tammy's slim figure, in a pale green that matched her eyes, which gazed adoringly at Hugh. She'd curled her straight hair and piled it on her head. She looked as if she already owned the Chamberlain house.

As for Hugh, he was his father's son. In looks, anyway. He had to be thirty-five at least, because he had graduated from high school by the time Olivia was a freshman. He had an abundance of dark, wavy hair and Martin Chamberlain's handsome face, softened by an easygoing nature. When Tammy left the group to fetch a tray of hors d'oeuvres, Hugh's eyes followed her for a moment.

Olivia was refilling her sherry glass when the doorbell rang. She took one more smoked salmon canapé before selecting a chair that would give her the best view of everyone present.

Bertha reappeared, accompanied by Aloysius Smythe, a wispy thin man with thinning gray hair and hunched shoulders. Olivia recognized him from the Chatterley Café, where she sometimes went for a late lunch while Maddie minded the store. He always arrived around two, the slowest time for the café, carrying a bulging briefcase. He would settle at a table for four and spread papers all over, giving the impression he intended to stay all afternoon.

Olivia's first impression of the attorney as elderly and foggy changed in an instant as he surveyed the room. He had quick, dark eyes that, when they reached Olivia's face, seemed to bore into her mind. No wonder Clarisse had thought the world of him. When he began to push a small desk toward his audience, Hugh leaped up to help. Tammy smiled as Hugh lifted the desk as if it were a stage prop.

Olivia stole a quick glance at Edward, who was scowling in Hugh's direction. Edward sat at the edge of his seat, as if he had intended to spring forward to help but wasn't quick enough.

The attorney placed a small stack of papers on the desk in front of him and cleared his throat. "Good evening, all of you. As you know, you are here to hear the last will and testament of Clarisse Chamberlain. I was her attorney, as well as her husband's, for over forty years, and it is with great personal distress that I fulfill my final professional service for her."

Looking directly at Olivia, he said, "Ms. Greyson, you are the only person present to whom I have not been formally introduced, although I certainly know of you and your place of business from the many times Clarisse spoke of you. She always did so with great admiration and affection, which is why, three months ago, she added a codicil to her will naming you as an added beneficiary."

Olivia swallowed hard as a ball of grief hit her in the solar plexus.

"By the way, as my full name is rather a mouthful, not to mention pretentious, everyone calls me by some version

of my middle name, Willard. Some people call me Mr.
Willard—or plain Will, possibly because of the irony. I
would be pleased if you do so, as well."

After a moment of confusion, Olivia got it. Will . . .
Lawyers write wills. She decided on Mr. Willard; it was
less likely to make her giggle.

"Now, to the business at hand," Mr. Willard said, glancing down at the papers in front of him. "I will summarize
most of Clarisse's bequests, but I will also read certain sec-
tions that she asked me to read aloud."

A rustling sound replaced the silence as Clarisse Chamberlain's family and friends shifted in their seats, prepar-
ing themselves to hear what she thought of them. Olivia
deposited her half-full glass of sherry on the side table next
to her chair so she wouldn't down it in one gulp.

Mr. Willard picked up one sheet of paper, again cleared
his throat, and began. "The bulk of Clarisse Chamberlain's
personal estate is left to her two sons, Hugh and Edward,
to be divided equally between them."

Olivia heard sighing that sounded like relief, but she
couldn't tell where it had come from. When she shot them
a quick glance, both Hugh and Edward showed impassive
expressions. Tammy's hand slid over Hugh's intertwined
fingers.

Mr. Willard consulted a second sheet of paper and continued. "This includes the house and grounds, as well as
savings, investments, and so forth, all of which total an
estimated worth of over one million dollars, after the
subtraction of Clarisse's other bequests. However, she
stipulated that the property may be sold and investments
liquidated only with the free consent of both brothers or
their beneficiaries should one predecease the other."

The attorney's eyes sought out each brother, as if he

were transmitting a silent message. "As for the Chamberlain businesses, Hugh and Edward, your mother wanted you to continue as you have been, working as a team. Profits and losses are to be split evenly between you. Either of you may buy out the other by joint agreement, but you must do so formally, as you would when acquiring any existing business. Should one son predecease the other while still a co-owner, his share will pass to his heirs, unless he has provided other arrangements in his own will. If he has no heirs, the businesses pass to the remaining brother or to his heirs."

Interesting, Olivia thought. Assuming they knew the contents of their mother's will, neither Hugh nor Edward appeared to have a compelling reason to kill Clarisse. Unless she had hinted that she intended to change her will before she died.

Olivia studied Hugh and Edward as long as she dared, which amounted to about fifteen seconds each. Neither betrayed any particular emotion. Edward stretched out his legs and crossed them at the ankle. Hugh bent toward Tammy as she whispered something in his ear. He nodded but said nothing in return. They looked resigned and bored. All in all, that was about what Olivia would expect from two brothers with little in common who have been shackled together for life by their deceased mother.

"Clarisse made a number of bequests to charities, which include several animal rescue organizations, national groups committed to caring for the poor, the Chatterley Heights Food Shelf, and Johns Hopkins University School of Medicine for research relating to heart disease."

How like Clarisse, Olivia thought. She was successful, healthy, and tougher than granite, but she knew others had not been as lucky.

"We are almost finished," Mr. Willard said, "and I don't know about you, but I'm famished." Faint tittering greeted his sudden shift to informality. He picked up the third and final sheet of paper on his borrowed desk.

"Clarisse made two bequests to individuals outside her family. First, to Bertha Binkman, income for life, to be adjusted for inflation, and a home for life, as well, should she wish to stay here. At any time after her sixtieth birthday, or earlier in the case of illness, Bertha may retire with full benefits, including retirement income, long-term care insurance, and other supplemental health care coverage, as needed. At retirement, she may choose to stay in the house or have the use, for life, of the guest cottage."

Bertha burst into noisy tears. Edward checked his watch, pushed to his feet, and began to wander. He selected a magazine from a stack on the table near the parlor doorway and leaned against the wall to leaf through it. Hugh and Tammy had their heads together, deep in whispered conversation.

As Bertha's sobs subsided, Mr. Willard once again cleared his throat. He looked at Olivia and said, "Now we come to the codicil. It is short and simple. Clarisse wanted me to read it aloud."

Mr. Willard paused, but no one besides Olivia paid any attention. Only Bertha had a good excuse, since her outburst had brought on a wheezing attack. Mr. Willard gave up and spoke directly to Olivia.

"Clarisse had the greatest liking and respect for you, as I'm sure you know," he said. "Here is what she wrote: 'With deep admiration and with gratitude for our many hours of conversation, I bequeath to Olivia Greyson the sum of one hundred and fifty thousand dollars, to use as she sees fit. I hope she will invest some of it in her business, which has given me many hours of pleasure. In addition, I leave her my entire cookie-cutter collection, which at the time of this writing is valued at approximately thirty thousand dollars.'"

A magazine hit the parquet floor with a slap, breaking the utter silence that followed Mr. Willard's reading of the codicil. Olivia couldn't bring herself to look at anyone, so she picked up her sherry glass and stared at the amber liquid. Then she emptied it down her throat.

Chapter Fourteen

❦

"Clarisse left you *how* much?" Maddie's voice came through distorted, due to the fact that she was yelling into her cell phone.

"You heard me," Olivia whispered. She was calling from the upstairs bathroom at the Chamberlain house, after excusing herself to Bertha as the group began to wander toward the dining room.

"Clarisse left me upwards of one hundred and eighty thousand, if you count her entire cookie-cutter collection. Maddie, are you sure no one can hear you? You're completely alone?" She feared Lucas might be lurking nearby, absorbing her information. Not that Lucas was the type to blab; however, as far as Olivia was concerned, he was still in the running for suspect number five. Or maybe number six, if she counted herself. One hundred and fifty thousand dollars plus an incredible cookie-cutter collection might be considered worth killing for.

"Wow," Maddie said. "So does everyone hate you now?"

'"I'm sure they are plotting my demise as we speak."
Olivia turned on the overhead fan and flushed the toilet.

"What's all that noise?" Maddie asked.

"Never mind, I don't have much time. Where are you?"

"Dinner with Lucas was short but sweet, so now I'm
back at The Gingerbread House, inventorying the kitchen
supplies. Why?"

"Because I want you to do something for me," Olivia
said. "We'll be back at work tomorrow morning, so we
need to use this evening well. You're better at Internet
searches than I am. I want you to use my laptop to find out
anything you can about Hugh and Edward, as well as the
Chamberlain businesses. Get financial information, if you
can. See if there's anything about Tammy, too."

"I'll start with Tammy," Maddie said.

"Why am I not surprised?"

O livia hurried downstairs, hoping the group wasn't
already seated in the dining room. She hopped off
the bottom step to find Tammy, arms crossed tightly across
her chest, leaning against the parlor doorjamb.

Startled and breathless, Olivia said, "I hope I haven't
delayed dinner. I was just . . ." She gestured upward.

"Livie Greyson, I thought we were friends." Tammy
came about as close to hissing as the human voice can
manage. Her eyes were narrowed to ice green slivers, and
she must have been running her fingers through her hair
because her elegant pile of curls was tumbling.

"Tammy, of course we are friends. We've been friends
so long I don't even remember how we met. What's wrong?"
Olivia had a good idea what was wrong, but she wanted to
hear Tammy's interpretation.

Tammy unglued an arm from her chest, grabbed Olivia's, and yanked her into the parlor. She closed the door behind them.

"Shouldn't we be getting to the dining room?" Olivia asked.

"You've already been gone long enough for everyone to notice," Tammy said. She released Olivia's arm and glared at her. "How *could* you?"

"How could I what? Tammy, I honestly don't get why you're so angry with me. If it's about Clarisse's will—"

"Of course it's about the will. Clarisse must have been going soft in the head to hand over all that money to you. She'd only known you for a year." Tammy plunked a fist on each hip. "Unless . . . How did you get her to write that bequest?"

"All right, that's enough." Olivia's even temperament did have its limits. "I had no idea Clarisse was leaving me so much as a dime. If I'd had a clue, I would have tried to talk her out of it. I'm sorry if you don't believe me, but it's the truth."

Olivia expected Tammy to explode, but instead her lower lip began to quiver. Olivia instinctively reached out to her. Tammy noticed the gesture, and tears gathered in her eyes. "Oh, Livie, I'm sorry, it isn't your fault, and it isn't even about the money. Although the least you could do is let Hugh have the cookie-cutter collection. It belonged to his mother, after all."

"And to Edward's," Olivia added, and immediately wished she hadn't. Quickly, she continued. "What did you mean? What isn't my fault?"

Tammy shrugged. "Oh, you know, that Clarisse loved you like a daughter and couldn't stand me." She walked to an ornate mirror hanging on the wall over a marble-topped chest of drawers. "She hated me, you know. She told me in no uncertain terms." Leaning toward the mirror, Tammy took a bobby pin from her hair, reworked a curl, and moved on to the next.

"But why would she dislike you?"

Tammy frowned at a repaired curl. "Because of Jasmine." She yanked the pin from the offending curl and started it again. "Because Clarisse thought I'd gotten Jasmine to run away and disappear forever. Believe me, if I could have done that, I would have, but Jasmine was tough. I almost liked her." Jabbing the pin back in place, she added, "If I hadn't hated her so much for trying to take Hugh away from me. Then she left, simply disappeared into the air, and Clarisse blamed me. Would you believe, she threatened to write Hugh out of her will if he insisted on marrying me? It's true. She said it to my face."

Holding a lock of hair twisted around two fingers, Tammy swiveled her head toward Olivia. "Without her precious Jasmine around, Clarisse wanted Hugh to marry you, you know."

"Hugh, but not Edward?"

"I can't see why she'd want you to marry Edward. She never seemed to worry much about him. I think it's because Hugh is the elder son, and Clarisse was old-fashioned enough to care about that kind of thing."

Olivia doubted that but kept it to herself.

"Anyway," Tammy said, "Hugh reminded Clarisse of Martin, so she had a soft spot for him."

That, Olivia could believe.

Tammy finished repairing her hair and nodded her satisfaction to the gilt-edged mirror. "None of that matters now, though. There's nothing Clarisse can do to keep Hugh and me apart."

* * *

The dining room was nearly empty by the time Olivia and Tammy arrived. As it turned out, no one had missed them. Due to a wheezing fit, Bertha had kept the corn chowder on simmer while she searched for her inhaler. Edward was in Clarisse's office with the door closed, taking a cell phone call from a manager at one of the Chamberlain companies. Mr. Willard and Hugh sat at one corner of the dining room table, an open bottle of Glenlivet Single Malt Scotch between them. Olivia recognized the bottle because her ex-husband had begun drinking it as he became more successful. He always left the bottle on display.

Tammy walked right over to Hugh, slid onto his lap, and planted a kiss on his cheek. Mr. Willard's welcoming smile faded. He looked so uncomfortable, Olivia felt it her duty to rescue him. Perhaps he would be grateful enough to answer a few questions. She caught his eye and nodded a greeting. Mr. Willard responded at once by slipping out of his chair with as little movement as possible and joining Olivia by the sideboard.

"Young love can be a bit much," Olivia said, as if she weren't exactly the same age as Tammy.

Mr. Willard raised his eyebrows and sighed.

"I notice the remainder of those lovely appetizers ended up here," Olivia said, admiring the sideboard. Several bottles of wine, both red and white, stood open and ready for pouring. "I don't know about you, but I'm starving. I'd love a glass of wine, but I'd better put something in my stomach first or I can't guarantee my ability to remain upright." She selected a tiny egg and watercress sandwich.

Mr. Willard's trapped-animal stance relaxed. He abandoned his glass of scotch and picked up two olive-cheese balls. Holding one in each hand, he said, "I prefer the classics. As a small child, I used to steal these delicious little darlings right off the guests' plates when my parents hosted a cocktail party." One of the darlings disappeared into his mouth.

Olivia was beginning to like Mr. Willard. If and when she needed an attorney, he'd be her first choice.

While Mr. Willard enjoyed his second olive-cheese ball, Olivia glanced over at Hugh and Tammy, still engrossed in one another. Good. Lowering her voice, Olivia asked, "I wonder if you would mind answering a question. It's about Clarisse's bequest to me."

Mr. Willard's narrow face assumed its legal-professional look, marred somewhat by a crumb of cheese crust at the corner of his mouth. Olivia couldn't keep her eyes away from it, which prompted him to wipe his mouth with a paper napkin. "I wondered if you might have questions," he said.

"Clarisse never mentioned her will to me."

"Clarisse and I were in agreement that the less said about wills, the better. They tend to complicate relationships among the living."

"Really, Clarisse said that? Then I wonder why . . ." Olivia checked the romantic duo again. Hugh and Tammy were whispering to each other, forehead to forehead.

"What are you wondering?" Mr. Willard asked. "Of course, in my profession there are secrets I must protect, but you've piqued my curiosity."

"Tammy and I were talking earlier, and she said Clarisse threatened to cut Hugh out of her will if he married her."

Mr. Willard's thin eyebrows bunched together. He picked up two more olive-cheese balls and tossed both in his mouth at once. How did the man remain so wraithlike?

Maybe he didn't eat at home. Olivia was sure she'd noticed a wedding ring, but she didn't want to be obvious. Presumably there was food in the larder.

"Your information disturbs me," Mr. Willard said finally. His hand hovered over the last smoked salmon canapé but came away empty. "Clarisse possessed enormous self-control, as I'm sure you know."

Olivia nodded her agreement.

"If she actually delivered such a threat, she must have been under a great deal of stress. I feel comfortable telling you that she spoke recently of writing a new will, but her stated intention was to divide the family businesses between her two sons. She always hoped the boys would work together, melding their differing skills, but Hugh and Edward . . ." Willard sighed and shook his head. "Oil and water, those two. Oil and water."

The Chamberlain's formal dining room table had been shortened as much as possible, but it still provided plenty of room for a party of twelve. Since they were only six that evening, Bertha had set the places to cluster everyone toward one end.

Tammy had other plans. "Let's see now," she said, one finger to her freshly lipsticked lips, "Bertha, you sit at the kitchen end, of course, so you can serve and clear."

Olivia lowered her head, lest her eye rolling become obvious. Not only was Bertha a beneficiary and therefore an equal part of the group, but she clearly struggled with her breathing as she brought in a soup tureen. Willard took the tureen from her and delivered it to the table.

Tammy scooped up a place setting. "I'll sit at the other end," she said as she laid out the plates and silverware.

"Hugh will sit on my right, of course. Mr. Willard, you are here, with Edward and Olivia across from you." She created a single, lonely space for Willard in the middle of one side. Edward and Olivia's seats, on the other side, were so far apart, they'd have to fire off paper napkin airplanes to communicate.

The group watched in silence as Tammy examined her arrangement and found it satisfactory. "Now I'm going to freshen up," she said, "and then we can begin."

The moment she disappeared from sight, Mr. Willard slid his plate and utensils back to their original position catercorner from Bertha, whose round face lit up. Simultaneously, Olivia and Edward scooped up their place settings and moved them closer to Bertha, across from Mr. Willard.

Four sets of eyes focused on Hugh, who stood at the other end of the table. He offered an expressive shrug and a grin that was both abashed and charming. "She isn't usually like this, you know," he said. "I mean, she's a take-charge woman, no doubt about it, but right now she is . . ." Hugh took a quick look over his shoulder. "It's been tough on her. She and my mother weren't the best of chums, and after what's happened, well . . . She isn't someone who can fake grief, and it makes her feel uncomfortable. When she's uncomfortable, she takes charge." His smile broadened to reveal perfect teeth. "When you think of it, that's a good way to handle a classroom full of first-graders."

Hugh's understanding of Tammy impressed Olivia to the point of speechlessness. She knew for a fact that Tammy didn't know herself as well as Hugh seemed to, and his description rang true. An ability to read people could be an advantage in the business world, especially for manipulating others.

Certainly Hugh had charmed everyone at the table

except his brother. Edward's expression, as he'd listened to Hugh, could best be described as stony.

Tammy reappeared beside Hugh and took in the table rearrangement. Olivia could almost hear everyone's breath halt. Hugh slid his arm around Tammy's waist, kissed her forehead, and said, "Sweetie, this has been a rough evening for all of us, and we wanted to sit closer together, you know, as friends and family. How about it? Shall we join them?"

Tammy gazed up into Hugh's face and said, "Okay. If it would make everyone more comfortable."

"Great, let's do it," Hugh said. As he and Tammy moved to two chairs across the table from Olivia, Hugh said, "The soup looks delicious, Bertha. You've outdone yourself, and that takes some doing."

Once Bertha had filled everyone's soup bowl, quiet descended, interrupted only by murmured appreciation or the occasional slurp. Olivia cherished the peaceful moments. She had a feeling they wouldn't last.

At the end of the soup course, Bertha left to fetch the main course and side dishes. Mr. Willard gathered up the soup bowls and nearly empty tureen and followed her into the kitchen. Olivia watched his back disappear with the uncomfortable sense that she was now on her own in enemy territory.

"Olivia, I feel as though I barely know you." Olivia's head snapped around in surprise as she realized it was Edward who had spoken. "Although now it appears you were my mother's best friend for the past year."

"I don't know about that," she said. "And do call me Livie. Everyone does."

"That is quite a large inheritance for someone who doesn't know if she was a best friend."

"My brother is inclined toward bluntness," Hugh said, in his smoothly modulated voice. "He doesn't actually know he is being rude. What Edward means is that Mother's bequest to you caught us all by surprise."

"What I meant was, you had to have known about it. Which makes me wonder how much influence you had over her and whether she was really of sound mind." Edward fixed her with a stare that felt like a mind probe. Intense— wasn't that the word she kept hearing when anyone tried to describe Edward?

"Really, Edward, is this necess—"

"Yes, Hugh, it is necessary. How do we know she didn't take advantage of Mother? Obviously, given how she died, she must have been slipping mentally."

"Edward!"

"Maybe you figured that out, Livie?"

"That's enough, Edward." This time the voice belonged to Tammy. The take-charge Tammy, not the love slave. "Livie is our guest, and I've known her practically my whole life. She would never, ever do such a thing." This was also the Tammy who earlier had accused Olivia of practically the same crime. Okay, Tammy had only questioned Clarisse's mental faculties, not Olivia's intentions. But it had felt the same.

Ignoring Tammy's attempt at intervention, Edward kept his razor eyes aimed at Olivia. It was time, she decided, to take the offensive. In a nice way, of course.

"It seems to me," Olivia said, "that if Clarisse had been slipping mentally, someone in the family would have noticed it before her death, not after. She taught me a great deal about business, and I can promise you that her mind was sharp and clear." Before she could think better of it, she added, "However, I did notice that she seemed worried

the last few days of her life. She certainly wasn't failing
intellectually, but something had upset her deeply. Any
idea what it was?"

"Livie," Hugh said, "I promise you, we had no idea
Mother was upset. Perhaps we should have been more observant, but—"

"You seem to be the only one who thought Mother was
upset," Edward said.

"No," Olivia said, "Bertha thought so, too."

"What did I think?" Bertha pushed the kitchen door
wide with her ample posterior to allow Mr. Willard to
deliver a large platter holding a generous roast, surrounded
by potatoes and carrots. Bertha followed him to the table,
carrying a gravy boat and a loaf of bread.

"We were discussing Mother's state of mind last week,
before her accident."

Trust Edward to be brutally blunt, Olivia thought.

"Oh, let's not talk about that," Bertha said. "Not tonight."

I n deference to Bertha's request, dinner conversation had
been minimal and dull. The meal itself was superb and
gave Olivia an unaccustomed longing to learn to cook. She
could bake nearly anything, but the cooking of wholesome
food had never interested her. Maybe she could take les-
sons. Or she could simply adopt Bertha.

Her taste buds might be delighted, but Olivia longed to
probe for more information. At least she had observed some
suggestive family dynamics, especially between Hugh and
Edward Chamberlain. However, she needed more if she
wanted to pin down the circumstances of Clarisse's death.

After several glasses of wine and many compliments
about her cooking, Bertha radiated content. "It's time for

dessert," she announced. "No, no, I'll bring it myself," she said as Mr. Willard pushed back his chair to help her. "I worked on this all day yesterday, as a special tribute to Ms. Clarisse, so I expect you all to have at least one."

Once Bertha was out of earshot, Tammy groaned and said, "I suppose I'll have to eat one, but I won't be able to fit into my new dresses."

"A bite is all it will take to keep Bertha happy. She understands how small you are," Hugh said, soothing but with an undercurrent of paternalism.

Bertha opened the kitchen door, once again by pushing with her backside. "Ta-da," she warbled as she turned around. With a happy, loopy grin, she presented a large platter holding a precarious pyramid of decorated cookies.

Olivia was too stunned to speak. There was silence all around, interrupted once by a titter that sounded like Tammy's voice. Mr. Willard frowned in the direction of the dining room ceiling, his thin fingers tapping a silent rhythm on the edge of the table. *He knows what happened to Sam Parnell*, Olivia thought, *but he wasn't expecting this to happen.*

Across the table, Hugh tried to look composed and benign but couldn't stop himself from shifting in his seat. Tammy's eyes grew wide at the sight of the cookies. She quickly dropped her head and began drawing light little circles on the tablecloth with one pink fingernail. Because everyone had faced toward the kitchen when Bertha emerged with dessert, Edward was behind Olivia. She couldn't see his face. He hadn't made a sound since Bertha's arrival.

Bertha lowered the heavy platter to the table. "Now, I know this isn't a traditional dessert, but Ms. Clarisse dearly loved her cookie cutters, so I borrowed a few. Not any of the valuable ones, of course. I found some recipes you must have given her, Livie. I used the one with the grated orange zest in the dough. Took me right back to my childhood, it did."

It was very clear to Olivia that Bertha had heard nothing about Sam Parnell. On the other hand, she was sure that Hugh, Edward, and Tammy had, and the presence of the cookies made them distinctly uncomfortable. Whether they were squirming because the cookies had been made by the very cutters that now belonged to Olivia or because one of them was being reminded of what they had done to Sam, not to mention Clarisse, Olivia couldn't be sure. But if one of the guests around the table—or two or even three of them—murdered Clarisse, she began to wonder if cookies and cookie cutters might be her best tools to catch a killer.

Chapter Fifteen

It was ten p.m. by the time Olivia returned from dinner at the Chamberlain home, and all she could think about was the soft, cool feel of her sheets as she slid into bed. There was Spunky, of course; he'd be whining to go out before she got her key in the lock. However, if he wanted a run, he was out of luck.

Olivia unlocked the front door and found the light on in the foyer. Maddie must have forgotten to turn it off when she left. They'd have to repeat that little talk about the energy bill. As she reached for the light switch, she noticed the corner of a piece of paper sticking out under the door to The Gingerbread House. She knelt down and managed to claw out a four-by-six recipe card, with The Gingerbread House imprinted at the top and a color drawing of a gingerbread woman holding a large spoon. In the space provided for a recipe, a scrawled note read, *If this note is here, so am I. Come in & talk to me. M.*

Maddie had an annoying habit of using recipe cards for everything, including notes to herself. She could go through a package in a week. Another waste of money. Then Olivia remembered: she didn't have to worry quite so much about money anymore. What a strange feeling.

Maybe bed could wait a bit. Spunky, however, could not. Olivia heard whimpering and scratching before she was halfway up the stairs. She opened her apartment door and squatted down quickly to intercept Spunky before he could race downstairs. Holding the squirming dog against her hip, she grabbed the leash she kept near the door. She hooked it on Spunky's collar and hurried back outside barely in time to avoid a puppy accident.

After Spunky finished his little tasks, he growled and strained at the leash.

"Sorry, kiddo," Olivia said. "Unlike you, I haven't been napping all evening. After what I've just been through, it would take a fire to get me to run with you."

Spunky began to plead in his pathetic puppy way. As Olivia reached to pick him up, he peered toward a cluster of three arborvitae at the edge of Olivia's property. His small body went rigid, ears perked up and nose quivering.

Olivia knew this stance. Spunky had heard a noise he didn't like. Probably nothing more than a bold bunny. On the other hand . . . Olivia's ears were not as acute as Spunky's, but when she held her breath, she did hear something. A snapping sound, or maybe a click. Could be anything. Squirrels made all sorts of odd noises when they were defending their territory.

Spunky decided the threat warranted action. He yapped with the fierceness of a much larger creature and pulled at his leash so hard Olivia worried his little neck would snap. She grabbed the puppy around the middle and held his squirming body against her stomach while she fumbled with the front door, thanking providence that she'd chosen to live in a well-lit area of town.

Olivia got the door open and slipped inside. She flipped the dead bolt, turned around, and rested against the door to catch her breath. Spunky stopped yapping at once and wiggled to free himself from his mistress's death grip.

The door to The Gingerbread House opened. "Don't tell me," Maddie's ironic voice said. "The zombies are at the door, and you barely escaped."

Half an hour and a hot cocoa later, Olivia had described her dining experience in detail to Maddie. For his valor in the face of danger, whether real or imagined, Spunky was allowed to stay with them in the store kitchen. He had spent the first twenty minutes sniffing every inch and attempting to taste the sugar canister, the floor, and the lemon soap at the sink. Finally, he flopped down on a towel Olivia had put out for him. In moments, he was out.

"Okay, my turn," Maddie said. She gathered a stack of notes—written on blank recipe cards, of course—that she'd left on the small desk holding Olivia's laptop. "My evening wasn't as fraught with human drama as yours, but I found a few suggestive tidbits. I'm sure a private detective could ferret out a lot more. I found annual reports online fairly easily, which surprised me because Chamberlain Enterprises isn't answerable to stockholders."

"Clarisse was a stickler about being open and above-board," Olivia said. "She always said that when the product has to do with health, trust is crucial. However, you won't find any trade secrets in those reports."

"Let's hope trade secrets won't be important in this instance," Maddie said. "So first, this is a list of the businesses owned by the Chamberlain family. I'm sure they are familiar to you, but I never had occasion to learn what they all are." She laid one recipe card in front of Olivia, who nodded as she read the list.

"Do you notice anything about that list?" Maddie asked.

Olivia read through it again and it came to her. "Most of them have something to do with health care. The family's first company, and their biggest by far, is Chamberlain Medical Supplies. Clarisse told me that when Hugh and Edward reached their teen years, Martin started them out as stock boys in that company. They worked in the warehouse, they learned to fill orders, handle problems with customers, everything."

Maddie snatched the list out of Olivia's hand. "Even better," she said, "the Chamberlains own a walk-in clinic in Chatterley Heights, plus several drugstores here and in various nearby towns, and a pharmacy clinic that delivers medications to shut-ins. Hugh and Edward would definitely know their poisons. They could easily have slipped Clarisse some sleeping pills in a higher dosage than her usual prescription, for example. Or injected some sort of tasteless poison into our cookies before leaving them for Sam. Or maybe they put something in the cookies that would interact with his insulin?"

Maddie paused in her usual dramatic fashion. "You haven't yet heard my truly cool discovery, my coup d'état."

"I think you mean pièce de résistance," Olivia said. "Coup d'état means overthrow of the state."

"Language nerd." Maddie sorted through her recipe-card notes, selected one, and held it to her chest. "Tell me, did you ever wonder how Tammy Deacons and Hugh

Chamberlain first met? Hugh is five years older than we are, so he was a year out of high school before Tammy even started. Their families certainly ran in different circles, too."

"I don't remember Tammy mentioning to me how she met Hugh. It was after I left town, that's all I know."

Olivia reached for the recipe card, but Maddie twisted away.

"I will explain all," Maddie said. "As you may be aware, Tammy attended a small college nobody ever heard of in the DC area, where she got her elementary school teaching degree. She spent summers back in Chatterley Heights, where she worked at Chamberlain Drugs. During the first summer, none other than Hugh Chamberlain was her supervisor. I expect he gave her some hands-on training."

"That doesn't mean she learned anything about drugs or poisons," Olivia said. "She was probably a salesclerk."

"But wait! There's more!" Maddie's emerald eyes sparkled, and her hair had twined into corkscrews.

"Speaking of medications," Olivia said, "you might want to consider something for that incipient bipolar disorder."

"You're just jealous," Maddie said. "Tammy Deacons wanted to stay in town, presumably because she'd met the love of her life, but she couldn't find a teaching job right away. So she trained as a pharmacy assistant and kept working at Chamberlain Drugs. Ha! Now tell me she wouldn't have learned anything about drugs."

Olivia digested Maddie's information and found herself growing more and more puzzled. "Maddie, this is a wonderful find, and I take back every snide comment I've said this evening, but really, how on earth did you dig up all this fairly personal background information in such a short time?"

Maddie gave her a sheepish look. "I confess to a love-hate relationship with Internet social networks. It occurred to me that Tammy might be on Facebook, so I checked, and she is. You wouldn't believe the amount of personal information people reveal on those sites, and Tammy is not one to hold back."

"Wait a minute," Olivia said. "Only in an alternate universe would you and Tammy be Facebook friends. How did you gain access to her page?"

With a light laugh, which to Olivia sounded nervous, Maddie said, "Interesting story, actually. You're right, never in a gadjillion years would Tammy 'friend' me, or me her. However, I figured she would have invited you, her dear childhood buddy, to be her friend."

"I don't remember getting such an invitation."

"Oh, Livie, I know how you are about emails. If it isn't about business or cookie cutters, it goes through your eyes and out the back of your head. So I checked back aways, and there it was, more than six months ago, an unanswered email from Tammy inviting you to be her Facebook friend."

"You . . . you checked my email? You *hacked into my email?* How could you do that?"

"It was easy, really. FYI, don't use pet names for passwords."

Olivia heard a choking sound come from her own throat. She breathed in deeply, then said, "What I meant was, how could you do that to *me*?"

"Desperate times, Livie, desperate times. And look how fruitful it turned out to be." Maddie bit the bottom of her lip. "Am I unfriended?"

Olivia heaved a giant sigh. "If you ever do anything like that—"

"I won't, I promise."

"At least ask first. Now, if I don't get some sleep, you'll be alone at the store tomorrow."

"Understood. Except . . ." Maddie's teeth captured her lip again.

"What?"

"You might want to check your email before you lose consciousness. Del wants to talk to you tomorrow. He says he left messages on your cell and your home phone. He's willing to come to the store, but it's important that he talk to you."

"Tell you what," Olivia said, dragging her unwilling body out of her chair. "For penance, you can email him from my account. Tell him to come midmorning. Maybe I can get rid of him before the lunchtime shoppers start showing up."

"Absolutely," Maddie said.

Olivia lifted Spunky, who melted into her arms. "Do it tonight. First thing tomorrow, I change all my passwords. I'm thinking some obscure phrases from Proust, in the original French. Good luck with that."

Chapter Sixteen

Olivia's hope for a quiet Tuesday, the beginning of her workweek, evaporated the moment she opened The Gingerbread House for business at nine a.m. A small group of her local regulars had already gathered on the store's lawn, and all the prime parking spaces contained cars she recognized as belonging to antique dealers and collectors from out of town. Olivia forged a welcoming smile as she held open the front door.

Before the dealers and collectors could reach the store entrance, Olivia slipped past her customers, avoiding eye contact, and escaped to the kitchen. At the worktable, Maddie was piling decorated cookies on a platter. Behind her, the Mr. Coffee spat out its second pot of the morning. The kitchen door slapped shut behind Olivia, and Maddie looked up. Her smile of greeting melted when she saw the look on Olivia's face.

"You told Lucas, didn't you? Maddie, how could you?"

Olivia began to pace around the kitchen. "The store is filling up with dealers and collectors and plain old busybodies." She raked her fingers through her hair, which threw her off balance enough to bump into the table.

"Livie, take a deep breath and stand still. You're bruising yourself and, more important, ruining your hair." Maddie took a cookie from the platter and held it out to Olivia as she paced past. When Olivia waved it away, Maddie said, "Look, if you think I told Lucas anything about your inheritance, you are wrong. I said not one word about you last night. In fact, I haven't even talked to Lucas since our quick dinner. It wasn't easy to get away last night, you know. Lucas wanted me to come over and watch a DVD with him. Something about football bloopers, sounded like fun, but no, I spent the whole evening doing your bidding and awaiting your arrival. I had to fudge and say I was way behind on paying invoices so he wouldn't think I was blowing him off. I knew he'd understand if it was business."

Olivia heard the hurt in Maddie's voice. "Then how . . . ?"

"How do you think?" Maddie's arched eyebrows and clear disgust said it all.

"Are you saying . . . *Tammy?*"

Maddie nodded. "Yep, I'm saying Tammy. Mind you, it could have been anyone who was there last night, but really, does anyone else fit the bill? Tammy is the one who spills huge amounts of personal information all over the Internet. She probably checks her Facebook account first thing every morning and last thing before bed. She probably spilled the whole story as soon as she got home last night. Unless she stayed over, in which case she'd use Hugh's computer."

The din beyond the kitchen door had reached an insistent level. "I need to get out there," Olivia said, nodding her head toward the sales area. "We have a business to run."

"We do, but let me handle it for a while," Maddie said. She whipped off her apron and lifted the platter of cookies. "You need to figure out how to answer the questions you'll be getting. Besides, no one will buy anything if you're there. I suggest you check Tammy's Facebook page and see exactly what deeply private thoughts she has shared with her online nearest and dearest."

"How do I . . . ?"

"I'll set it up for you," Maddie said. She slid the plates on the kitchen table. "Come over here and watch me." She sat down and opened the computer lid. Her fingers flew across the keys, leaving Olivia confused. "Play around with it," Maddie said. "I'm out of here."

As she settled at the computer, Olivia felt a surge of resentment. She wanted her life back. She wanted to nestle in the warm, gingerbread world of cookie cutters and decorated cookies and making a living with her best friend. But here she was, hiding from customers and hunched over a Facebook page that had invaded her privacy.

Tammy's latest most recent entry had been posted at one o'clock that morning:

You will not believe what happened at the will reading. Mostly it was what we expected, Hugh and Edward got most of their mom's estate, split in half, and so on. But then we found out their mom had added an extra part that said Olivia Greyson—dear friend Livie—got $150,000 AND Clarisse's whole huge collection of antique cookie cutters!! She's supposed to use the money for her cookie-cutter store here in town, The Gingerbread House. (A little plug for your store, Livie.)

Of course, Livie thought, this entry was written after Tammy discovered Olivia had "accepted" her Facebook invitation, which would explain the gushing.

A number of responses had been posted throughout the night and into the morning. Olivia began to read:

Lucky lady. She sure knows how to pick her friends.

Yeah, rich ones who are about to kick off.

Makes you wonder, doesn't it?

What about that postal carrier? Wasn't he poisoned by her cookies?

What do you really know about her, anyway? She could be a serial killer.

At that point, Olivia signed off and snapped her computer shut. Her hand pressed hard on the laptop lid as if it might fly open and spew out more accusations against her. Not that it mattered; the damage was done.

There was only one path through this quagmire. Clarisse's killer and Sam's attacker—Olivia was convinced they were one and the same—had to be identified and arrested as soon as possible. Somehow she had to convince Sheriff Del. If she couldn't do so, she and Maddie would have to find the killer themselves, but it would be so much easier if Del would cooperate. Although he would undoubtedly order her to stay out of it, which she couldn't do.

Olivia wanted to escape out the back and into the alley, but instead she stepped into the store. The Gingerbread House had taken second place for too long, and Maddie needed help. The sales floor teemed with customers.

Maybe they were there for the wrong reasons, but publicity sometimes took a strange form.

Maddie stood in front of her, behind the sales counter, moving at warp speed as she rang up and bagged sales. As Olivia moved into the room, she heard the volume of chatter lower, then a whoosh as customers tried to reach her first. She recognized a few Chatterley Heights residents, as well as several antiques dealers and cookie-cutter collectors. At least half the faces were unfamiliar.

A tall, thin woman of about thirty, wearing a tight sweater, skinny jeans, and combat boots reached Olivia first. She stuck out her hand, and said, "Ms. Greyson? I'm Anita Rambert, representing the Rambert Antiques Mall. We've never met, but perhaps you've heard of me?"

Olivia had heard of her, through Maddie, who had made the rounds of antiques malls when they'd first opened The Gingerbread House. Maddie had described Anita Rambert as a barracuda cookie cutter, all sharp angles and hungry eyes. When she smiled, Olivia noticed her incisors were on the pointy side.

"I'll get right to the point," Ms. Rambert said. "I'll take the Chamberlain collection off your hands for a fair price, in cash. I'll need to see a complete listing of the cutters, of course, and verification of their authenticity."

"That's an interesting offer," Olivia said, "but at this early stage, I'm not yet considering my—"

"You won't get a better one, I assure you. I know all the players in the cutter world, and not one of them has sufficient cash on hand to buy the Chamberlain collection, at least from what I've heard about it."

Ms. Rambert had impenetrable eyes that matched the sleek blue-black hair she wore tied back at the nape of her neck. She possessed all the ingredients for exotic beauty, but somehow they formed a forbidding presence.

Since she was almost the same height as Ms. Rambert, Olivia looked straight into those eyes and asked, "Where did you hear about the collection?"

Ms. Rambert's eyebrows lifted in a startled expression. "On the Internet, of course. It's tough to keep information about a collection secret, unless the collector is a complete hermit. Unlike some art collectors, cookie-cutter collectors love to share. Really, Ms. Greyson, I'd expect you to know that already."

"Call me Livie," Olivia said, pasting a smile across her face.

Olivia glanced over Ms. Rambert's shoulder to see Maddie waving at her. When they made eye contact, Maddie, who was in the middle of unpacking an upscale professional mixer to show two customers, mouthed, "Help," and pointed toward the register. Six customers, their arms full of potential purchases, fidgeted and peered around the store looking for help. Olivia excused herself from Ms. Rambert and hurried to the sales counter.

Heather Irwin, the new, fresh-out-of-college librarian for the Chatterley Heights Public Library, stood at the front of the line clutching a dozen individual cookie cutters in her small hands. With evident relief, she dumped them on the counter. While Olivia removed tags from the cutters and rang up the charges, Heather leaned forward and said, "It's so exciting about you inheriting Ms. Chamberlain's whole antique cookie-cutter collection. I've heard it's amazing. Would you consider letting the library host an exhibit? It would be great publicity for The Gingerbread House, after all, and maybe more people would think about supporting the library." Heather's sweet, young voice tightened in frustration when she mentioned support for the library.

"We'll see," Olivia said. "I honestly haven't had time to take it all in."

"Really? You mean you didn't know that Ms. Chamberlain was leaving her—?"

A male voice from the end of the ever-lengthening line called out, "Could we save the chat for later? Some of us have work to get back to." *Must be a dealer*, Olivia thought. She wouldn't be surprised if he'd come for the same reason as Anita Rambert—to make an offer for Clarisse's collection.

Another pile of cookie cutters clattered onto the sales counter. Olivia noticed an animal theme, specifically fish, bones, cats, dogs, rabbits, and one lone ferret. "I decided to leave the pony until later," said a round-faced young woman. "We're hoping to get some land outside of town so we can expand."

"Gwen," Olivia said with genuine pleasure. Gwen Tucker and her husband Herbie ran the local no-kill animal shelter, Chatterley's Paws. They were responsible for leading Olivia to the Yorkie rescue website where she'd found Spunky. "I didn't know you were interested in cookie cutters."

"I didn't, either," Gwen said. "But then I got this idea for making animal treats and decorated cookies as a way to tempt people to come see the animals. If their kids are with them, so much the better. How many parents could say no to bringing home a cat or a dog after watching their kid feed it a treat?"

"Especially parents who are nibbling on decorated cookies themselves," Olivia said as she wrapped the cutters in tissue paper and slid them into a bag.

"Exactly! I figure this is the perfect time to try out my idea, now that everybody in town is talking about cookies and cookie cutters. What an incredible stroke of luck that you should inherit Ms. Chamberlain's collection. If it contains any animal figures, would you mind if Herbie and I took pictures of them to post around the shelter? Cookie cutters are such homey things, aren't they? We thought the pictures and the cookies and treats would put people right in the mood to complete their families with a pet or two."

Gwen's request sent Olivia's mood on another trip down the slide. Everyone seemed so eager to cash in on Clarisse's death, and Olivia's own "stroke of luck" had happened for the same reason. She felt a sudden urge to take a shower, pack up the car, and move with Spunky to an undisclosed location.

Avoiding eye contact, Olivia worked through the line of customers in silence. If anyone started to ask a question, she pretended not to hear. By two o'clock, The Gingerbread House began to empty as cars and vans carted off four or five passengers at a time, hoping to beat the worst of the Baltimore and DC rush hours.

With only a few stragglers left in the store, Olivia gestured to Maddie that she was taking a stack of receipts into the kitchen. Once the door closed behind her, Olivia dropped the receipts in a heap on the table, sank into a chair, and let her forehead drop onto her folded arms.

Clarisse's death and Olivia's growing conviction it was murder, Sam's hints about a grandchild, Sam's possible poisoning, the inheritance from Clarisse—too much had been happening, much too fast. And now she was smack dab in the middle of the mess and well on her way to joining the suspects list.

Olivia took Spunky on a quick run in the alley behind The Gingerbread House, then sped through the receipts. Not a bad take, and the day hadn't ended. Having finished business, she began to search the Internet for references to the Chamberlain cookie-cutter collection.

When she heard the kitchen door open and close behind her, Olivia called over her shoulder. "Hey Maddie, come here and see what I've found."

"Livie, we need to talk." The voice did not belong to Maddie.

"Del!" Guided by instinct, Olivia clicked closed the website she'd found, lowered the computer lid, and twisted around in her seat. "You surprised me. I was expecting . . ."

Del wasn't his usual low-key self, and Olivia felt her muscles tighten. "What's up?" She tried to keep her voice light and casual. As Del stepped around the corner of the kitchen table, she noticed he was carrying a rolled-up newspaper. "Spunky has more or less grasped the whole housebreaking thing, if that's what you've brought the paper for." Okay, that was pathetic. She instructed her mouth to stay shut.

Del unrolled the newspaper and held it out for her to see. "Did you know about this?"

Olivia recognized the front page of the local paper, *The Weekly Chatter*, which usually came out every Wednesday.

"Where did you get this?" she asked. "It's only Tuesday."

"It's late on Tuesday, and I'm the Sheriff. Binnie always drops off an advance copy."

"That's mighty cooperative," Olivia said, "for a newspaper editor."

Del shrugged and shifted his gaze toward the cupboards. "Binnie used to babysit me when I was a kid."

Olivia stifled an urge to laugh, but her amusement dissipated when she read the banner, "Chamberlain Death Suspicious." She yanked the paper from Del's hand. A photo accompanying the article showed Olivia dressed in the black pants and gray sweater she'd worn to the will reading.

She was standing next to her Valiant, talking with a man whose back was to the camera. The photo caption read, *"Olivia Greyson, heir to fortune, consults with her lawyer."*

"What the . . . ?" Olivia muttered. "*My* lawyer? Heir to fortune?"

Del said nothing. He pulled a kitchen chair near her and sat down, his legs crossed in a casual way, one ankle resting on the opposite knee. Olivia's peripheral vision registered the rapid wiggling of his left foot.

According to the byline, Binnie Sloan wrote the piece and Nedra Sloan was credited with the photos. Dread lay like a waterlogged tennis ball in Olivia's stomach as she forced herself to begin reading the article. Binnie's take on her surprise inheritance appeared to depend on comments from several "confidential sources," who offered quotes such as:

Ms. Chamberlain was a healthy, successful woman with a ton of money and a couple grown sons under her thumb.

It's the same old story, an elderly woman gets taken in by a young con artist and leaves her a bundle, but the con artist gets impatient because the old lady won't die fast enough.

That Greyson woman, she runs this little store with cookie cutters, and all of a sudden she's inherited five million dollars and another million in antique cookie cutters? All I can say is, where there's smoke, there's fire.

Olivia heard a high-pitched whimpering sound and realized it had erupted from her own throat. The newspaper dropped on her lap. She glanced over at Del, who watched her with a thoughtful expression, as if he wasn't sure what her reaction meant.

"Del, I check my phone messages and emails all the time, and Binnie never even tried to interview me."

"There's more," he said. "Go to page five."

With a deep groan, Olivia did so. She found two more photos. The first showed her with Spunky in the store's side yard. That explained the disturbing clicks they'd heard. The caption read," Heiress Olivia Greyson enjoys a break."

In the second photo, Bertha stared at the camera, her eyes so wide the whites encircled her pupils. The article continued with a quote from Bertha: "*I can't believe Ms. Olivia would hurt her. Why, Ms. Clarisse treated her like a daughter.*" Olivia groaned again. She could hear Bertha saying those words in all innocence, but written down they could be read as conveying shock.

It came as no surprise that the attorney Mr. Willard, along with Hugh and Edward Chamberlain, had refused to comment. Tammy Deacons was not mentioned. Either she wasn't there at the time of the so-called interviews, or she was one of the "confidential sources."

Olivia sprang out of her chair and slapped the newspaper down in front of Del. It made a satisfying thwap, but Del barely blinked.

"When you first barged in here, you demanded to know if I knew about 'this.' If you think I'd have anything to gain from this kind of exposure, you're nuts." Olivia hauled herself up onto the table so she could look down at him.

Del uncrossed his legs and sat up straighter. "By 'this,' I meant the bequest Clarisse made to you. And by the way, I'm aware it wasn't five million dollars plus a million in antique cookie cutters."

"How do you know?"

"I called the Chamberlain house and asked. Apparently, I have more influence than the editor of *The Weekly Chatter,* because Edward answered the phone and assured me you'd received only one hundred fifty thousand dollars and a collection estimated to be worth about thirty thousand."

"It won't make much of a dent in his inheritance, or Hugh's," Olivia said. "Although it sounds huge to me, and it might look like a good motive for murder."

"It probably would."

"At any rate, the answer to your question is a definite no. I had no hint that Clarisse planned to leave me anything at all. When Mr. Willard called to tell me she had made a bequest to me, I assumed it would amount to a few of her favorite cookie cutters, the ones with sentimental value. I was stunned when Mr. Willard read the codicil. That's why we were talking outside afterwards, when that photo was taken. He assured me that Clarisse had wanted the bequest kept secret. You can ask him, if you don't believe me."

"I already have," Del said with a faint but definite smile. "However, he couldn't know if you'd found out from another source. I needed to hear it from you."

He didn't add that he now believed her, and she didn't ask.

According to the clock over the sink, it was five. Maddie would be straightening up the chaos left behind by a crowd of excited customers. On the one hand, Olivia wanted Del to leave so she and Maddie could get back to their own investigation. On the other hand, maybe this wretched newspaper article had opened Del's mind a bit.

"Del, remember that conversation we had at the café right after Clarisse's death?"

Del nodded.

"You seemed so certain it was an accident. In fact, you wouldn't even talk about the possibility of suicide. I couldn't believe it had been either one, but the possibility of murder didn't occur to me then. Now it has. I've thought for some time that Clarisse was murdered, and now I'm convinced she was. Only I don't know by whom."

Del leaned forward, elbows on knees, and stared at the kitchen floor for what felt to Olivia like an hour. Anyway, it was long enough for her to move through a string of emotions from intense anxiety to curiosity to embarrassment that the floor hadn't been swept in a week.

Finally, he looked up at her and asked, "What makes you so sure?"

She should have known he'd ask her that question. How could she be convincing without involving anyone else?

"And before you tell me," Del said, "let me add that I already know Cody shared his so-called crime scene photos with you. We had a serious discussion about that."

"Oh dear," Olivia said, cringing. "I hoped I wouldn't get him into trouble, but you were so insistent it wasn't a crime, you can't really blame him. Blame me, if you want, but not Cody. He's serious about his job, and I, for one, think he's on to something."

"So do I," Del said.

"You do? Really? When did . . . I mean, how . . . ?"

"Give me some credit, Livie. I realize television mystery series present small-town sheriffs as buffoons or bullies, but most of us speak in complete sentences and take pride in our jobs."

"Um, I—"

"Furthermore, I am not required to tell you, at any time, what I might know or suspect in a certain case. It makes my job a lot harder when private citizens start asking dangerous questions and putting themselves in harm's way because they think they are smarter than I am."

"Wait a minute, I never, ever thought I was smarter—"

"I'm not finished, Livie. I'm saying this because I care about you."

"Well, you have a strange way of—"

Del sprang from his chair and grabbed Olivia by the shoulders. He looked into her eyes with an intensity that sent a distracting shiver through her.

Del released her as the kitchen door opened.

"I'll finish closing up," Maddie said quietly, her eyes darting from Del to Olivia. "Then I'll be heading on home." The door clicked shut.

Del slid back onto his chair. "Now having said all that, let me add that I think you are intelligent, insightful, and I want to hear everything you, and I presume Maddie, have discovered."

An hour later, Olivia had shown Del the financial information Maddie had gathered, the websites they'd searched, and Tammy's notorious Facebook page. She told him that Sam Parnell delivered to Clarisse a letter he thought was from a private detective, and she urged him to connect the attack on Sam with that letter.

However, as she prepared to tell Del about the letters from Faith and Clarisse, his cell rang. He turned his back on her and answered. All she heard was, "I'll be right there." He turned around and said, "I've got to take care of something."

Del slid an arm in his uniform jacket sleeve. "I want you to delete those photos of the scene." When Olivia opened her mouth to protest, he added, "Not because I'm the sheriff and I think you shouldn't have them. Although you shouldn't. I don't think it's safe for you to have them."

Del picked up his hat and reached for the alley door. In a lighter tone, he said, "I'd count it as a personal favor if you wouldn't go all Miss Marple on me."

"You needn't worry," Olivia said.

With a nod, Del opened the door.

"I'm really more the Tuppence Beresford type."

"Really? The young Tuppence or the older one?"

Before Olivia could draw in enough breath for a comeback, Del was gone.

Chapter Seventeen

If Wednesday morning dawned clear and sweet with the scent of lilacs, Olivia Greyson didn't notice. She barely noticed Spunky's insistent tug on his leash, indicating his longing for a run. Lost in her own thoughts, she ran on automatic pilot back and forth along the alley behind The Gingerbread House. She wasn't eager to show her face outside the store. Not yet, anyway.

"Come on, Spunks," Olivia said as she nestled the squirming dog under her arm. "I'll make it up to you, I promise. Tell you what, you were so good yesterday, why don't you stay with Maddie and me today in the kitchen? In fact, I'll move your spare bed and bowls down there. You have to promise to stay in the kitchen, though." *Sure, that'll happen.* At least if he escaped into the store, customers would make a fuss over him, which in turn would delay him long enough to ensure his recapture.

It was seven thirty a.m. when Olivia, with Spunky on a

leash, let herself into The Gingerbread House, carrying a dog bed and water bowls, food, treats, and a few toys. She opened the door with the two fingers that weren't already holding on to dog paraphernalia. With a whimper, Spunky whipped the leash from her other hand and bounded into the store.

"Spunky!"

"It's okay, Livie, I heard you coming. I've captured the little scoundrel."

"Maddie?" Olivia scooted inside and slammed the door with her rear end.

"Nice moves," Maddie said.

"What are you doing here so early? Not that I'm complaining. We have work to do." Olivia deposited the dog food and treats in the kitchen. Choosing the corner farthest from both doors, she set up Spunky's second home.

"Couldn't sleep," Maddie said. She released her hold on Spunky, who raced around the kitchen in frantic circles, pausing now and then for a quick sniff. "After you called last night and told me about your conversation with Del— and by the way, I saw actual sparks in the air—anyway, I was too wired to sleep for long. So here I am, my skills and my laptop at your disposal." She pointed to a PC on the worktable.

"Mine isn't good enough for you?"

Maddie shrugged. "I figured you'd changed all your passwords. I can't read French, and I doubt I could read Proust even in English translation. Also, I brought along my printer, and it would take time to get it to talk to your little MacBook thingie."

"Great," Olivia said. "We can both do some searching before the store opens and take turns when business is slow."

Maddie wrapped her foot around a chair leg and dragged it to the table. While her computer booted up, she said, "By the way, I've made an executive decision. I realize business was fabulous yesterday, and far be it from me to quell such success, but I sent an email to everyone on our mailing list announcing that, at the current time, the Chamberlain antique cookie-cutter collection is not for sale. I asked everyone to hold their enquiries until further notice."

"Might not work, but it's worth a shot," Olivia opened her laptop and pressed the start button. "My first order of business is to hunt down some background information on the editor of *The Weekly Chatter*, Ms. Binnie Sloan. I intend to have a meaningful chat with that woman. I want to know her sources, if any, even if I have to—"

"Don't say it," Maddie said. "I might be called upon to testify under oath."

Olivia's opportunity to talk with Binnie Sloan came sooner and more easily than she'd anticipated. Twenty minutes after The Gingerbread House opened, Maddie poked her head into the kitchen and said, "Binnie Sloan is here. She wants to talk to you. What should I say?"

"Tell her I'll be out in a minute."

"Will do."

Olivia had skimmed the editor's biography and a few of her most recent articles in *The Weekly Chatter*, all of which she'd found on the newspaper's website. Her search had left her confused about Binnie. Her official photo showed a plump, middle-aged woman with large round glasses, a friendly smile, and a gap between her front teeth. Her straight, short graying hair looked unstyled, and she wore a flannel shirt for a formal photo.

Her newspaper articles, all written in a conversational style, covered town issues ranging from the need to clean bird poop off the town founder's statue to the underrepresentation of chocolate at the last PTA bake sale. Binnie Sloan didn't seem the type to take on a controversial topic. Or perhaps Olivia's predicament had offered Binnie her first opportunity to dig her teeth into a story.

Olivia realized she'd spent much of her time the past year working on and in The Gingerbread House, discussing business with Clarisse Chamberlain, or hanging around with Maddie. She knew about all the bake sales her best friend had held while she was in Baltimore and how Maddie worked hard to make ends meet while still doing what she loved. But Olivia realized she'd lost touch with her home town. She vowed to get to know Chatterley Heights much better in the coming year.

However, first things first. She entered the store and spotted Maddie helping a customer. With a tilt of her head, Maddie pointed toward the antiques cabinet. Binnie stood in front of the glassed-in display, moving her head slowly as she examined each row of cookie cutters. Olivia joined her.

"Ms. Sloan? I'm Olivia Greyson. Everyone calls me Livie, and I hope you will, too." She tried for her best warm-yet-confident smile, though the clenched teeth weren't helping. At first glance, Binnie Sloan looked like everyone's grandmother, but her article had revealed another side.

"Your store is marvelous," Binnie said. "I can't believe I haven't come in before now—I really should have, it was remiss of me. I love these old cookie cutters. They remind me so much of my grandmother. Oh, she made the most wonderful cookies. Everyone calls me Binnie, by the way." She focused pale blue eyes on Olivia's face.

"Ms. Sloa—Binnie. About your article," Olivia said. "I have to say, I wasn't thrilled by it." This was an understatement of gigantic proportions, but if she wanted a retraction, she'd better keep her temper.

"Oh, I'm so sorry you feel that way. Usually folks around here love to see their names in the paper, but, of course, you lived in the city for so many years." Binnie's gaze wandered around the store.

"You never talked to me to find out the truth. That's . . . that's unprofessional."

With a dismissive wave of her hand, Binnie said, "We're not trying to be the New York Times."

"Well, you did practically accuse me of murder without even checking in with me. I think most folks might find that upsetting."

Binnie offered a wide, gap-toothed smile. "Really? Based on the popularity of all those reality shows, I believe people crave attention, even when it brings public humiliation." She shrugged. "Anyway, there's no such thing as bad publicity anymore. Why, I peeked in your store yesterday, and it was packed with customers! So really, you have to admit my article was good for your business."

Binnie looked so pleased with herself. Apparently, she expected Olivia to be gushing with gratitude, not whining about her threatened reputation and her silly privacy.

Olivia opened her mouth and closed it again. Was there any point in trying to reason with Binnie Sloan? She was so agreeable, so sure of herself, and so not of the planet earth.

Suppressing a sigh of frustration, Olivia said, "Look, Binnie, I know you're only doing your job, but I have two requests. These may not seem important to you, but I would truly appreciate your cooperation. First, print a retraction in next week's paper making it clear that the quotes you printed about me were inaccurate and not from knowledge-able sources. And second, stop taking photos of me with-out my permission. Especially on my own property."

Binnie's eyebrows shot up in astonishment. "Oh, I'm sure Ned wasn't on your property, if that's what you're so upset about. I specifically instructed her to stay in the arborvitae, which are actually on your neighbor's property. I looked up the plat map to be sure."

"Ned?"

"Nedra, but she likes to be called Ned. She's my assis-tant. Well, really my niece, my brother's daughter, but also my new assistant. Fresh out of journalism school and full of energy. Well, it was actually a correspondence course online, but they said she was the best student they'd ever had."

"Uh—"

"I'm glad we've cleared all that up. Now, I'm here to ask you a couple questions for next week's issue. You'd be amazed how much interest you've stirred up in this quiet little town. Everyone wants to know everything about you, but of course I have space limitations, so I'll stick to the most important issues. First and foremost, what do you plan to do with your five-million-dollar inheritance and Clarisse Chamberlain's million-dollar antique cookie-cutter collection?" Binnie dug into one of the many pockets of her safari jacket and extracted a handheld tape recorder with a cracked plastic cover. "Speak into this, dear," she said in that benign and terrifying voice.

Olivia's vocal chords froze, along with her blood. She would have welcomed a customer about then, but they must have worn themselves out the day before. Olivia struggled to form a comment.

"Really, Livie, it can't be that difficult," Binnie said. "You must be fantasizing about how to spend all that money. Will you sell the store and travel around the world? Buy a villa in Italy?"

To her right, Olivia heard a slight click, followed by a creaking sound. She turned to see the kitchen door edge open and a furry little head pop through. When he spotted Olivia, Spunky yapped with joy. He cleared the entrance a moment before Maddie's arms reached out to capture him.

Spunky escaped to the cookbook nook, from which came the thumping sound of books hitting the floor, followed by the clattering crash of metal pans and cooking utensils. Olivia ran toward the nook, arriving as Spunky bolted through the entryway and back into the main part of the store.

Binnie remained near the antiques cabinet, a bland smile on her face. She was holding her tape recorder toward the sales area to record the sounds of destruction. Spunky paused when he saw her. Ever the curious puppy, he tilted his head up toward the tape recorder. Olivia recognized the stance. He thought Binnie was offering him a treat or a toy.

"Binnie, put that down," Olivia yelled. Binnie winked at her. A smug wink.

Spunky raced toward Binnie, with Olivia and Maddie in pursuit. Olivia reached out, grabbed the end of his tail. It slipped through her fingers.

To avoid capture, Spunky leaped onto a table, landing in the midst of an elaborate display of farm animal cookie cutters. The cutters sprayed out in various directions, some of them flying at Binnie. Her jaw dropped, along with her tape recorder, which hit the floor and cracked open.

Spunky lost traction on the slick table, skidded toward the edge, and landed in Olivia's waiting arms. She held him firmly and rubbed the fur on his neck to calm him. As he relaxed in her grip, she whispered soothing words in his ear. Something about a week of extra treats for a job well done.

By midafternoon, The Gingerbread House had received only half a dozen customers. Olivia worried that fallout from *The Weekly Chatter* article had begun to accrue.

"Stop fussing," Maddie said when she emerged from the kitchen to chat with Olivia on the sales floor. "Yesterday was a lucrative fluke. It's inevitable things would quiet down."

"I guess."

"Anyway, since there's no one here right now, I'll catch you up on what I've found out." Maddie hiked herself onto a sturdy display ledge. "Okay, the first thing I did was call my friend Kate—she's a nurse at Montgomery General in Clarksville, where Sam Parnell is. Kate sneaked a peek at his file and called back from her car during her break."

"I can't believe she did that for you," Olivia said.

"What can I say, I'm adored by one and all." Maddie lifted her chin, crossed her jeans-clad legs, and fluffed up her mass of red curls from behind. "Anyway," she said, dropping her pose, "I promised to set her up with Lucas's cousin, who is almost as lovable and yummy as Lucas. Now, stop interrupting. Here's the scoop: Sam's blood glucose level was way off, but there was no evidence of any poison in his system. Kate said they can't measure insulin in the body. Kate didn't see any notes in the file about tests on the cookie crumbs from the bag. We'd have to hack into—"

"No hacking, I beg of you," Olivia said. "If there was no poison in Sam, there probably wasn't any in the cookies.

However, I don't think this was an accident. Someone left that bag of cookies to implicate us somehow."

"Why?"

"To warn us off, maybe? Or to stop Sam from spreading rumors? I wish I hadn't pushed him so hard about that letter Clarisse got. I'm afraid I convinced him he was on to something really important, and it would be like him to drop hints all over his route."

"Sounds like our Snoopy," Maddie said.

Olivia checked the store clock, designed to look like the witch's edible house in Hansel and Gretel. It wasn't the easiest clock to interpret, but Olivia's mother had given it to her when the store opened. The time was somewhere between two and two fifteen, at least three hours from closing.

"Did you find out anything about Hugh and Edward's alibi for the night of Clarisse's death?" Olivia asked.

"Spunky's little adventure interrupted me, but I did identify the conference they should have been attending. There was only one national business conference that week in Baltimore, so it wasn't hard. It was held at the Rockwell Hotel, which is still newish and trying to corner the convention market."

Olivia remembered reading about that conference. She'd thought of going, but Maddie would have needed help to run the store.

"I wrote the hotel phone number on a recipe card next to my computer," Maddie said. She slid off her perch and stretched. "By the way, we need to order more recipe cards."

"My name is Ms. Clark, and I am an administrative assistant at Chamberlain Enterprises in Chatterley Heights." Olivia had come up with a story that she hoped would elicit information about Hugh's and Edward's whereabouts the evening and night of Clarisse's death. "I am calling on behalf of Mr. Hugh and Mr. Edward Chamberlain concerning the conference for small business owners they attended at your hotel last week."

Thank goodness she had remembered to block her phone number from caller ID.

"Yes, Ms. Clark, how may I help you?"

Olivia's throat was going dry from nervous excitement. "The Chamberlains asked me to inquire about the session they attended the evening of Thursday, April 23. They are concerned about some materials a member of the panel loaned to them and which they wish to return. Unfortunately, they seem to have lost the presenter's card, and neither can remember his name. Mr. Hugh Chamberlain thinks it was something like Robinson, and Edward insists it was Thomlinson. They are hoping someone at your hotel might be able to supply the correct name and business address."

Olivia had found the conference website online and purposely picked one name from a Wednesday session and a second, similar name from the Saturday morning session. The website had also stated that, because space was limited and conference attendance had exceeded expectations, preregistration would be required for this very popular panel. Olivia was counting on the hotel's desire to go the extra helpful mile to maintain their competitive edge.

"If you can wait a few minutes, Ms. Clark, I'll ask the events director for you."

"Thank you so much," Olivia said. When the Kenny G. music started, she ran for the kitchen sink, poured herself a large glass of water, and gulped it down. She filled the glass again and returned to the phone as the music halted in midphrase.

The hotel concierge sounded tentative, as if he were concerned about irritating her. "Ms. Clark, I spoke with our events coordinator and she was a bit confused. You see, the two names you mentioned served on panels that took place on two other days, but they did not participate in the Thursday evening panel the Chamberlains mentioned. In fact, she also checked and found that Hugh and Edward Chamberlain had both preregistered for that evening, but apparently they didn't claim their seats. At least, their names aren't checked off. Our events coordinator wondered if the Chamberlains might be remembering a different panel?"

"Could you wait a few moments while I ask one of them?"

"Of course." Olivia could almost hear the concierge sigh.

Thank goodness Maddie had talked her into including a hold function with her store phone service. Olivia watched the clock for one minute, hoping it would feel like ten to the concierge. After several more gulps of water, she was about to reconnect when Maddie opened the kitchen door and poked her head inside. "It's quieted down out here, so could you—?"

"Hang on, I'm almost finished." Olivia pointed to the flashing red hold button on the phone.

Maddie wedged herself between the door and the jamb, so she could watch the store and listen at the same time.

Olivia picked up the receiver and punched the hold button. "Hello? Yes, this is Ms. Clark again. I'm so sorry to have taken so much of your time," she said, relaxing into a more friendly, apologetic tone. "When I mentioned the other panels to Mr. Chamberlain, he suddenly remembered the right one, as well as the name of the presenter. Thank you for being so patient and helpful. Chamberlain Enterprises will certainly keep your hotel in mind for the future."

Whew. Olivia disconnected with a gratified concierge.

"Wow," said Maddie. "I didn't know you had it in you."

"Hey, I played a role in one of our high school plays, remember?"

"Yes, but that was Chatterley Heights High School theater. Anyone who wanted a part, got a part. However, what I heard sounded impressive. What did you find out?"

Olivia filled her in. "It isn't proof, of course," she added. "Hugh and Edward might have attended some other function, or the hotel might have made a mistake. But at least they don't appear to have a solid alibi at the moment."

"This would be a lot easier if we were cops," Maddie said. "But I'd miss the cookie cutters." She peeked into the store. "Gotta go. I hear someone coming in from outside."

"One more call and then I'll spell you."

Once Maddie had left, Olivia picked up the phone again. At least this call should be easier. She finally found time to dial her old friend's number. After two rings, a familiar cheerful yet no-nonsense voice answered. "Stacey?"

"Livie? You're a mind reader. I've been thinking about you ever since . . . Well, I don't need to remind you." Her voice became softer and a bit distorted, as if she were whispering with her mouth too close to the phone. "I'm in the outer office, and it's crammed with kids and teachers. Hang on." After a moment, Stacey's voice returned to normal. "There, that's better. I'm in my office. How the heck are you?"

Stacey Harald was another of Olivia's since-kindergarten friends, though their lives had taken different turns after graduation. At the age of nineteen, Stacey married her high school sweetheart, with whom she'd had two children. When Olivia returned home, she'd discovered that Stacey and her husband had split. During the summer, she and Stacey had squeezed in several lunches and reconnected over their tales of divorce. Stacey did not look down her nose at a bit of discreet gossip. Best of all, after her divorce, Stacey had brushed off her secretarial skills and worked her way up to office manager at Chatterley Heights Elementary. She knew Tammy well and wasn't especially fond of her.

"I'm good," Olivia said. "Considering the situation."

"Looks like one big, messy situation from where I sit."

With a rueful laugh, Olivia said, "About that . . ."

"Spit it out, Livie."

Olivia smiled to herself. Stacey's directness was legend throughout Chatterley Heights. Beating around the bush would only irritate her. "Okay, between you and me," Olivia said, "I'm trying to save my own skin. Sheriff Del wants me to stay in the store and bake cookies, but I need to find out what's been going on around here. If you know what I mean." She didn't want to be too explicit on the phone.

"I know what you mean."

"Maddie is helping, but I need to talk to someone more . . ."

"More in daily touch with, say, one of the main players?"

"You are so quick, it's scary." Olivia glanced up at the kitchen clock. Three thirty. The Gingerbread House closed at five. "Any chance you're free for dinner?"

"As it happens, Tyler has basketball practice and Rachel will be studying at a friend's house, or so she claims."

"How about six thirty? My place? It's more private." The tables at Pete's Diner were so crowded together that Olivia had heard complete conversations from three tables away.

"You aren't going to cook, are you? Because I've heard things. . . ."

"You wound me. No, baking is the only cooking I do

willingly. I'll order a couple of the Chatterley Café's finest pizzas. You can take home the leftovers."

"It's a deal. And Livie, don't be too hard on Del. I dated him for a brief time before marrying what's-his-name. He's levelheaded and honest. I always thought I'd made the wrong choice."

As she hung up, Olivia felt a stabbing sensation in her chest. "Careful, kiddo," she murmured. "That felt suspiciously like jealousy."

Chapter Eighteen

Olivia made it home, after picking up a few groceries and two pizzas, with five minutes to spare. Her front doorbell rang precisely at six thirty. She ran down the stairs in her stocking feet, carrying a yapping Spunky.

"You sound out of breath," Stacey said as she walked into the foyer. "I'm not early, am I? I hate it when guests are early. My ex used to be early for dates. I'd make him drive around the block and come back later."

"I'm out of shape, that's all," Olivia said.

Stacey's sandy hair fell forward as she knelt to massage Spunky's ears. "What a sweet noisy little critter you are," she said. Spunky wriggled his head in ecstasy. "I love dogs," Stacey said. "Cats, too. So much easier to live with than men." She gave the puppy a final pat on the head and said, "To be continued once my strength is restored by pizza."

"And red wine," Olivia said as she led the way upstairs.

"An excellent combination."

Once upstairs, Stacey gave the pizzas a quick warm-up in the oven and set the table. Olivia poured wine and unpacked her groceries, which included a hunk of parmesan cheese, bagged salad, and some fresh Caesar dressing from the Chatterley Café. She chopped a few olives for the salad and scavenged for some cocktail tomatoes that hadn't yet shriveled up.

By the time they sat down to eat, their wineglasses required refilling. Stacey selected a slice from the veggie and cheese pizza, while Olivia went straight for the three-meat with extra mozzarella.

"This might be why I'm out of shape," Olivia said.

"Naw, you're just too busy, like me."

"Or too lazy."

After savoring her first bite, Stacey said, "Bribe accepted. What do you want to know?"

Olivia sipped her wine and gathered her thoughts. "Keep this conversation to yourself, okay?"

"Of course."

Olivia selected a second slice of pizza, one with less meat and more olives. "I think Clarisse Chamberlain was murdered," she said.

"I wondered about that myself. I knew Clarisse. She was way too sharp to accidentally poison herself."

"I just wish I could prove it," Olivia said. "I think Del believes that Clarisse was murdered, too, only he doesn't want me involved."

"But you can't help yourself." Stacey reached for a pizza slice with the meat and the fewest olives.

"You saw Binnie's article about my so-called inheritance from Clarisse? She made me look like a murder suspect. The entire piece is a fabrication, but I still have to protect my reputation." Olivia picked a sliver of kalamata off her pizza slice, popped it in her mouth, and washed it down with a sip of wine.

"That article was hysterical." Stacey rested her chin on her laced fingers, all attention. "So," she said, "two questions. How can I help? And would you reach the wine bottle for me?"

Olivia laughed, which felt good. As she filled Stacey's glass, she said, "I'm trying to track down alibis for the most likely suspects—Edward and Hugh Chamberlain, Tammy Deacons, Bertha the housekeeper, and maybe Lucas Ashford."

"Lucas? Really? I guess you never know with the quiet ones. And he has been stressed these past few years, what with his dad dying and his mom so sick, doctor bills, you name it. Everyone has a breaking point."

"How well do you know Lucas?" Olivia asked.

"He volunteers at school. Fixes the furnace on a regular basis, donates parts, even changes those fluorescent bulbs no one else can reach. Nice guy. Maybe too nice. He does too much free work for someone with financial pressures."

Stacey speared a tomato from her salad. "Although his financial situation certainly has improved," she said right before the tomato disappeared into her mouth.

"It has? How?"

Stacey held up her fork for a time-out while she finished chewing. "Okay, this is secondhand," she said, "but one of our fourth-grade teachers is married to a shop teacher at the high school, who is good friends with Lucas. I think they fix things together. Anyway, the story I got is that since Clarisse's death, her sons have restructured the terms of the loan she made to Lucas. The way I heard it, they've cut his interest rate by half and forgiven the interest he owes on payments he missed while his dad was dying."

"Really." If true, it would explain the sudden lightening of Lucas's mood after Clarisse's death. "I wonder why Hugh and Edward would do such a thing?"

"You mean such an uncharacteristically kind act toward a fellow human being? Haven't a clue. What's for dessert?"

"Hm?" Olivia's mind was broiling with possible reasons for Hugh and Edward's largesse. Maybe they conspired to murder their mother, and somehow Lucas found out about it and blackmailed them. Or Lucas conspired with them to kill Clarisse, maybe even did the deed himself, and the loan restructuring was payment. Lucas didn't seem capable of such behavior, but how well did anyone really know—

"Earth to Livie," Stacey said. "Dessert? The tasty stuff that follows dinner?"

"Dessert. Right. Decorated cookies, of course." Olivia scraped back her chair and began to clear the table.

"Oh goodie, that's what I was hoping for." Stacey flipped closed the lids on the pizza boxes and stuffed them in the refrigerator. "Where are they?"

"On top of the fridge." Olivia finished filling her Mr. Coffee and pressed the on button.

Stacey lifted down a covered cake pan and slid off the lid. "Heaven," she said. "Forget the serving plate." She placed the pan in the middle of the table and settled in her chair. Her hand hovering over the cookies, she said, "So I imagine you want to ask about Tammy Deacons, too?"

Olivia delivered coffee cups, cream, and sugar to the table and joined Stacey. "I certainly do."

"Then you have bribed the right person."

"I'm hoping to pin down Tammy's whereabouts on April 23, day and night. You might not know about that whole time period, but—"

"I know all," Stacey said. "Except how you can make

such delectable cookies and not be able to boil an egg." She selected a second cookie, shaped like a baby carriage and decorated with pink and white icing. "However, we'll save that for another evening. Tammy. On Thursday and Friday, the twenty-third and twenty-fourth, classes were cancelled for a teachers' conference. Tammy was supposed to be there, but she called in sick. Left a message on the office machine. She should have left some information about her classes, but she didn't. I called and called her home number. No answer. The vice principal asked me to go to her house and see if I could get her class information from her. Which I did. No one answered the door. The house was closed up tight and her car was gone."

Stacey bit off a baby carriage wheel and closed her eyes as she chewed. Olivia understood. After a sip of sweet, milky coffee, Stacey said, "Playing hooky is one thing. Leaving town while claiming sick time is another."

"Are you sure she left town?" Olivia's resolve cracked, and she selected a cookie shaped like a cat with an arched back and electric purple fur.

"Where would she go in Chatterley Heights without being seen? I called all my sources. What can I say, I got curious, and well, you know that she's not my favorite person in the world. A few people saw her at Lady Chatterley's, trying on dresses, so I figured she must have been planning some illicit getaway with Hugh. Anyway, by Friday it was too late to use her class information, so I didn't check her house again."

Olivia nodded, remembering Tammy's dramatic appearance at The Gingerbread House on Friday morning. She must have spent the night with Hugh, then returned to Chatterley Heights, while Hugh went back to his conference. So Tammy and Hugh could alibi each other for

Thursday night, or they might both have been involved in Clarisse's death.

"However," Stacey continued, "I didn't mention it to the vice principal, but on Thursday afternoon I also called the Chamberlain house. Bertha answered, no Tammy. Bertha gave me the phone number of the hotel Hugh and Edward were staying at in Baltimore. I called. No Tammy. Also no Hugh. The concierge told me Hugh and his fiancée had ordered a rental car and wouldn't be back until the next day. Edward was there but on some panel or other."

"How on earth did you get the concierge to tell you all this?"

"Charm." Stacey had managed to finish off the baby carriage and was nibbling on the ear of a red and purple striped bunny. "Also, guile. I told the concierge I was the Chamberlain housekeeper and Clarisse had asked me to get some information from Hugh as soon as possible and his cell was turned off."

"You're good," Olivia said. She pushed the pan of cookies closer to Stacey. "Did you find out where they went?"

"The concierge didn't know. I figured they were sneaking a night together, given that Hugh called Tammy his financée. Now I realize there was another possibility."

"Indeed," Olivia said. "Can we keep this our little secret for now?"

"My lips will unseal only to take in food. Specifically, your cookies." Stacey checked her watch. "My daughter is supposed to be home in half an hour. I want to be there to make sure it happens."

"I'll give you the whole pan of cookies plus the leftover pizza for one more piece of information."

"You are a goddess." Stacey gathered the cookie-laden pan to her bosom. "What do you want to know?"

"Who would know a lot about Hugh and Edward?"

"Like what?"

Olivia leaned back in her chair and stared at a stain on the kitchen ceiling. A plan had been forming in her mind. It might not work, could even make the situation worse. On the other hand, with so little evidence available, her idea might flush out a murderer.

"I need to find out more about their private lives, their pasts," Olivia said. "I want to talk to someone who can help me understand who Hugh and Edward are when they aren't being businessmen."

"Ah," Stacey said, "you want the real scoop. Well, two names occur to me off the top of my head, and one belongs to someone on your suspects list. Bertha, the Chamberlain housekeeper. She helped raise those boys, and there's nothing like raising a kid to tell you his strengths and weaknesses."

Stacey stood up and stretched. "I'm truly sorry to have to give you the second name." She slid the lid on the cake pan and snatched it up, as if she were afraid Olivia would take back the cookies when she heard the name.

"The guy you should talk to is the perfect informant. Unfortunately, he's also my ex-husband, Wade. He grew up near enough to Hugh and Edward that they were playmates, and he double-dated with Hugh sometimes."

"Can I trust anything Wade might tell me?" Olivia piled the pizza boxes on top of the cake pan in Stacey's arms.

"Probably not," Stacey said. She checked the kitchen clock and said, "Okay, I'll tell you the story, but I'll have to make it quick." While Olivia retrieved her coat, Stacey said, "The three boys did their underage drinking together. During that period, they went joy riding one night and smashed into a tree. Hugh and Edward claimed Wade was driving, which he denies to this day. Strings were pulled; there wasn't an investigation. Wade took the fall, and the brothers Chamberlain came off as innocent victims."

"Wade is still angry?"

"An understatement. However, I can assure you he has an alibi for Thursday and into Saturday. He had the kids. Thursday evening, they went to a monster truck show, instead of doing their homework. Where did I go wrong?"

Chapter Nineteen

❧❧❧

Olivia sat cross-legged on her living room sofa, staring at the small screen on her laptop. She'd been looking at the photo of Clarisse Chamberlain's desk for almost an hour, with Spunky curled next to her, dozing off the effects of a good run in the chill of early morning. Olivia closed her eyes and leaned her head on the sofa back. Images of cookie cutters glowed on the inside of her eyelids.

Olivia's cell phone vibrated against her hip. Spunky's ears perked up, but he was too sleepy to raise his head. She dug the phone out of the pocket of her hoodie and checked the caller ID. "It's Mom," she said. Spunky must have understood; he relaxed his ears and resumed snoring.

"Hi, Livie," Ellie said, "I just returned from my morning jog and got your message. Sure, I can help in the store today. I have my yoga class at four; maybe I could slip away for that?"

"No problem."

"This will be fun," Ellie said with far too much energy for eight or so in the morning. "I'll get to spend more time with my daughter."

"About that, Mom . . . I'll need to be out for chunks of the day."

"Oh, well then, I'll get to spend more time with Maddie. Maybe I'll adopt her."

"Ouch. Look, it's too complicated to explain right now, but I promise I'll fill you in when I can. Anyway, the store might be busy today. The DC cutter collectors often make the rounds in groups, and if they come to The Gingerbread House, it's usually on a Thursday. I really appreciate this, Mom."

"I know that, dear. I'll be there at nine, dressed in some appropriate yet exotic outfit."

Olivia ended the call and checked the time on her computer. Eight fifteen. She still hadn't showered, and the store opened at nine. Maddie was probably there already. Olivia reset her cell to her favorite ring tone—Maynard Ferguson's trumpet caressing a lyrical phrase from *"An Offering of Love," Part 1*—and placed it on the coffee table, next to her laptop. Leaving Spunky to snooze and snore on the sofa, she headed for the shower.

By opening time, cars and vans had already begun to arrive from DC. Thursday was beginning to look like a repeat of Tuesday, which would be fine if it brought in anything close to Tuesday's profit. Some out-of-town customers asked about the Chamberlain cookie-cutter collection, but apparently Maddie's email announcement had done its job.

Around ten thirty, a customer who was leaving held the

door open and in walked Bertha, wheezing heavily. Olivia rushed over to her.

"Ms. Olivia, now . . . *wheeze* . . . don't you worry . . . *wheeze* . . . about me. I'm . . . *wheeze*—"

"Bertha, don't try to talk. Would a glass of water help? Nod or shake your head."

"Wheeze." Bertha shook her head and handed Olivia her large pocketbook. Olivia thought about patting Bertha's back, but she couldn't remember if that would help or hurt. She'd been married to a surgeon, for goodness' sake, shouldn't she know what to do?

"Wheeze." Bertha's face was reddening at an alarming pace.

Ellie materialized at Olivia's elbow. "Livie dear, I think Bertha has an inhaler in her pocketbook. Why don't I look for it?"

When her mother tried to take the pocketbook from her, Olivia realized she was clutching it to her so tightly her hands stuck to the stiff patent leather. With calm focus, Ellie located the inhaler within seconds and folded Bertha's fingers around it. Olivia made a silent vow to find a first-aid class and take it until she passed.

"Thanks, Mom," she said. "You were amazingly calm. How did you do that?"

"Meditation, dear. Three classes a week and practice every day."

Olivia added a meditation class to her mental list.

"Oh, Ms. Olivia, your store is so lovely," Bertha gushed as her eyes roamed around the table displays and across to the baking area. She gave a small gasp of appreciation when her gaze lifted to the cookie-cutter mobiles. "My goodness," she said, "look at that one. Those are all different baby carriage cookie cutters."

Olivia gazed up at the strings of cookie cutters jangling lightly in the circulating air. The baby carriages were similar in design, but some were antiques with wooden handles, some with metal or no handles, and others were plastic. One shiny tin cutter sparkled in the light, and Olivia remembered Clarisse's sadness as she looked at the cutter display of baby items. That gave Olivia an idea. Bertha might know about Jasmine Dubois.

Olivia stretched her arm around Bertha's shoulders. "You've never been here before, have you? I'd love to show you our little kitchen at the back of the store. Would you have time for a cup of coffee?"

"Now, Ms. Olivia," Bertha said, "I can see how busy you are, but I would love a cup of coffee, if you can really spare the time. I've been feeling terrible ever since that dinner on Monday evening. About those cookies, I mean."

"Cookies?" Olivia cupped Bertha's plump elbow with a guiding hand and steered her toward the kitchen.

"I honestly didn't know about what happened to Sam."

Ah. *Those* cookies. Olivia was amazed she'd forgotten that episode even for a moment. "Bertha, believe me, it never occurred to me you'd done that on purpose. You aren't like that." She closed the door to ensure some privacy.

"Have a seat," Olivia said. "I'll start some fresh coffee for us." She filled a glass with water and gave it to Bertha. Over the clatter of cups and spoons, she said, "I'm glad you dropped by. I've been hoping to have a chance to talk with you."

While Mr. Coffee dripped the last of its brew, Olivia delivered cream and sugar to the table. "You know, Clarisse never once hinted about leaving me anything in her will. When I heard how much, not to mention her entire cutter collection, I couldn't believe it. I thought Mr. Willard must have read it wrong."

"I know what you mean," Bertha said. "She always said she'd take care of me, but I never dreamed she meant she'd take care of everything for the rest of my life. Health expenses, even? I about fainted dead away." She chuckled, ending in a cough. "Of course, if I'd died of shock, that would have left a lot more for the boys."

Yes. It would. Olivia filled their cups as Bertha's plump face puckered up, and she began to sniffle. She rifled through her huge pocketbook. "My mother used to carry a handkerchief in her sleeve." Tears trickled down her cheeks. "Seems like a good idea about now."

Olivia never knew what to say when someone was crying. Phrases like "there, there" or "it's all right" always sounded silly or insulting, and asking what was wrong felt like skipping through a minefield. So she opted for practical silence and hopped up to locate a box of tissues. She found one on the counter and delivered it to Bertha.

"Thank you, dear," Bertha said. "I'm not usually this way, you know, but Ms. Clarisse was like a daughter to me." She put three tissues to her nose and blew with enthusiasm. "I'm grateful she left me so well fixed, don't think I'm not, but I'd rather have her back. The house isn't the same anymore. It doesn't feel right." Bertha plucked another tissue from the box. "It's mostly Ms. Clarisse being gone, but it's more than that." She spread her strong, wide hands on the table. The knuckles were red and thickened by arthritis.

"You know, I think it was those cookies," Bertha said. "I felt better making those decorated cookies, using some of Ms. Clarisse's favorite cookie cutters. It felt like she might walk in any moment and smile." Bertha's lips compressed. "But instead the boys and Ms. Tammy got all uncomfortable and started treating me differently after that night. I helped raise those boys, and I liked Ms. Tammy." Bertha's shoulders slumped, and her hands fell onto her lap. "But they're not actin' like the people I thought they were. None of this would be happening if my Clarisse was still alive."

Hearing Bertha mourn her Clarisse convinced Olivia to take her off the suspects list—and add her to the informant list. But besides hurt feelings, would Bertha be willing to share anything really negative about the boys she mothered? Or anyone, for that matter? Olivia figured she'd never get a chance like this again. Maddie and her mother seemed to be handling the store without her help, so it was now or never.

Olivia emptied the remaining coffee into their cups. With a light laugh, she said, "You know what suddenly popped into my mind? I was imagining Clarisse arguing with that painting of Martin in the study. Remember you told me about that?"

Bertha brightened. "My goodness, yes. She'd be so wrapped up talking to that picture, you'd think it was answering her."

"Is that how they argued when Martin was alive? I never knew him."

"Oh my, yes. They were so close, those two, but when they disagreed about something, well, I'd stay in the kitchen and wait for the house to crumble around me." Bertha looked like her cheery self again.

"What was their worst argument? Do you remember?"

Bertha clapped her hands together. "Do I! It was about a year before Mr. Martin died so sudden." Her smile faded. "But he died of those cigarettes, not from arguing, not a chance," she said, perking up again. "He loved to argue.

They never fought about business, though. It was always about the boys." With a sigh, Bertha lapsed into silence.

"Did they disagree about how to rear the boys?" Olivia prodded.

"When it came to those boys, they disagreed about *everything*. Should they be required to dress for dinner? When and how to punish them, how many rules to give them, who they could date . . ."

"Who they should marry?"

"You hit the nail on the noggin. The worst argument I ever heard between Ms. Clarisse and Mr. Martin was about a young woman both boys liked. Such a pretty girl, with that lovely black hair. Feisty, too. She had a flower name, now what was it? Violet? Camellia? No, I think it started with a 'T' or maybe a 'J' or . . . It certainly wasn't Jewelweed," Bertha said with a hoarse laugh. "I'm always trying to get that out of the garden."

Olivia bit both lips and her tongue trying to avoid blurting out the name. She knew she'd sound too eager.

Bertha straightened so quickly her body jiggled. "Jasmine," she said. "Her name was Jasmine Dubois. I got to know her because she waitressed at Pete's Diner. I used to treat myself to dinner there sometimes when the family would be out. I liked that girl. She had a mind of her own. I wonder where she went."

"What do you mean?" Olivia felt so keyed up she was having trouble remembering to breathe.

"Well, she was there one day and gone the next. That's what they were arguing about, Ms. Clarisse and Mr. Martin. Ms. Clarisse liked Jasmine and thought it would be nice if she married Hugh or Edward. She was smart, that's what Ms. Clarisse said about Jasmine. She was smart and honest, and she'd be an asset. Mr. Martin thought she wasn't good enough for one of his sons. A menial laborer, he called her. Oh, that made Ms. Clarisse mad. She was poor growing up, you see. Worked two jobs to put herself through nursing school. Mr. Martin came from money; he didn't understand."

"Could Martin really stop Hugh and Edward from marrying anyone they wanted?"

Bertha pondered for a few moments before saying, "I don't believe Mr. Martin would have cut off either of those boys, I really don't. But when Jasmine disappeared, Ms. Clarisse accused him of getting rid of her." With a little gasp, Bertha put her hand to her mouth. "I don't mean Mr. Martin had her killed her or anything, Ms. Clarisse never said that, but maybe he bribed her to leave? Mr. Martin told her not to be ridiculous, he'd never waste money that way."

"Martin said that?"

"I remember like it was yesterday," Bertha said with an emphatic nod. "I think Ms. Clarisse believed him, too. That man never wasted a penny."

Chapter Twenty

After Bertha left The Gingerbread House, Olivia and Maddie huddled together in the cookbook alcove to compare notes and plan their next moves. The alcove's two small armchairs, placed so customers could glance through baking books, allowed Olivia and Maddie to keep an eye on the store. If Ellie needed help, one or both of them could spring into sales mode.

"So as I understand it," Maddie said, consulting the notebook on her lap, "you want me to go to the library and find out from Heather how to search obituaries in Baltimore papers, right?"

"Or any mention of Jasmine Dubois. It's a long shot, but everything we've learned so far—the private detective agency's letter, the phone number on the note from Faith— it all makes me think Jasmine went to Baltimore after leaving Chatterley Heights."

"I wish we had a last name for Faith," Maddie said.

"I have a feeling we'll find Faith when we figure out what happened to Jasmine."

Olivia reached in the pocket of her linen slacks and pulled out her cell phone. "It's eleven thirty. The noon crowd will be arriving soon. I have an appointment with Mr. Willard at one fifteen, his office, so I should be back by two thirty at the latest. Then you can split for the library, but be back by four. Mom has a yoga class."

"Of course she does."

Ellie Greyson-Meyers's petite form appeared in the alcove entryway. "Customer alert," she said. "A van pulled up out front, and five women are heading up the walk. They look like they mean business. Oh, and Sheriff Del called. He's on his way over to talk to you, Livie."

"Uh-oh," Maddie said after Ellie left. "What did you do this time?"

"Smirking is not attractive."

"But I do it so well."

An errant wave fell over Olivia's eye and she slid it behind her ear. "Stow my notes in the kitchen for me, would you?"

"Sure." Maddie took a moment to smooth the wrinkles out of her form-fitting black jeans. "You do realize that Del will find out you are asking questions. Chatterley Heights is a rumor mill, and a darned good one."

"Your civic pride is duly noted."

"I'm only saying, Del might not be in the best of pro-Livie moods."

Olivia shrugged with a nonchalance she didn't feel. "I never actually promised to stop asking questions. Del can be as mad as he wants; I don't intend to stop until I know who killed Clarisse."

* * *

Sheriff Del arrived in uniform, which put a damper on cookie-cutter commerce. Everyone in The Gingerbread House, including Maddie and Ellie, watched with open curiosity as Olivia led him into the cookbook alcove. He hung his hat on a display stand mixer, pursed his lips, and strode around the perimeter of the alcove.

"Del, please, stop pacing and sit down." Olivia pointed to the chair Maddie had vacated. "A lot of our customers lately are overly curious right now, and I'd rather not invite more rumors."

"I was hoping for more privacy," Del said.

"I told you, I need to keep an eye on the store in case—"

"In case Maddie and Ellie need you, I know."

Del paused in midpace and glared at a large rolling pin made of shiny marble with two-tone gray swirls. It was one of Olivia's favorite pieces. She kept it on a low shelf near the cookbook browsing table. She didn't take Del's frown as disapproval of her pride and joy, since she doubted he even saw it.

"I'll make it quick," Del said, dropping into an armchair. "I just drove back from Howard County General." He was speaking so quietly that Olivia had to lean toward him to hear. "Sam came out of his coma."

"That's great news. Will he be okay?"

"Looks like it."

"Was he able to remember anything?"

Del shifted in his chair so he could face Olivia. "He remembers finding a bag of cookies on his front porch when he got home for lunch. The bag said The Gingerbread House—he remembers that, too. But nothing afterwards. I checked with Polly at the Food Shelf. She couldn't tell if any of the cookies you delivered went missing, but the bag didn't. She took that home."

"Lots of folks keep those bags," Olivia said. "My mother has piles of them."

"I'm not accusing you, Livie. I have to ask, were you aware of Sam's schedule?"

With an attempt at a smile, she said, "Would you believe me if I said I wasn't?"

"I see your point. Maybe I'd want to, but as a sheriff I'd have to apply a grain or two of salt."

"As it happens, I did know Sam's schedule, more or less. I suspect everyone in town does. But I did not know about his diabetes."

Del's half smile lasted a picosecond. "That's the problem. Sam lives on a dead-end street with only four houses. No one else was home all morning, so no witnesses."

Olivia leaned her back against the velvet-covered back of her armchair. "I truly had nothing to do with this. I wish you could believe me."

Del leaned forward, elbows on his knees. His gold-flecked brown eyes had turned to granite. "I never believed that you attacked Sam," he said. "But I think you had something to do with it."

Olivia felt the heat of anger flush her face as she sprang from her chair. She towered over Del's chair, arms crossed over tight fists.

Unmoved by her reaction, Del said, "You told me about the letter to Clarisse that Sam delivered, remember? From a private detective agency?" Del's eyes narrowed. "What I suspect you did not tell me was that Sam knew something about what that letter contained."

Olivia stiffened. "Sam Parnell likes to keep secrets, when it suits him."

"On Monday morning, he was late with his route, and he hinted it was because he'd had a long talk with you. He also indicated that he had discussed the contents of an important letter with you, and you repaid him with cookies."

Olivia's legs went wobbly. She took a deep breath and released it slowly, as her mother was always telling her to do. "Did Sam actually tell you all of that or was it someone else? How do you know your informant was reliable?"

"My informant was your close friend, Tammy Deacons. Sam told her when he dropped off her mail."

So Tammy was home on Monday.

Olivia sank back in her seat. "Remember, you were called away while we were talking about the letter to Clarisse."

"You could have called and told me later."

"I've been a bit busy, in case you haven't noticed." Olivia knew she was being stubborn, but Del's high-handed treatment made her seethe. It reminded her of her ex-husband.

Del stood up and reached for his hat. "I won't keep you from your customers any longer," he said. "I still don't know you all that well, Livie, but I have a bad feeling right now. My instincts tell me you're holding something back. I want you to promise me that if you find out anything relevant to Clarisse's death—or the attack on Sam, for that matter—you'll come straight to me." Del stared hard at her. With mesmerizing precision, his right hand rotated the rim of his hat through the loose grip of his left thumb and forefinger.

"If I find anything solid," Olivia said, "of course I'll pass it on to you." She meant it, too. She had suspicions, observations, and, okay, that note from a "Faith" and the letter from Clarisse, but nothing that qualified as solid. That little prick of guilt wasn't strong enough to pierce her anger.

As Del headed toward the alcove entrance, Olivia said, "I do need something from you."

Del turned and gave her a wary look. "And that would be?"

Olivia lowered her voice slightly, to ensure she would not be heard outside the alcove. "I need to know if you consider Lucas Ashford a suspect."

"Livie—"

"Maddie and Lucas are dating. I need to know if my best friend and business partner is becoming serious about someone who might be a murderer. If I'm not convinced Maddie is safe, I'll investigate him by myself, so you might as well tell me."

With an exaggerated sigh, Del plopped his hat on his head. "All right, no, I do not consider Lucas a suspect in Clarisse's death. He spent that afternoon and evening at a friend's house, helping to fix a complicated plumbing problem. The friend and his wife confirmed this. The job wasn't finished until past midnight, and the couple insisted Lucas sleep in their guest room. And before you ask, both witnesses got up in the night to visit the facilities, and each heard Lucas snoring. Are you satisfied, or should I insist on a lie detector test?"

"Not necessary," Olivia said. "Those tests aren't admissible in court, anyway. Thanks, Del."

"Don't mention it. Ever."

Olivia watched Del's back disappear into the main sales area of the store. Lucas's alibi sounded solid enough, and she was inclined to drop him from her suspects list. However, there was still the question of why Hugh and Edward lowered the interest rate so significantly on Lucas's loan from Clarisse. Even if he hadn't murdered Clarisse, Lucas could be guilty of blackmail.

Mr. Willard's law office occupied the top floor of a narrow, two-story Georgian-style building on the east side of the town square. The building's ground floor housed Olivia's second favorite store, after The Gingerbread House—the Book Chat bookstore. To reach the stairs leading up to Mr. Willard's office, she had to walk through the cookbook section and then the mysteries. It took all her willpower not to slow down and skim the titles. One of the downsides to running a store of her own was that she couldn't linger in other shops during normal working hours. She consoled herself by breathing in the crisp smell of new books.

Olivia rejected the new-looking elevator in favor of the wooden stairs, well worn in the middle. At the top, she came to Mr. Willard's frosted glass door, left ajar. The hinges squeaked as she edged the door inward.

"Come on in," Mr. Willard's voice called from an inner office. The outer office must once have been for a secretary, but today no one occupied the chair behind a battered wooden desk. An old electric typewriter, unplugged and forlorn, hinted that the office hadn't served its original purpose for many years.

Olivia made her way toward Mr. Willard's voice, past floor-to-ceiling bookcases filled with law books. Without thinking, she dragged a finger across several spines and collected a layer of dust, which triggered a sneeze.

The inner office door opened and Mr. Willard's head appeared. "I am so sorry for the state of my office," he said. "I've done all my own administrative work for years, so I haven't needed staff. However, a regular housekeeper might not be a bad idea." He gestured for Olivia to enter. She couldn't help noticing his almost skeletal hands, with the joints protruding from long, thin fingers. He looked as if he could use a few decorated cookies.

"Thank you for seeing me on such short notice," Olivia said, taking a seat across from Mr. Willard's desk. A quick glance told her the real work was done in his office. A new model laptop sat on his desk, closed and pushed to one side, and neat piles of legal-size papers covered at least half of the work space. File cabinets lined three walls. A large laser printer stood at the ready on a side table.

"My time is my own, so I am really quite flexible." Mr. Willard's smile added a moment of fullness to his cavernous cheeks. "What can I do for you, Ms. Greyson?"

"Call me Livie, please." She took a moment to gather her thoughts. She had thought through what she wanted to discuss with him, but she had to proceed with care. "I have one simple request, but there's more, much more, that I'd like to discuss with you. Whether I can do that depends on . . . well, on a possible conflict of interest. I know I'm being vague, but . . ."

Mr. Willard sat up straight, his eyes bright. "In fact, I am intrigued," he said. "Might my potential conflict of interest have to do with the Chamberlain family, by any chance?"

Olivia had been concentrating so hard on how to approach the topic, she'd been holding her breath. She released it so fast her cheeks puffed out. "Yes, it would, absolutely."

"Then you may put your mind at rest. My long association with the Chamberlain family ended with Clarisse's death. Hugh and Edward preferred to hire the services of a large law firm in DC, so I am not privy to any confidential legal information about them."

"Good, then I want to hire you. Or put you on retainer, if that's the right term."

"It is. Consider yourself my client. What may I do for you? I hope Sheriff Del has not designated you a suspect in Clarisse's death? I'm not a criminal attorney, of course, but I can certainly recommend an excellent one."

"No, nothing like that."

"Good." Mr. Willard scraped back his chair. "May I offer you a cappuccino? I was about to make some when you arrived."

"Cappuccino? I think I hired the right lawyer."

Mr. Willard's laugh was deeper than Olivia would have expected, given his thinness. "While the machine performs its magic," he said, "why don't you start with the simple request you mentioned?"

"All right, I need a list of the cookie cutters in Clarisse's collection, and I need it right away." When Mr. Willard's eyebrows arched, she added, "I'm so glad you are my attorney because now I can explain."

Mr. Willard held up one hand. "Let me froth the cappuccinos and we can discuss this in a comfortable fashion. Something tells me it will be complicated."

Now that she knew she could talk over her plans with Mr. Willard, Olivia could hardly wait to start. Besides, she needed to get back to the store soon, or Maddie wouldn't have time to visit the library.

Cups finally in hand, Olivia began. "I've been doing some digging into Clarisse's death. Yes, I know it could be dangerous, but I don't care. Clarisse was my dear friend. Besides, now someone is trying to implicate me. So if you're going to try to talk me out of it, you can save your breath."

"Then I shall save my breath. Please go on."

"Maddie Briggs is the only one who knows what I'm doing. She has been helping. I don't want to put her in danger, but if you knew Maddie . . . Anyway, I started with five suspects and have more or less eliminated two—Lucas Ashford and Bertha Binkman. Unless you know something about them that I don't?"

Mr. Willard shook his head. "I'd be surprised if either of them was guilty of murder, especially Bertha."

"So that leaves three suspects."

"Let me guess," Mr. Willard said. "The brothers Chamberlain and Hugh's fiancée, Tammy Deacons."

"Wow, you're good."

"It wasn't that difficult. Why Ms. Deacons, if I may ask?"

Olivia sipped her cooling coffee. "Tammy is an old friend of mine; it isn't easy for me to think of her killing someone. She has always been intense in her emotions. Also determined. She has been in love with Hugh Chamberlain since . . . Well, I don't even know since when, but she has never wavered. She hated Clarisse for turning Hugh against her—at least, that's how Tammy saw it. I don't really know what happened."

Mr. Willard cleared his throat. "I thought of Clarisse as an old friend as well as a client, and I believe it was in friendship that she discussed with me her problems with Ms. Deacons. In fact, Clarisse liked the young woman for her strength of will and her persistence. However, Hugh became intrigued by another woman, and, as I recall, Clarisse thought her more suitable."

"Jasmine Dubois?"

"Precisely. When Ms. Dubois left town abruptly, Clarisse confronted Martin, thinking he had driven her away. He denied doing so, vehemently. Clarisse then became convinced that Ms. Deacons had somehow threatened or tricked Ms. Dubois into leaving. Another cappuccino?"

"What? Oh, no thanks, I need to get back to the store." Olivia handed over her empty cup. "Did Clarisse ever find any evidence that Tammy was involved?"

"Not that I am aware of. Clarisse never spoke of it again." Mr. Willard pulled open a packed file drawer and began shuffling through the hanging files. "Here it is," he said as he lifted out one thin, buff folder. "This is the list of cookie cutters in Clarisse's collection. We keep it updated for assessment and insurance purposes." He placed the file on his desk, in front of Olivia. "You don't have to tell me why you need this so urgently, of course. . . ."

Olivia slid the file closer. "Actually, I'm hoping for your help." She outlined her plan to host a memorial on Sunday. "Clarisse was looking at some of her cookie cutters when she died. I think those cutters are clues to her murder."

As Mr. Willard's thin face tightened with growing concern, Olivia steeled herself for an argument.

"My dilemma," she concluded, "is how to make sure all three suspects attend. I might be able to convince Tammy that she and Hugh should for appearance's sake, but I doubt Edward would care. I wondered if you might have some ideas?"

Even Mr. Willard's gray eyebrows were thin. When they shot up, they nearly disappeared into a fold of skin. He reached across his desk, retrieved the cookie-cutter file, and opened it. He turned the pages one by one, all the time tapping one long forefinger against his lips. He seemed to be thinking rather than reading.

Olivia was reminded of being sent to the principal's office in the fourth grade. The experience of watching the principal read through a teacher's report of her transgression, which Olivia now had forgotten, was more than enough to kick her back to the straight and narrow. Sort of. Anyway, she learned how not to get caught.

Mr. Willard closed the file and pushed it back across the desk. "I believe it would not be difficult for me to convince Hugh and Edward to attend your memorial," he said. "I will do so on one condition."

Olivia waited.

"My condition is that you involve the sheriff in this event. Hear me out," Mr. Willard said as Olivia opened her mouth to object. "If you are successful in eliciting a reaction from the guilty party—or even worse, guilty parties— there is the possibility of violence on their part. At the very least, you will have put yourself and Maddie in danger."

"Yes, I realize that, but—"

"Let me finish." Mr. Willard stood and began to pace slowly, his hands clasped behind his back. "You are an intelligent woman, Olivia. If I may call you Olivia?"

"Livie, please, I beg of you."

"Livie, then. Your plan might work. I say this because I, too, am aware of Clarisse's propensity for discussing problems with inanimate objects that had meaning for her. And I am sure you do realize the danger involved. I ask you to consider that you may be underestimating Sheriff Del. He might find your proposal worth considering, especially if you make it clear to him that you are aware of the dangers and wish to take precautions."

Olivia doubted this, but it might be worth a try. Del had resources she didn't, so he could dig up background information faster. The danger worried her, too, particularly since she'd be luring innocent others into it.

Olivia picked up the file and stood. "Thank you,

Mr. Willard. I'm open to a compromise. If you can assure me within the next twenty-four hours that Hugh, Edward, and Tammy will attend the memorial, then I will tell Del what I've told you." She didn't add that she would host the memorial event with or without Del's presence.

"Agreed. I will attend, as well, if I may." He held out his hand, and Olivia shook it. "Perhaps I can be helpful, though I will be armed only with my wits."

"And your powers of observation," Olivia said. "Bring those along, too."

Chapter Twenty-one

Thursday evening found Olivia sitting cross-legged on her living room sofa, hunched over her laptop, with Spunky snoring at her side and a turkey on stale rye within reach. And coffee, lots of coffee. Her eyes felt hot and gummy after two solid hours of staring at the little screen, trying to identify the cookie cutters on Clarisse's desk. She closed her eyes to rehydrate them. Bed sounded lovely. Maybe she could get up an hour or two early and finish.

A light ding told her a new email had arrived, but she was too tired to care. She was reaching for the close button on her computer when the trumpet call of her cell phone startled her. She checked the number. Maddie. So much for bed.

"Hey, Maddie."

"Hey back. Checked your email lately?"

"Must I? Oh, all right."

"Stop grousing, Liv, and prepare to be amazed."

Olivia reopened her email program and spotted Maddie's address. The brief message, "I am a genius," included an attachment.

"Well?"

"Hang on a minute." Olivia put her cell phone on the coffee table and double-clicked on the attachment. A newspaper article appeared on the screen. The headline read, "Body Found in Patuxent Park." Olivia skimmed the short article, dated March 2, 2004:

> Early Thursday morning, a hiker contacted Park Police to report finding the body of a young woman at Patuxent River State Park. The remains have been sent to the Montgomery County Medical Examiner's Office in Baltimore to determine cause of death. Montgomery County detectives have not yet identified the victim. Estimated to have been in her midtwenties, the victim is described as approximately five foot seven, slender build, with shoulder-length black hair.

Underneath the article, Maddie had pasted a brief update, dated a week later, titled, "Patuxent Park Death Ruled an Accident." The victim still had not been identified, but the medical examiner's office had concluded she died of exposure after sustaining serious injuries from a fall. The autopsy also revealed that she had recently given birth.

Olivia studied the sketch that accompanied the article, which looked like a reconstruction. Presumably the victim's face had been damaged beyond recognition. However, the sketch showed a beautiful young woman.

"What makes you think this is Jasmine Dubois?"

"I'm not absolutely, positively certain," Maddie said, sounding testy. "The description is right, she had given birth, plus the timing works—about ten months after she disappeared from Chatterley Heights. If no one has heard from her in over six years, it makes sense she died early on. As I recall, that was your idea." Definitely testy.

"Okay, but what about obituaries? Did you search those?"

Huge sigh. "I have been hunkered over my computer all evening searching for any mention of Jasmine Dubois anywhere in the whole, entire country. It's like she never existed. I found a couple references to other Jasmine Duboises—two, to be exact—but one is an eighty-year-old black woman living in Georgia, and the other died fourteen years ago in some little town in Ohio."

"What was the name of the town?"

"Why on earth would that be—?"

"Please, Maddie, humor me, okay? Anything might be important."

"Okay, give me a sec."

Olivia heard a clunk, like the sound of Maddie's cell phone hitting a hard surface, but the line remained open.

"I'm back," Maddie said. "The town was McGonigle, in southwestern Ohio. Population miniscule. That Jasmine died in a car wreck. Sad, really. She was seventeen and driving under the influence. Anyway, unless we've uncovered an undead situation, this is not our Jasmine."

"I'm amazed that you found an obituary fourteen years old from a tiny Ohio town."

"I didn't, exactly. The girl's story turned up in newspapers off and on for years—sort of a cautionary tale for teens. Anyway, my guess is our Jasmine managed to slip through the Internet cracks, which was easier then. Maybe Jasmine isn't her real name. Can I go home now?"

"Where are you?"

"Home. What I meant was, Lucas wants me to come over for a late, late dinner. He picked something up from Pete's, and we haven't had any time together for at least a century. Please?"

"I'm not actually your boss, you know. Only could you do one more thing for me? If you'd send me some guidelines for searching newspaper archives, I'll keep looking. You know how backward I am when it comes to the Internet."

"Enough with the buttering up, I see right through it. I'll shoot you an email. Then I'm gone."

"Thanks, Maddie," Olivia said, even though the connection had broken halfway through her first word.

When her kitchen phone rang, Olivia glanced at the time on her laptop. Eleven p.m. She did not need another call from her ex-husband, and who else would call her so late? She really needed to order caller ID for her private line.

Spunky opened his eyes and sat up as Olivia grunted her way off the sofa. With muted enthusiasm, he yapped once and followed her to the kitchen. She took her time, hoping the ringing would end before she got there.

At the beginning of the seventh ring, she answered.

"I am so sorry, Olivia—Livie, I mean—"

"Mr. Willard? Don't worry, I wasn't even in bed yet."

"Still, I apologize for the lateness of my call, but I've only now returned from dinner at the Chamberlain home. We spent much of the evening discussing details concerning Clarisse's will and the family's private service for her on Saturday, but I was able to convince Hugh and Edward, as well as Ms. Deacons, to attend the Sunday memorial event you are planning for all of Chatterley Heights."

"I'm impressed. May I ask how you did it?"

"It was not too difficult," Mr. Willard said with a hint of pride in his voice. "I merely reminded them of their mother's lifelong involvement in the community, which benefited both the town and Chamberlain Enterprises. She and Martin served on local committees, contributed to local organizations—an example being the Food Shelf—and as a result, the town council was receptive to their requests for rezoning. And so on. I had a long history with Martin and Clarisse to draw upon."

"I'm glad you're on my side," Olivia said. "I'll keep my part of the bargain. Tomorrow I'll talk to Del."

"I'm relieved to hear that. I will sleep somewhat better tonight."

The next morning, Olivia poked her head into The Gingerbread House a few minutes after opening. Maddie and Ellie were already helping customers, so she waved her travel mug at them and slipped away. Only two days left until Sunday, when she and Maddie would be hosting a cookie-cutter memorial service for Clarisse—and hoping to reveal her killer.

Before crawling into bed the night before, she had finished a nearly complete list of the cookie cutters she needed for Sunday's memorial. Her energy surged as she drove toward the Chamberlain house. She felt more in control of her fate, no longer buffeted by events, especially those nasty attempts to cast suspicion on her for Clarisse's murder. Now she had a direction, plans, cookies to decorate. . . . By the time Bertha met her at the front door, Olivia was floating in adrenaline.

As they climbed the stairs to the second floor, Olivia

asked, "Were you the one who put away the cookie cutters Clarisse was looking at the night she . . . ?"

Bertha paused on a step, took a wheezy breath, and nodded. "I figured it was my job. Usually Ms. Clarisse did that, but, well . . ."

"Of course. I don't suppose you remember where you put them? In which drawers, I mean?"

"Bless you, dear, I don't even remember what they looked like. I was so upset and teary, I could barely see to find the room. I put those cookie cutters back anywhere I could find a free space. Why? Is it important?"

At the tone of alarm in Bertha's voice, Olivia back-pedaled. Bertha had sworn an oath of secrecy concerning Olivia's visit; that was enough of a risk. The less she knew about the details, the better.

"Oh no, I'll find plenty of cutters for Sunday, don't worry."

They reached the second floor, and Bertha opened the first door on the left. "Well, here we are, dear. I'll leave you to it."

Clarisse Chamberlain's cookie-cutter collection filled an entire spare bedroom. Olivia had visited it on numerous occasions during her visits to the Chamberlain home, yet each time she entered the room a quickening rushed through her. Even now, with Clarisse gone, Olivia felt like a child crossing the threshold of a toy store.

Once Bertha closed the door behind her, Olivia turned in a slow circle, taking in the bureaus and cabinets that lined all four walls. She knew the history of each one. The older, smaller cabinets had belonged to Clarisse's working-class family, while the Victorian-style walnut dresser had survived through several generations of Martin Chamberlain's well-to-do family. Other pieces were antiques, which

Clarisse had purchased for her growing cookie-cutter collection.

During the year she and Clarisse had shared their passion for cutters, Olivia had seen perhaps a third of the collection. She had no more than half an hour to find the pieces she needed for the memorial event, so she couldn't afford to dawdle. When her mother agreed to help out at the store yet again, she'd made it clear she did not intend to miss her book group at ten a.m.

Clarisse had loved both the cookie cutters and the act of organizing. Olivia knew that she would at times amuse herself by dismantling part or all of her collection and then reorganizing it. So even though Olivia had seen the insides of many drawers, their contents might have changed since then.

Olivia checked her short list of vintage cookie cutters, culled from the longer list of cutters on Clarisse's desk. These were shapes she could not reproduce from the store's inventory:

1. Dancing Snoopy *

2. Gingerbread Boy with Crown *

3. Gingerbread Man Running *

4. Gingerbread House *

5. Gingerbread Woman and Girl *

She remembered that Clarisse usually reserved the chests from her own family for her mother's modest collection, as well as other cutters from the 1940s and 1950s. The walnut dresser and an old cedar chest were the only pieces from Martin's family, and they had also contained some antiques.

Olivia began with the cedar chest. The heavy lid creaked as she lifted it, and she caught a fleeting whiff of mothballs. Inside, she found wooden trays lined with velvet and stacked on top of one another. The cutters were spaced evenly in rows across the trays. Each cutter bore an easily read identification tag. *Bless Clarisse and her obsessive organization.* She worked her way to the bottom two trays. There she found gingerbread figures, including the woman and the girl from her list.

One cookie cutter down and four to go.

Olivia turned to the walnut dresser, which had three large drawers and a mirror in a carved frame. Beneath the mirror lay a marble insert, flanked on each side by a small drawer. She pulled open the right drawer. It contained only one cookie cutter—a gingerbread house with a chimney. The shape was on her longer list, so she took it. She could have used a similar shape from the store, but it was good to have the well-used original.

She opened the small drawer on the left. It was empty. Naturally it wouldn't be that easy.

Olivia moved on to the large drawers. In the top one, she found a maze of various-size boxes, arranged as tightly as possible. Some had clear plastic lids, several were collections with pictures of the cutters on the top, and the rest would have to be opened. Olivia said good-bye to the remains of her adrenaline rush.

By the time she'd reached the bottom of the top drawer, Olivia was in despair. So far, only two cutters matched her list. She checked her watch. If she didn't leave in fifteen minutes, at the latest, Maddie would be on her own in the store. Maybe she'd be all right for a while, but not for too long.

Olivia tried to think of a way to shorten her search. She still needed three cookie cutters: gingerbread boy with crown, gingerbread man running, and the 1971 Dancing Snoopy, from a Hallmark collection. In a pinch, she and Maddie could make templates, but it wouldn't be the same. She looked at the tightly packed second drawer of the walnut dresser and remembered Bertha's comment that she'd put the cutters back wherever she could find room.

Olivia stood in the middle of the room and studied the remaining pieces of furniture. *If I were Bertha, I'd make it easy on myself.* Then she saw it—a small bureau in a sleek Scandinavian style. It screamed 1970s, and it was right next to the door. In the second drawer, she found an extensive collection of Hallmark Peanuts cookie cutters, including a rare Snoopy sitting on a pumpkin. Unable to help herself, Olivia picked it up, caressed it with her thumb, then yelled at herself for wasting precious time.

Within seconds, Olivia located the Dancing Snoopy she had sold to Clarisse. Snoopy was resting between the boy with a crown and the running gingerbread man. She checked her watch. If she left now, she should arrive at the store as her mother left for her book group.

Olivia stuffed her loot into a cloth bag she'd brought along and ran for the stairs. As she passed the living room, she saw Bertha wielding a vacuum cleaner. Olivia waved to catch her attention, then mouthed "Thank you." Before Bertha could turn off the vacuum cleaner, Olivia escaped through the front door.

Only seven miles separated the Chamberlain home from the town of Chatterley Heights. However, the twists in the road and the hilly terrain could make the trip feel much longer. Propelled by a growing sense of urgency, Olivia had sprinted from the Chamberlain's front door to her dusty old Valiant. Her tires spit gravel as she accelerated hard down the long driveway. Before turning onto the main road, she made a rolling stop and swung right.

Questions bounced around in Olivia's head, forming an overwhelming to-do list. Was Jasmine Dubois truly the dark-haired dead woman found six years earlier near the Patuxent River? If so, was her death an accident or was she murdered? Had Clarisse found out about a murder as well as a grandchild?

Of course, there were other possibilities. Maybe Clarisse once gave up a child for adoption, or Martin Chamberlain fathered a child, who grew up and decided to extort money from Clarisse, or . . . Following a curve in the road, Olivia swerved over the center line into the ongoing lane. She corrected at once, and no traffic was coming toward her, but it shook her. She realized that the more her thoughts raced, the harder her foot pressed the accelerator. She eased up, placed both hands on the wheel, and gave herself a lecture.

"Stick with the evidence, Livie, stick with the evidence." There were times that called for talking to oneself, and this was one of them. "The evidence I have is a cryptic note, from someone named Faith, claiming the existence of a grandchild. Clarisse initiated an investigation, probably through a detective agency. Clarisse sounded hopeful in her letter to me, written shortly before her death. Yet even Bertha reported that she was distracted and upset on the last evening of her life."

Olivia came to a straight stretch in the road, but instead of speeding up, she decelerated to well below the speed limit. Maddie could handle the store for a while. She needed more time to think. She was certain that Clarisse had been murdered, despite the lack of clear forensic evidence. She also felt sure that whoever killed Clarisse also,

somehow, caused Sam's diabetic coma. Maybe that bag of
cookies had been laced with something that threw his insulin off. The Chamberlain brothers would know all about
what drugs might do the trick.

Tammy stayed home from school on Monday, so she
had no alibi for the period preceding Sam's collapse. Olivia
remembered that on Mondays, Clarisse made the rounds
of her businesses, to keep tabs on operations. She'd mentioned more than once that the boys did the same. So Hugh
or Edward also had opportunities to leave those cookies
for Sam.

Olivia couldn't shake the conviction that Clarisse had
learned something about Jasmine's fate. Something that
disturbed her deeply. And she was killed to keep her quiet.
Olivia stretched her hand toward the passenger's seat and
touched the small bag that held Clarisse's cookie cutters.
It was made of soft cloth to buffer the cutters against an
ungentle world.

A glance in her rearview mirror revealed a car gain-
ing on her fast. Her first instinct was to speed up, but she
hesitated. The next patch of road had several curves, one
of which had sent many a drunk driver into the ditch. The
driver behind was clearly in a hurry. He'd try to pass her.
If she sped up, he might do so, too. She decided to slow
down, let him pass.

Olivia took her foot off the accelerator and slowed to
twenty-five miles per hour. Then to fifteen. The car seemed
to be flying closer, as if the driver hadn't noticed her. Olivia
wasn't skilled at identifying a car's make and model, but
the one behind her looked like a beater. Probably a teenager, maybe talking on a cell phone—or worse, texting.

She edged to the side of the road. There was no shoulder, only a culvert. As she headed up a hill, the drop-off

deepened. She was going so slowly, she had to accelerate to get up the hill. Maybe it was for the best. If the kid didn't come to his senses in time, he'd rear-end her.

On her descent down the hill, Olivia picked up more speed. She was heading for the final hill, the bane of drunk drivers. Beyond that she would hit a straight stretch, a good place for passing. She increased her speed, hoping to put more distance between the two cars. She'd have to slow down a bit to take the treacherous double curve that began just over the crest, but she'd done it many times before.

The car continued to gain on her. Olivia nudged her accelerator as she began to ascend. For the first time, she could see the driver in her rearview mirror. The quickest of glances showed curly hair on a bobbing head. The driver's shoulders seemed to be dancing. It was a kid all right, lost in an iPod world, swaying to the music. And she was a girl, not a boy.

Olivia had no time to ponder her misdirected sexism. She was about to crest the infamous hill. She tapped her brakes to slow down, so she could accelerate into the curve. Her speed didn't change. She pumped the brakes. Nothing happened. Finally, she jammed down, and the pedal hit the floor without resistance. That's when she knew. She had no brakes.

Olivia gripped the steering wheel with all her strength. She hovered her foot above the accelerator, letting the engine drag slow the Valiant. Only when she'd entered the curve did she press lightly on the accelerator, figuring she'd have more control. She focused so intensely on the road that her mind noted the cracks in the pavement, each telling dent in the low guardrail. She didn't dare blink.

Despite a deep swerve into the oncoming lane, Olivia managed to navigate the first curve. However, she was now going downhill, picking up too much speed. She couldn't afford to keep her foot on the accelerator. All she had left was her steering wheel. She was clutching it so hard her fingers began to cramp as she headed into the second curve.

At the sound of screeching tires, Olivia's eyes flashed to her rearview mirror. She noted with relief that the car behind her had cleared the first curve and slowed enough to make a rear-end crash unlikely. A split second later, she saw the front end of her car rush toward a badly damaged section of guardrail. Her last thought was how unfair it was. She wasn't even drunk.

Chapter Twenty-two

❦

The voice sounded close. Was someone in the
house? In her bedroom? Not a threatening voice, though . . .
Concerned, maybe . . . And young, very young.

"Wake up, please wake up," the voice said. "Please
don't be dead. I can't handle that."

Olivia recognized the words but couldn't figure out how
they went together. Where was she? She opened her eyes.
Through a window she saw tree tops and trunks, with sky
behind them.

"What happened?" Olivia's voice sounded weak, but at
least it worked.

"You're alive! Oh, thank God! Does anything hurt?
Well, of course, everything must hurt. No wait, don't move,
the paramedic said not to move you unless the car was on
fire, which it isn't."

"Para . . . ?"

"I called 911. They said to stay with you, so I did. Don't you remember anything at all?"

The voice, Olivia realized, belonged to a woman, but it wasn't familiar. "Nothing." She leaned her head back as exhaustion flooded through her. The feel of the headrest triggered a thought. "I'm in a car," she said.

"Right, you were driving. I'm Julie, by the way. You don't have to remember that, just relax." Sirens whined in the distance. "Oh good, here they come. Sit still, okay? It won't be long. I'll be right here."

Olivia began to drift, but the siren screamed until it filled her head. Then it stopped. She groaned, closed her eyes, and gave up trying to understand. A light touch on her shoulder brought her back.

"Livie, don't try to move yet. The paramedics are arriving. They'll take care of you." It was a male voice, familiar, gentle. A nice voice.

"I'm fine, really," Olivia insisted. She dragged herself to a sitting position in her hospital bed." A few bruises, that's all. Something knocked the breath out of me."

"Crashing into a guardrail will do that," Del said.

"Is my car salvageable?"

"It's a mess, but not as bad as it could have been. Those old Valiants are solid . . . Jason towed your car back to the garage. He'll look it over and see what he can figure out."

"Figure out?"

"What's the last thing you remember?"

Olivia closed her eyes and tried to think back. She remembered leaving the Chamberlain house, driving toward Chatterley Heights. Something about a car behind her had caught her attention, worried her. Then it went blank. "Nothing specific."

"Your brakes went out," Del said, "and I want to know why. Jason swears those brakes were in great shape when he tuned your car a month ago."

"Can't brakes simply give out?"

Del snorted. "Your brother is a first-rate mechanic, not to mention a perfectionist. If there's a mechanical explanation for those brakes croaking, he'll find it."

"What other explanation would there be?"

"I want you to stay here in the hospital for a while," Del said. "Now don't argue. It's only for a few hours. Cody will be here until we can locate Ellie and Allan to come get you."

"That I do remember. Allan is out of town on business until Monday evening, and Mom is in Clarksville at a kung fu competition. She would have left right after her book group and probably forgot to turn her phone back on."

"Well, Maddie, then. She was trying to rush down here when I told her what happened, but I asked her to wait so I could talk to you. She can come after the store closes."

"Lay off, will you? I'm a big girl, and I feel fine. I've had all the X-rays; nothing is broken or lacerated. I'm a little bruised, that's all."

Del frowned at the floor, a worry wrinkle between his eyebrows.

Olivia tried to push to a sitting position and winced at the pain that seared through her shoulder. "Del, do you suspect my accident wasn't really an accident? Is that why you're so eager to hear what Jason finds, you think someone tampered with my brakes?"

Del shrugged into his uniform jacket. "I'll tell you what. If Jason says it was an accident, I'll let Cody drive you home. Otherwise, I want you here overnight, under guard. So stay put for now."

When Olivia's cell phone rang, she was dressed, sitting up in her hospital bed, and losing her seventh game of hearts to Deputy Cody. She stretched toward her cell, blessing the medication the doctor had given her. She was aware of the pain, she just didn't care.

"You okay?" Cody asked.

"Fine." She clicked on her phone. "Jason? Speak to me."

"I live to obey you."

Cody signaled to Olivia that he was stepping out of the room for a moment. She nodded as Jason said, "Del's on his way, and I wanted to give you a heads-up. Your car had no brake fluid; that's why the pedal went to the floor without resistance. I found a nice, clean hole, enough to cause a slow leak. No scratching or anything, so it wasn't done with gravel or rocks."

"So you're saying . . ."

"Someone tampered with your brakes, Liv. This is serious."

"I see. Listen, did you find a bag of cookie cutters on my front seat?"

"Yeah, miraculously unhurt. I swung by the store and left them with Maddie."

"Good." Olivia hung up before Jason could resume his lecture. She swung her legs off the bed. Wobbly, but serviceable. She grabbed her jacket and headed for the hospital room door.

No one was in the hallway. Olivia hurried to the stairwell, went down the one flight, and exited through a delivery door at the back of the hospital. Bless those summer weeks she'd spent as a teenage volunteer at Chatterley Heights's small hospital.

A young orderly stood on the delivery platform, lighting a cigarette. He glanced at Olivia, but his eyes didn't linger. Her bruises were hidden by clothing, and at thirty-one, she was beyond his interest.

The hospital was four blocks north of The Gingerbread House. Olivia zipped up her jacket and tried to look as if she were out for a spring walk. Two teenage girls, deep in conversation, passed without glancing at her. Once she was alone on the sidewalk, Olivia pulled her cell from her jacket pocket and speed-dialed Maddie's number. The call went to voice mail. Olivia tried the store number next.

"Gingerbread House, how may I help you?" Maddie sounded less perky than usual.

"It's me."

"Livie! What's going on? I've been so worried that—"

"I'll be there in five minutes. Are any customers in the store?"

"One woman looking at cookbooks, but she keeps checking her watch. I think she's waiting for someone."

Olivia shot her wrist out of her jacket sleeve and checked her own watch. "It's almost five. See if you can shove her out the door, gently of course, then lock up. I'll come in from the alley and stay in the kitchen until you've cleared the store."

"Ooh, mysterious." Maddie sounded more like herself.

"And one more thing. Del will be heading our way. I have a head start, but to be on the safe side, get the store closed fast."

"Won't he come to the back door?"

"I want to slow him down so you and I can get to the same page. Look, I'm a block away. We'll talk soon."

*   *   *

Maddie was waiting in the kitchen and rushed toward Olivia when she arrived. "Are you sure you should be here? Are you really okay? Is anything broken?" Maddie asked, watching as Olivia shook two pills from a bottle of ibuprofen and washed them down with coffee.

"I'm fine, really. These things are great for a simple headache," Olivia said, clutching the pill bottle in her hand." I'm not sure how much help they'll be right now, but it's worth a shot." She reached in her pocket and pulled out a prescription bottle of Vicadon. "The doctor gave me these for pain. They're great, but they prevent coherent thought." Her shock had worn off, to be replaced by aching ribs, a painful shoulder, and a headache. Neck pain would probably follow, according to the doctor who had examined her at the hospital.

"Let me get this straight." Maddie hoisted herself onto the worktable and swung her legs. "You were just banged up in a car crash and snuck out of the hospital. Del is about to arrive here via the warpath, ready to order thee to a nunnery, or at least a safe house for the duration. But you and I will co-opt him into helping us flush out whoever killed Clarisse and attacked you and Sam. Have I got that right?"

"Basically." Olivia opened a drawer next to the sink and deposited the prescription bottle. If Del saw it, he'd use it as ammunition to keep her out of the action.

"Not to cast doubt on your master planning skills, but how are we supposed to accomplish all that?" Maddie asked.

A sharp, imperious rap on the alley door ended their discussion. "Show time," Olivia said. "Follow my lead." She held open the door as Del barged into the kitchen.

Del glared at Maddie, then zeroed in on Olivia. "I should have told the nurse to lock up your clothes."

"It's good to see you, too."

Maddie slid off the table and took a clean mug from the sink strainer. "We made a fresh pot of coffee," she said.

"I don't want coffee." Del crossed his arms over his chest.

Maddie offered him a filled cup. "Let me take that jacket. It looks snug across the shoulders. Been working out, have you?" Del ignored her. Maddie opened the freezer door, extracted a decorated cookie in the shape of a cardinal, put it on a small plate. She placed the coffee and cookie on the counter next to Del. "Frozen cookies are great for dunking. Sure I can't take that coat?"

"Stop talking and leave. I need to talk to Livie alone."

Maddie resumed her seat on the table. "I don't think so. Over to you, Livie."

"We have a couple items to show you," Olivia said, "and some information we think you'll want to hear. So sit down, dunk that cookie, and unclench those jaw muscles while I get organized." When Del didn't budge, she picked up the cup and plate and plunked them on the table. Pulling out a chair, she said, "Sit. I'll be right back."

Spunky met her at the door with frantic yapping and whining. She'd forgotten all about him, poor little guy. She noticed he'd had an accident of his own, though he had used a puppy pad.

From the small safe in her office, Olivia removed the bag of Clarisse's cookie cutters Maddie had stowed away after Jason had delivered them. Olivia also retrieved Clarisse's letter, dated shortly before her death, and the letter from Faith she had found in the store's antiques cabinet. She gathered up all the other information she and Maddie had printed off the Internet, including the article about a black-haired dead woman. After dropping all the items into a bag with handles, she picked up her desperate pet and returned to The Gingerbread House.

The silence was palpable when Olivia and Spunky entered the kitchen. At least Del's cookie had been nibbled and he had surrendered his jacket. Spunky wriggled out of her arm and raced around the kitchen, conducting a frenetic sniffing exploration. Olivia noticed Del's eyes following the process, and she was sure his tight expression softened.

While Maddie refilled mugs with coffee and a plate with frozen cookies, Olivia spread her evidence on the table. Del read the letter from Clarisse first. Then he moved on to Faith's note. "Who is this Faith?"

"Not a clue," Olivia said. "At first I thought it might not be a person but rather a closing for the note—like 'Keep the Faith' or something. In her letter, Clarisse mentioned Faith might be a blackmailer. But I'm not so sure. To me, this looks like part of a letter, the end. I suspect Clarisse wanted me to know what was going on, in case something happened to her. She was supremely confident, but realistic, too. I think she sensed danger."

Del put the note aside and turned to the two articles about an unidentified, dark-haired woman found dead in the Patuxent River State Park. When he finished, he stared at nothing for some time. Olivia clenched her teeth to keep from interrupting his thoughts. Even Maddie kept still.

Finally, Del gathered the papers into a pile and placed his palm over them. "Why didn't you turn these over to me?"

"I just did," Olivia said evenly.

"You know what I mean."

Olivia shrugged. "Clarisse entrusted me with those letters, and she didn't want her privacy violated. She wouldn't

have wanted it violated after her death, either. You kept
insisting she died either by accident or by her own hand. I
figured you would argue that someone was trying to blackmail her and that's why she was upset. The letters alone don't
really prove she was murdered. It was those articles Maddie
found that began to point me toward a possible motive."

"I don't see the significance of the articles," Del said.

"We haven't found anyone who has heard from Jasmine
since she left town so suddenly."

"Jasmine?"

"Jasmine Dubois." Olivia was trying to keep the impatience out of her voice. "If Clarisse did have a grandchild,
Jasmine was most likely to be the mother."

Del looked genuinely puzzled. "The name sounds
vaguely familiar, but . . ." He lifted his hand and picked up
one of the articles about the dead woman. "Ah, I see. This
happened six years ago. Eight years ago, my marriage broke
up." He dropped the paper back on his pile and went silent.

Del had never mentioned his broken marriage to Olivia.
Not that she was curious, of course. But if Del began to feel
self-conscious, he might not explain what his divorce had
to do with Jasmine. With a slight shake of her head, Olivia
warned Maddie to stay quiet.

Del said, "I needed to get away for a while, so I took a
deputy job in a little town in northern Minnesota for two
years. Learned a lot. Then the sheriff here retired, and I
got the job. End of story. So, who is Jasmine and why is
she important?"

Olivia's energy had begun to flag; she needed a few
moments to regroup. She shot a pleading look at Maddie,
who gave her an understanding nod.

"Here's the scoop," Maddie said. "Hugh, Edward,
and Clarisse all thought Jasmine was wonderful. Daddy

Chamberlain and jealous girlfriend, Tammy Deacons, begged to differ. One moment Jasmine was a fixture at Pete's Diner, raking in tips from admiring customers and hanging out with the Chamberlain brothers. The next moment, she had disappeared, leaving confused and broken hearts, never to be heard from again. Those who knew her seem vague about where she came from in the first place."

"I see," Del said. "So you suspect this unidentified victim might be her? Why?"

"Timing, long black hair, age about right. Also, as you will note, she had given birth."

"That's a lot of circumstantial evidence."

"Agreed, but it's the best we've got. Also, if you'll look more closely at my Internet searches, you will notice I couldn't find any evidence that she ever existed. Sort of makes you wonder." Maddie lifted the last cookie on the plate, a chartreuse bunny rabbit. His ear became history.

"Six years ago, ordinary people were a lot less likely to find their names on the Internet," Del said. "We weren't drowning in social networks."

Olivia felt some energy return and jumped in. "What Maddie is trying to say is there are too many unanswered questions and coincidences. Clarisse was murdered; the attacks on Sam and me are indirect proof of that. So who was most likely to murder her, and why? It has to be Hugh or Edward or Tammy. Or some combination of them, including all three working together."

"Livie, you're going off on a—"

"I think you believe us, but you want us to back off. You intend to take this information and pursue your own investigation. If we stop asking questions, you hope the killer will relax and stop trying to murder people. Am I close?"

Del rubbed his forehead. He looked more tired than

Olivia had ever seen him. "I don't want anyone else to get hurt. You two aren't police officers or trained investigators."

"But that's—"

"I'm not insulting you, Livie, I'm stating the facts. You are smart, both of you, and you've done some good investigating so far. But I'm the one with the training and the resources, not to mention experience."

"And a gun," Maddie said.

"Which I prefer not to use, but yes. I do agree with your list of suspects, although I doubt Tammy Deacons would know how to tamper with your brakes. Still, she might be involved, as you've pointed out. Arguably, Hugh, Edward, and Tammy all have motives, so two or all three of them could be working together." Del ran his fingers through his hair. "I want you to cancel the memorial for Clarisse, Livie. It'll only make both of you vulnerable to another attack."

Olivia and Maddie exchanged quick glances but said nothing.

"Listen, Livie, whoever tampered with your car isn't going to give up. You are in real danger. So are you, Maddie, and maybe your families, too."

"I gave Aunt Sadie an early birthday gift," Maddie said. "A spa getaway in DC. She accused me of wanting the house to myself, but she left anyway, this morning. Won't be back until Wednesday."

Del sank back in his chair. "Have you two listened to a word I've said?"

"You've expressed your concerns quite clearly," Olivia said, "and we aren't ignoring you. We see the situation differently, that's all. We need you, but you also need us. Okay, go ahead and roll your eyes, but at least hear me out."

Del made a show of checking his watch.

Olivia reached for the bag of Clarisse's cookie cutters

and emptied them onto the table. "These are why I went to the Chamberlain house in the first place. Somehow, my attacker knew I was there, although Bertha swore up and down she didn't say a word. My guess is she acted nervous or asked a question that made our suspect or suspects suspicious. Anyway, what matters is that these little babies survived intact. We have three suspects for Clarisse's murder, a cold murder case, two attacks, and maybe a missing child. What we don't have is a clear, quick way to figure out who among the three suspects is responsible for what."

Del said, "As sheriff, I can interview—"

"You can investigate like crazy," Olivia said, "but that will take time, probably lots of it, and even then you might not succeed. Maddie can't keep sending her aunt out of town, and I don't want to hire a bodyguard for who knows how long. Maddie and I have devised a plan that might flush out the guilty party, or parties, much faster."

"How many painkillers have you consumed?"

"Just ibuprofen. Listen, cookie cutters had meaning for Clarisse. She used them to help her work out problems. I didn't figure this out until last night—early this morning, really. I was trying to identify the cutters in the photo of her desk—"

"Which I ordered you to delete, as I recall."

"And I remembered Bertha telling me that Clarisse would talk things out with the portrait of her husband, the one that hangs over her office fireplace. Then it hit me. Sometimes when Clarisse picked out cookie cutters at our store, she'd make an offhand remark, like . . ." Olivia picked up the running gingerbread man cutter. "When I sold her this one only a few weeks ago, she said, 'Run, run as fast as you can.' That's a quote from the old Gingerbread

Man fairy tale, so I didn't think anything of it at the time."
Olivia picked up the Dancing Snoopy. "She bought this
one the last time I saw her. It's such a joyful cutter, but I
thought Clarisse was going to cry when she looked at it. I
remember wondering why she bought it if it made her feel
so sad."

Del had stopped interrupting. Olivia glanced up to find
him studying the cookie cutters. He picked up the baby
carriage. "So you're thinking these might represent people
in her life?"

Olivia nodded. "People, events, I haven't had time to
figure them all out. Maddie and I plan to arrange the cookies in different designs that will look random to anyone
who isn't involved. But we're hoping to tease a guilty reaction out of those involved in Clarisse's death."

"In other words, it's one big, potentially dangerous
experiment? I can't let you do this, either of you." Del
dropped the baby carriage cutter on the table and stood up.
"I forbid you to try this stunt." He grabbed his jacket and
hat and strode toward the alley door.

"It's our store and our risk," Olivia said. "We aren't asking for permission. Or for protection. We'll hold the memorial as planned, whether or not you take part. It's up to you."

Del's shoulders dropped. "Livie Greyson, you are the
most stubborn woman on the planet." He turned to face
her. "You know perfectly well I'll be here. If something
happened to you—or Maddie—I'd never forgive myself."

"Thanks for the afterthought," Maddie said.

Del waved the papers Olivia had given him. "I have
work to do. Tomorrow we will discuss how to keep you two
from getting yourselves killed." He slapped his hat on his
head and opened the alley door. "Meanwhile, Cody will

check on the store as often as he can. If you hear anything suspicious outside or inside, don't explore on your own. Call my cell. I'll keep it with me. If for some reason I don't answer, call 911. Got it?"

"Got it," said Olivia.

"Yes sir," said Maddie.

"And lock this door behind me."

As Maddie locked the door, Olivia said, "Okay then, to work. We need to cut and bake the cookies tonight so they will be cool enough to decorate tomorrow after closing. I'll dig out the additional cutters we'll need."

"Hold it," Maddie said with authority. "You will not be digging or cutting or baking anything, not tonight."

"Stop fussing."

"I do not fuss. I command. Go upstairs, and take that noisy creature with you." Maddie pointed to Spunky, curled in a snoring ball on his blanket. "Then take a warm bath, eat something, and relax with a good book. Having completed those tasks, fall into bed and sleep as long as you can. Frankly, Livie, I've never seen you look so awful."

"Thanks ever so much." She had to admit she felt exhausted, not to mention sore and stiff. "However, you are right, my friend."

"I am?"

"I need all my strength to get through the next couple days, and my reserves are depleted. Promise me, though— if you need me for anything, even if you're having trouble finding those extra cookie cutters, give me a ring."

"I know the location of everything in this store," Maddie said. "Do not set your alarm and do sleep all day. Here's your cuddle toy," Maddie said. She lifted a sleepy Spunky, blanket and all, and slid the bundle into Olivia's arms. "Now go away."

Chapter Twenty-three

For some reason, Olivia's alarm had switched from a gentle beep-beep to a high-pitched whine. Also, her body was being used as a punching bag. She slogged through the quicksand of sleep until she could identify Spunky as both whiner and assailant. He was expressing his displeasure at being cooped up too long. Given her soreness after her recent accident, Spunky's five pounds felt like five hundred. She lifted him off and rolled onto her side. "Remind me why I thought adopting a puppy was such a good idea?"

Spunky responded by bouncing off her sore shoulder.

"Would you give me a break?" Olivia reached over him for her cell phone. She had defied Maddie's order to sleep all day by setting her cell's alarm for eight a.m. She hadn't heard it go off, but it must have, given the bright daylight edging her bedroom curtains.

Olivia squinted at the upper-right corner of her cell. "Four o'clock!" She sat up. "Ouch!" Spunky leaped backwards with a nervous yip. Olivia rubbed her eyes and checked the time again. Four o'clock all right, with a little "p.m." following behind. She'd slept through her alarm and then some.

Instantly she thought of Clarisse and how close she was to learning the truth. The thought cleared Olivia's head and muted her awareness of pain. In the next thirty-six hours, she intended to find out who had killed her friend.

After a shower, a cold slice of sausage pizza, and a couple extra-strength ibuprofen, Olivia took Spunky downstairs for a quick visit to the side yard. When he'd finished, she tucked him under her arm and entered The Gingerbread House. Over by the antiques cabinet, Maddie was deep in conversation with two women, who were exclaiming over some vintage cutters. Maddie spotted Olivia and winked at her over the customers' bent heads.

At the sales counter, Olivia's mother handed a small Gingerbread House bag to another customer, a husky woman who looked familiar. When the woman turned to leave, she recognized Binnie Sloan, editor of *The Weekly Chatter*. Binnie's tight mouth expressed displeasure. As soon as she saw Olivia, however, a predatory smile spread across her face. Spunky squirmed in Olivia's arms, but she held on tight, feeling in need of his protection.

"There you are, Livie, just the person I wanted to see." Behind Binnie, Ellie waved to get Olivia's attention and shook her head in silent warning.

"Hey there, fella," Binnie said, reaching her hand toward Spunky's head.

Spunky responded with a low growl. Olivia could feel his muscles tighten. She backed up a step to prevent him from biting Binnie's outstretched fingers.

Binnie dropped her hand. "Not very friendly, is he? Anyway, I dropped in to let you know I'll be covering your little memorial service tomorrow for the newspaper. Your mom tells me it's private, which is why it's so important for me to report on it. Everyone who knew Clarisse Chamberlain needs a chance to grieve her loss."

It took a chunk of willpower for Olivia to keep her eyes from spinning toward the ceiling. "I'm afraid the memorial will be closed to the press," she said. "It will be a time for Clarisse's family and close friends to remember her in private. I'm sure you understand." She managed a tight smile. Spunky growled in his throat.

Binnie gave Spunky a wary glance. "Have you considered how the rest of Chatterley Heights will react to being excluded from her circle of 'close friends'? They might feel deeply hurt, don't you think? Maybe even angry?"

And if they don't feel hurt or angry, you will urge them to do so. "As an experienced journalist," Olivia said, "surely you can help the town understand our need for privacy. It will be a quiet, simple get-together, nothing newsworthy. If anything exciting does happen, I'll be glad to report to you afterwards." A rash promise, perhaps, but it was never a good idea to alienate the press in a small town.

Ellie appeared beside Olivia, providing a gentle air of support. "Livie dear, shall we begin closing? It's past five."

Binnie Sloan, however, was immune to hints. "On another topic," she said, "I hear you were involved in a single car accident yesterday. Ran right into that guardrail we locals like to call the Drunk Stopper. Care to comment?"

Alienating the press was starting to sound more appealing. Sensing his mistress's rising irritation, Spunky bared his teeth. Olivia had never seen him do that before. Ellie wove her fingers into the fur on his neck and stared into his eyes. Ellie must have lost her magical touch, though, because Spunky's growl turned menacing.

Without comment, Binnie headed for the door, her lips pressed into a thin line. When the door closed behind her, Spunky relaxed at once. Ellie rubbed his ears and said, "What a good, good boy you are. Olivia, are you quite sure that you're feeling all right after that dreadful accident? Your brother said—" Spunky's tail beat a staccato rhythm against Olivia's arm.

"Mom, I'm completely fine, I promise you. What just happened here?"

Ellie smiled. "Merely an experiment in dog whispering, dear. Now, if I hurry, I can make my poetry group on time. You two have fun decorating cookies this evening. Don't stay up too late."

The Gingerbread House kitchen smelled of orange zest, cookie dough, and pepperoni pizza, with an overlay of French roast coffee. Racks of cutout cookies covered half the worktable, and most of the remaining space was disappearing fast as Olivia gathered the ingredients for royal icing.

Maddie had brought along her Aunt Sadie's trusty twenty-year-old Artisan stand mixer. "This calls for the big guns." She gave it a loving pat. "So let me get this straight," she said. "You don't want me to have too much fun decorating these cookies?" Maddie was wearing jeans ripped across the knees and a tight T-shirt that said, "Born to Gambol," in case there was any doubt.

"I want the shapes to be recognizable," Olivia said. "If we hope to see anyone react to our designs, they'll have to know what they're looking at."

"So I could decorate a baby carriage with, say, magenta, as long as it still looks like a baby carriage?"

"Sure, within reason. But I have some ideas for specific cookies." Olivia pointed to the nearest rack, which held cookies in the shape of a hooded baby carriage on wheels. "Any color is fine, but make sure some are blue and some are pink. If there's a grandchild out there, we don't know the gender."

"Check." Maddie picked up the revised cookie cutter list Olivia had left with her:

CLARISSE'S COOKIE CUTTERS

1. Hooded Baby Carriage on Wheels

2. Small Angel

3. Dancing Snoopy *

4. Jasmine Flower (Added by Olivia)

5. Jasmine Vine with Flowers (Template added by Maddie)

6. Six-petaled Flower

7. Gingerbread Boy with Crown *

8. Gingerbread Man Running *

9. Gingerbread House *

10. Gingerbread Woman and Girl *

11. Coffin Shape

12. Witch's Hat

13. Round Tree

14. Dove

15. Nutcracker

UNIDENTIFIED

16. Shield? Coat of Arms?

17. Apple? Bell Pepper?

18. Flower? Grass in Wind? Head with Wild Hair?

"Those little angel shapes," Olivia said, "make some boys and some girls. And a few of each should have black hair."

"Aha. Like Jasmine, you mean." Maddie scribbled a note on her list.

"Exactly. Ditto for the gingerbread mother and daughter. But we should represent other hair colors, too."

"How about navy blue? Or violet?

"Uh, sure."

"Puce?"

"Have you been chewing coffee beans again?"

Maddie smirked. "Sorry, it's the excitement. Carry on."

Olivia wished she, too, felt the thrill of the chase, but all she could muster was fierce determination. Besides, the ibuprofen had barely touched the aching throughout her body. She rubbed her neck as she pointed toward the right side of the table. "The gingerbread boy wearing a crown—Clarisse must have acquired that cutter before I met her. It was distributed by Robin Hood Flour in the 1980s. She might have gotten hers that way. I wonder if she used it when Hugh and Edward were growing up. Her little boys." Olivia's legs felt spongy, and she braced herself against the table edge.

"Hey, you should be back in bed," Maddie said. She dragged a chair over and pushed Olivia into it. "Listen, tell me what you want, and I'll do the decorating. If you're serious about this unveil-a-killer event tomorrow, you'll need more strength than this."

Olivia knew her weakness had as much to do with sadness as with pain. "No, even you can't finish all this decorating and plan the event alone. We need to talk it through while we work. I can rest later, when this is over."

"Okay, but if anyone has to stay up most of the night, it's going to be me. Got it?"

"Won't be necessary." Olivia drained her coffee cup. "Okay. Gingerbread boy with crown. He could represent either or both of the Chamberlain brothers, or maybe a grandson. Make the crown stand out. I have a feeling that might be important."

Maddie refilled her own cup and Olivia's. "I'd better explain this shape," she said, pointing to a rack of cookies that looked like clouds. "I know you gave me an eight-petaled flower cutter to represent a jasmine flower, but I wasn't sure anyone would recognize it, even if we use white icing. So I made a roundish template with a stemlike bottom. I'll pipe icing into vine and flower designs."

"Good idea. If that doesn't work, we'll have to drop a hint." Olivia thought of her mother. She wasn't eager to put her mother in danger, but if anyone could drop a hint without raising suspicion, it was Ellie Greyson-Meyer.

"Any idea what the six-sided flower is supposed to be?" Maddie asked.

"That one puzzles me. I suppose Clarisse might have used it to represent Jasmine, but it doesn't seem the best choice. Jasmine flowers have so many petals; that's why I gave you the eight-sided flower shape instead of the six."

"Let's leave it for now and move on." Maddie started collecting measuring cups and spoons. "I need to move. You talk. I'll whip up a batch of icing."

Olivia retrieved her laptop from the desk, brought it to the table, and sank onto a chair. "Maybe we can get some ideas from this." She lifted the laptop lid to reveal Deputy Cody's photo of Clarisse's desk. "See that one?" Olivia pointed to a cutter shape in the lower-left corner. "That looks like Snoopy Dancing."

"Hallmark, 1971, red plastic," Maddie said. She cut open a bag of meringue powder and measured out four teaspoons.

"I'm almost positive Clarisse thought of Sam Parnell as Snoopy, like everyone else in town." Olivia touched the red image on the screen. "She bought this cutter right here, the last time I saw her. I remember she held it in her hand and said something like, 'So gleeful.' She was talking to herself, so it was hard to make out."

"You think she meant Sam or Snoopy?"

"Maybe both. Sam did look pleased with himself when he told me about seeing the word 'grandchild' in the private detective's letter to Clarisse."

"Vague enough for me," Maddie said. "Anyway, Snoopy is off to the side in the photo, so Clarisse probably hadn't thought much about it yet. In fact, look at this gap here." She drew her finger in a circle around the laptop screen. "It's like when I work a jigsaw puzzle. First, I group pieces that might go together. Then in the middle I put the pieces that suggest a design to me."

Olivia arched her eyebrows in surprise.

"What? I can be organized when it's really important."

In the interest of time, Olivia let that pass.

Maddie opened a new box of confectioners' sugar. "I'm

only saying, if Clarisse was using cookie cutters to work through a problem, wouldn't she single out the most important cutters first?"

Olivia zoomed in on the center of the photo. "Actually, you might be on to something. There are three cutters clustered in the middle—the crowned gingerbread boy, the running gingerbread man, and the gingerbread house. Hugh and Edward, maybe? And the Chamberlain home?"

"Which gingerbread man is which brother?" Maddie asked as she added two cups of confectioners' sugar to the mixing bowl.

Olivia leaned back in her chair and closed her eyes. Her head had begun to ache; time for another dose of ibuprofen. Nevertheless, she stayed put and forced her resistant brain to dredge up any judgments Clarisse had made about her sons. There hadn't been many. Clarisse had kept their less appealing qualities to herself, perhaps because she hoped Olivia would marry one of them. However, early in their friendship, Clarisse had made a couple of telling comments.

"Once when Clarisse was frustrated with Hugh, she said he expected everything to drop in his lap. He needed to work harder, she said, not depend on his charm to get by. She called it a 'sense of entitlement.'"

"So Hugh is the boy with the crown," Maddie said. "Lucas told me last night about when Hugh offered to adjust his loan. Lucas said he acted like it was his duty to take care of his inferiors, like Lucas wasn't smart enough to handle his own finances. Hugh never said one word about Lucas's mom and dad, how hard that has been."

"Noblesse oblige," Olivia said.

"Enough with the French, Livie. I have trouble with English."

"Sorry, only you described it perfectly. I'm convinced the crowned boy is Hugh. By the way, did Lucas request those loan concessions?"

"He did not." Maddie tossed a set of measuring spoons into the sink. "It would never have occurred to him. Hugh came to him, out of the blue."

"Really. Did Edward know about it?"

"Hugh said that Edward agreed. That's all I know. Now be quiet while I mix this icing to perfection."

Olivia relaxed to the familiar sound of a whirring mixer. Her attention drifted among the loose clusters of cookie cutters that surrounded the three central ginger-bread shapes. Dancing Snoopy frolicked in the lower-left corner, next to a witch's hat. If the gleeful Snoopy was Sam Parnell, might the witch's hat designate someone else who had disappointed Clarisse? Maddie would say the witch had to be Tammy Deacons, and maybe she'd be right.

Four images formed a semicircle along the right side of the photo: a lovely stylized dove, a nutcracker, a rounded shade tree, and two more gingerbread figures—adult woman and little girl. Mother and daughter. Did Clarisse know that Jasmine had given birth to a daughter, or was she guessing?

Olivia wasn't sure what to make of the dove, nutcracker, and tree. She herself knew that sometimes a certain cookie cutter evoked an emotion, so a dove might simply represent Clarisse's longing for peace in her family. The tree puzzled Olivia. And a nutcracker . . . She thought back to the nut-cracker story. Wasn't the nutcracker really a prince?

Maddie had finished mixing the royal icing and was collecting little bottles of gel paste food coloring.

"Hey, Maddie, do you remember the nutcracker story?"

"The nutcracker? I'm not sure I ever understood it

completely. Too many curses. All I remember is the nut-cracker guy was odd looking because he was under an ugly curse, but he was really a handsome prince. Then he does something heroic—like kill the evil mouse king or whatever—but the beautiful princess rejects him because he's ugly. Those beautiful princesses were mighty full of themselves, you know? Anyway, I think she changes her mind in the end, and the prince turns handsome again, and they live happily ever after in dolly land."

"I'm impressed," Olivia said. "Although I still wonder what the nutcracker meant to Clarisse. It must be related somehow to Hugh or Edward, or maybe even Martin."

Maddie didn't respond. She stood hunched over a small bowl, counting drops of coloring as they fell into a small container of icing.

If only she had a computer program for reading minds, Olivia thought. No, that would be scary. Only four more recognizable images to go, spread from the upper part of the photo and around the upper-left corner: coffin, baby carriage, small angel, and six-sided flower. Three more cutter shapes were partially obscured by shadows. One looked like the bottom of an apple or maybe a bell pepper. Next to it might be a flower or grass blowing in the wind— or a head with hair sticking out. Along the top-left edge, a bit of design could be part of a shield or coat of arms. Or almost anything.

Olivia leaned back and took a long, slow breath. Nice. She breathed in again, but her exhale erupted into a startled cry when she heard a loud pounding on the door to the alley.

"Déjà vu all over again," Olivia said when she saw Maddie bolt upright, holding a dropper of food coloring.

"Now *that* French I understand," Maddie said.

"Hey, you kids in there?" It was Del's voice.

"What are the odds?" Maddie said as she opened the door.

Del had bags under his eyes and a day's growth of stubble. He slid out of his jacket and slung it over a chair back. He caught sight of the photo on Olivia's computer screen, then glanced over the sea of cookies on the kitchen table. "So you're really going ahead with this memorial tomorrow? I can't talk you out of it?"

"Yes, we are," said Maddie. "And no, you can't even threaten us out of it."

"Then I have no choice. I can't let you kids do this all on your own. It's too dangerous." He gave Olivia a hard stare. "I'll be here the whole time, keeping a close eye on your guests."

"You'll scare them off," Olivia said. "You can come as a guest, but you can't be in uniform or carry a gun. And you'll have to give a speech about Clarisse."

"Livie, come on, I can't—"

"Teasing. But you can't wear a gun."

Del sighed loudly and sank into a chair. "Cody will be here, out of sight. Preferably in the kitchen, so I can give him a whistle if anything happens. And he will most definitely have his weapon."

Maddie gave a nod of approval, and Olivia said, "All right, we can live with that. Have you found out anything about Jasmine?"

Del ran his fingers through his hair, which explained its condition. "This is so wrong. I should be protecting you, not helping you with some harebrained—"

"Hey, could we move on? I'm tired, everything hurts, and I can't rest until I know who killed my friend. So what have you got?"

Maddie and Del both stared at her in mute astonishment

while Olivia swallowed an ibuprofen. Del cleared his throat and said, "Your information was very helpful. I contacted the Montgomery County PD, talked to a buddy of mine in the Cold Case Squad. Don't ask me how, but Roberta spent her Saturday tracing Jasmine back to a little town in southern Ohio. Parents deceased. And here's the kicker—Jasmine was supposed to be dead, too. Died in a car crash fourteen years ago."

"McGonigle, Ohio, right?" Maddie said. "I found that information online. Wow, I'm good."

"Jasmine's car went off a mountain road and burned," Del said. "Charred remains of a young woman inside. The authorities figured it was Jasmine and closed the case."

Olivia's latest dose of ibuprofen must have kicked in, because she felt better. "How did you determine that our Jasmine was the real one?"

"Dental records. Roberta managed to track down Jasmine's childhood dentist. He faxed us her records, up to age seventeen. The match was convincing. We may never know who died in Jasmine's car, or how she got there, but at least we know where Jasmine herself died."

"Do we know how?" Olivia asked.

"That's tougher. She was found near some rocks, but it was hard to determine if she fell, jumped, was pushed, or even whether she died elsewhere." Del slung his jacket over his shoulder. "Gotta get back."

Olivia refreshed her computer screen and stared at Clarisse's cookie cutters. "The autopsy revealed Jasmine had given birth. I'm willing to bet she had a daughter." She pointed to the gingerbread woman and girl. "There's no mother and son here, only a mother and daughter. Can your friend check with hospitals?"

"That would take a long time. We don't know when

Jasmine gave birth. She might have used another name or given birth at home. A name would help."

"What about Faith, the name on the note to Clarisse that I gave you?"

"Still a long, long shot. If this Faith was a friend of hers, then maybe Jasmine used her ID at a hospital, but we need a last name." With his hand on the doorknob, Del said, "Cody and I will be here tomorrow morning at eleven. Get some sleep."

"I'll probably still be decorating cookies at eleven," Maddie said.

Olivia didn't answer. She was staring at her computer screen, trying to tease out a thought. She heard the alley door shut behind Del, but it barely registered.

"Maddie, come look at this." Olivia pointed toward the left corner of the photo on her screen, then over to the right side.

"What?" Maddie pulled over a chair.

"Clarisse spoke some French, you know. A little, anyway. You see this tree shape, right above the gingerbread mother and daughter? What if Clarisse was trying to find a cutter that represented a forest?"

"You've totally lost me." With an air of boredom, Maddie began poking loose curls back under her bandanna.

"Dubois. The name Dubois loosely translates as 'of the wood' or 'of the forest.'"

Maddie dragged over a chair. "You think 'tree' is as close to 'forest' as Clarisse could get? That would imply the gingerbread woman is Jasmine Dubois, and the girl is her daughter, whose first name we don't know."

"Except . . ." Olivia pointed at the far left side of the screen. "What does that look like to you?"

Maddie twisted her head in several directions, trying to

find an angle that made sense of the partial image. "It looks sort of familiar. Not a flower shape, at least I don't think so. Can you zoom in a bit?" She touched the screen and traced the outline as best she could. "For some reason it reminds me of my first high school boyfriend, Matt."

"You mean Matt the do-gooder? The one who left you on the curb while he helped any woman over thirty across the street?"

"That's the one."

"Hang on." Olivia jumped up and rushed over to the desk, moving far too fast for someone who'd recently wrecked her car. She'd pay for it, but she didn't care. She grabbed her list of Clarisse's entire cookie cutter collection and flipped through it. "Yep, there it is," she said, poking a triumphant finger at one name.

"Hold still, will you?" Maddie followed Olivia's finger and read, "'Boy Scout insignia.' There's a Boy Scout cookie cutter?"

"Clarisse had this handmade when Hugh was a Boy Scout, so she could bake cookies for his troop. Well, so Bertha could bake them. Clarisse showed me a photo of a plate piled with cookies, all shaped and decorated like the Boy Scout insignia."

"Okay," Maddie said, "but what startling revelation does this lead to?"

Olivia quickly found a website that showed the Boy Scout insignia in its entirety. "What is that shape called?"

"Oh. It's another French thing, isn't it?"

"It's a fleur-de-lis."

"Livie, don't you dare ask me to guess what that means, or I swear—"

"Fleur means 'flower,'" Olivia said. "And 'lis' means 'lily.'"

A broad smile plumped Maddie's cheeks as she stared at the screen. "I knew I'd seen that somewhere before."

"I just told you—"

"No, not the fleur whatever, I mean that one." Maddie poked her finger at the six-sided flower to the right of the fleur-de-lis. She snatched the laptop off the table and put it on her lap. Her fingers flew until she pulled up the website of an online cookie-cutter vendor. "Look at that." She turned the screen toward Olivia.

And there it was, a six-sided copper cutter with pointed petals, labeled "lily flower." On Clarisse's list, the cutter was labeled simply "six-sided flower." Olivia wondered if Clarisse had obscured the name to protect her grandchild.

"I need your cell," Olivia said. When Maddie dug it out of her coat pocket and handed it to her, Olivia punched in a number. "Del? I may have something for you. Lily."

"The flower?" Del sounded groggy.

"Also a name. A flower name, like Jasmine. I think the child's name is Lily."

"What makes you think so?"

"It's complicated, I'll explain later, but I'm pretty sure I'm right."

"Okay, I'll . . ." Del yawned. "I'll call Roberta. Maybe it'll help. Bye." The telephone clunked and went silent.

Olivia handed the phone back to Maddie. "I hope our Lily doesn't show up in an obituary."

Chapter Twenty-four

The next morning as Olivia and Maddie finished readying The Gingerbread House for Clarisse Chamberlain's memorial, storm clouds began rolling in. Sheriff Del and Deputy Cody had already arrived. Cody had taken his position in the store kitchen, with the door slightly ajar. He would be the only one armed.

"Perfect," Maddie said, shutting the windows against the first spatter of raindrops. "It's a dark and stormy afternoon."

Olivia was so keyed up, she giggled.

Ellie and Jason Greyson arrived, shaking off raindrops. Ellie peeled her raincoat off an outfit that was unique yet appropriate—a tunic and loose pants of black silk with glistening silver thread work. A silver silk scarf draped loosely around her neck and over a shoulder. A single braid hung down her back, secured with a thin black ribbon.

Jason wore his best black jeans.

"Fill me in on my role, dear," Ellie said with a gentle tug at Olivia's arm.

"For this experiment to work, "Olivia said, "the guests need to understand what the cookie shapes are. You could drop a subtle hint here and there."

"I am the soul of subtlety."

Olivia led her mother to the cookbook nook, where Maddie had cleared space on a table by moving a display of pie-baking equipment to the main sales room. In its place was a large metal tray holding one each of the identifiable cookie shapes found in the photo of Clarisse's desk. They'd given up on two shapes.

"Never mind the icing colors," Olivia said. "First, tell me what you think the shapes represent."

Ellie pointed a silvery polished nail. "That is an angel in the upper-left corner. Then a baby carriage, a coffin, a bird of some sort?"

"A dove."

"Of course." Ellie hesitated at the next shape. "Oh, a nutcracker. And that must be a tree, despite the bright red trunk. Oh, a gingerbread woman and little girl. I grew up with a set like that. I wonder what happened to it."

"Time marches on, Mother."

"Yes, dear. Over here we have a witch's hat, that darling Dancing Snoopy with purple fur, a flower of some type. . . ."

"That's an important one," Olivia said. "It's meant to be a lily."

"Oh yes, I see it now. And the flower next to it?"

"A jasmine flower."

"Ah. So Lily is . . . ?"

"We think Lily is Jasmine Dubois's daughter. You mustn't say that to anyone, but do observe reactions."

"Of course." With a troubled glance, Ellie asked, "Are these two lovely flowers still blooming, do you know?"

"We have hope for little Lily."

"I see," Ellie said softly. "So perhaps dear Clarisse was not the only victim. How sad." Ellie straightened to her full four foot eleven. "This makes me angry, which is bad for my karma. I shall do my subtle best to help."

Olivia put her arm around her diminutive mother's shoulders. "Don't tell anyone else. Del and Cody know all, of course, but you are the only other person we are trusting with our suspicions."

"I am the soul of discretion."

"All those souls in one tiny body," Olivia said. "It must get crowded in there."

Hugh Chamberlain stood before the small group of mourners, holding a small glass of sherry. He looked both solemn and attractive in his dark suit and tie. Holding his glass aloft, Hugh bestowed a sad smile and said, "My little family wishes to thank you, Olivia and Maddie, for arranging this special memorial. To learn that our mother was so loved, as well as admired, touches us more than you can know." He even looked, Olivia thought, as if he meant it. Yet she found herself untouched by his words. *There's such a thing as too much eloquence.*

The attendees stood in a semicircle, since the store was too small and crowded for chairs. Olivia chose a place at one end, which gave her a view of the mourners. Jason fidgeted next to her. Next came Ellie, Maddie and Lucas, Mr. Willard, Bertha, Edward, Tammy, and finally Del, in a black suit and tie.

"We miss our mother very much," Hugh said. "And we always will. Edward, perhaps you would say a few words?"

Edward hesitated, as if he might refuse. With an abrupt nod, he lurched forward and took Hugh's place before the gathering. His dark blue eyes moved constantly. "My brother is right, our mother will be missed. However, I'm sure of one thing. She wasn't one to sit around and feel sorry for herself. She'd tell us to get back to work. I intend to work twice as hard, in memory of her." Head down, he rejoined Hugh.

Olivia marveled at how different the brothers were from each other. Edward had none of his brother's easy eloquence, but his words had rung truer. Had he known Clarisse better?

Olivia stepped forward. "To honor Clarisse, we have prepared decorated cookies using some of the cookie cutters that meant the most to her. There are trays of cookies all around the store, including the cookbook nook. We hope you will think of Clarisse as you enjoy them. Perhaps the cookies will bring out memories of her that you will share with each other. There is plenty of sherry, and fresh coffee set up by the antiques cabinet."

At a glance from Olivia, Maddie and Lucas positioned themselves near the front door. If anyone tried to leave right away, Maddie would talk at them until they gave up and escaped toward the cookies. Mr. Willard, in his role as sheepdog, stuck close to Hugh and Edward.

Olivia was ready to mingle, in a sneaky and targeted way, when she realized she didn't have her cell phone. Del had insisted they all carry one, in case of emergency. She must have left it attached to its charger when she changed into her black pants and gray silk blouse.

Jason stood nearby, eyeing a plate of cookies with longing. She tapped him on the shoulder and whispered, "I'll split the leftovers with you and throw in a pizza if you'll run upstairs and get my cell phone for me. I can't leave right now."

Jason grinned. "I'd have done it for nothing, but hey, I'll take the goodies."

"Thanks. It's on the dresser in my bedroom." As she felt in her pants pocket for her key, Olivia saw Edward, Hugh, and Tammy walk into the cookbook nook alone. Bertha had captured Mr. Willard. She handed the key to Jason and hustled after her three suspects. She figured her window of opportunity would be closing in fifteen to twenty minutes. It was a miracle that all her suspects were present, but they wouldn't stay long. Brief conversations, a glance at the cookies for the sake of appearances, and they'd be gone.

Tammy wiggled her fingers in a girlish wave as Olivia entered the nook. "Livie, it was so sweet of you to do all this, especially after we . . ." She shot a quick look at Hugh, who was talking with Edward. Both men were ignoring the cookie tray. Tammy lowered her voice. "I do want to apologize about how we treated you after we found out about your inheritance. I should never have said a word to that reporter Binnie. Oh, Livie, let's not fight anymore. I'm sorry I've been short with you lately. It's been so . . . Anyway, things are better now, and I have so much to tell you."

"Apology accepted." Feeling like a traitor, Olivia added, "You can make it up to me by touring our cookie trays with me. And make sure Hugh and Edward come, too."

"I can do that. Come on, boys," Tammy said, linking arms with Hugh and Edward. "Livie worked hard on these cookies. The least we can do is admire them." Hugh acquiesced with grace and a smile for Olivia. Edward looked irritated by the interruption, but he allowed Tammy to capture his arm.

The small group glanced over the cookies in the nook. "Lovely," Hugh murmured as he chose an angel with forest green hair. Edward made no comment, and Tammy said, "Yum." Olivia was disappointed but not surprised by the bland reaction. For the nook tray, she had repeated the design on Clarisse's desk, which hadn't shouted a clear message. In the main store were five additional trays with more suggestive designs.

Olivia guided the group out of the cookbook nook to the sherry. As Hugh and Edward refilled their glasses, Olivia saw Jason heading in her direction. Her cell phone. She shook her head at Jason to say she didn't want to be interrupted. He stopped and gave her a puzzled look. Ellie appeared at his elbow and spoke. He bent down to listen, shrugged, and snatched a cookie off a pile of extras.

The whole episode had taken only a few seconds, but when Olivia turned back to her charges, Hugh was staring at her. His sensuous lips curved, as always, in a good-natured smile, but his eyes were watchful. Alert. Curious.

In that instant, Olivia knew her lovely plan was doomed. It was too complex and time-consuming. She hadn't given enough thought to the human element.

It was now or never.

"Everyone, can I have your attention?" Heads swiveled toward her. Del, who had been lounging against a wall, straightened and reached into his pants pocket for his cell phone. "I know you're all busy, but before you leave, I'd appreciate your help. Would you all gather up here with me? Maddie, would you and Jason bring those three trays from the front?" She'd been vague, but Maddie would understand which ones she wanted.

With the trays arranged on three small display tables and the guests in a semicircle around them, Olivia said,

"Clarisse and I shared a passion for cookie cutters. Sometimes a particular cutter has a special meaning for me, and I know Clarisse felt the same. As I mentioned earlier, Maddie and I made these cookies from cutters that were special to Clarisse. I would like for all of us who cared for her to share our thoughts about what each of these shapes might have meant to her and the nice memories they must represent.

"Let's start with this one." Olivia selected two cookies in the shape of the crowned gingerbread boy and held them up so everyone could see. One had black hair, and the other, fire engine red.

"Goodness, that's Hugh," Bertha said. "When Hugh was little, Ms. Clarisse would have me make a batch of cookies for her 'little prince.' You wouldn't remember, Hugh, because she stopped when you were about four. She was afraid little Edward might think she loved you better." Bertha's face reddened as she realized the implications of what she'd said.

"Interesting," Hugh said.

Olivia couldn't see Edward's face, but he hung his head as if the revelation disturbed him.

"What about this one?" Olivia held up a running gingerbread man with bright red hair.

After a moment of silence, Tammy said, "If she wanted to be fair, wouldn't she choose a gingerbread man for Edward, too? Anyway, it looks like him. He's always on the go," she said with a teasing poke at Edward's arm.

Olivia picked up the gingerbread woman and girl. "And these lovely figures?"

After a moment of silence, Bertha sniffled. Ellie handed her a tissue, and Bertha dabbed at her eyes. "My poor Clarisse," she said. "She loved her boys but, oh, she wanted a girl so much. When that never happened, she started wanting a granddaughter."

Olivia sneaked a peek at her group of suspects. Tammy was checking her watch. Hugh's ever-present smile had disappeared. His head swiveled slowly as he studied each of the three cookie arrangements. Edward stared into space. Olivia decided to kick it up a notch. She picked up the two flower shapes. Both were iced with simple, realistic piped lines. The six-petaled flower had red stamens and dark pink, curving petals that came to a point. On the eight-petaled flower, numerous flowing white lines, spreading out from a pale yellow center, suggested a dense petal structure.

Olivia saw puzzled faces among the guests. Del took out his cell phone and edged away, as if he had a call. He strolled toward the front door, cell phone to his ear.

A slight movement caught Olivia's attention. It was her mother, adjusting the scarf over her shoulder. Ellie's raised eyebrows and serene countenance conveyed a message: *I'll move this along, shall I?*

"Livie, dear," Ellie said, "that lovely pink flower looks so familiar to me. Let me think a moment."

Del pressed a button on his cell and held it to his ear. He craned his neck to look behind Olivia. Shaking his head, he stabbed at his cell phone.

Olivia felt light-headed and realized she had stopped breathing. Cody must not be answering his cell. She tried to telegraph a warning signal to her mom, but Ellie gazed off to the right, as if racking her memory. "Yes, I think I'm right," she said. "I believe the pink flower is a lily. Possibly a stargazer, such a sweet scent."

Out of the corner of her eye, Olivia thought she saw Hugh and Edward both stiffen.

"Of course it is," Bertha said. "Clarisse loved her lilies. I knew that cookie reminded me of something. And now I think on it, that white flower reminds me of growing up in the South. We had such lovely flowers, and the fragrance on a summer's day, it was like perfume. That's it! That white flower is a jasmine, I'm sure of it."

Tammy gasped as she looked up at Hugh. "Hugh?" Her eyes widened as red blotches formed on Hugh's handsome face. "Hugh, what's wrong?"

"I haven't heard that name in so long," Hugh muttered to himself as his blotches were replaced with a ghostly pallor.

Olivia noticed a quick flash of something in Edward's eyes. It seemed like an uneasy mix of hatred and fear. He took one look at his brother's face and backed away. His lips were moving, but it seemed that he was unaware that a name had escaped them. The name released in a coarse whisper was "Jasmine."

"Edward?" Hugh was rubbing his chin now, seemingly deep in thought. Suddenly his perfectly modulated voice turned harsh as he locked eyes with his brother. "What is this all about? What's with this trip down memory lane?"

"I was about to ask you the same thing," Edward said. His dark eyes were wary.

The other guests spread away from the brothers. Del watched the brothers intently, looking uncertain. Olivia knew how he felt.

Hugh picked up the jasmine flower cookie. Holding it in the palm of his hand, he said, "Did you know that Jasmine wrote to me after she disappeared? Just once. She wouldn't tell me where she was. She said she was sorry but she had to leave, that my family would never forgive her."

"You know Father never approved of her," Edward said flatly.

"He also knew enough not to interfere," Hugh said. "But you . . . You couldn't stand it, could you? You never forgave her for loving me instead of you. You convinced her to run away, didn't you?"

"Why would I do that? Hugh, you're not making sense. And why do you care now, anyway? You've got a perky new wife while I still have what I've always had—nothing." Edward edged away from his brother, cast a glance at the kitchen door, and Olivia's doubts evaporated. She knew that Edward's emotions had always been so close to the surface. He and Hugh had tried to keep things civil while Clarisse was alive, but her little show with the cookies brought everything to a furious boil. Olivia was going for broke. She picked up the coffin cookie.

"You did more than scare Jasmine into leaving town, didn't you, Edward?" She'd kept her voice calm and soft. Her mother would be proud. She placed herself between Edward and the kitchen door. "You knew Jasmine was pregnant, didn't you? Did you offer to claim the child as your own if she would marry you? Did she refuse you?"

Hugh's head snapped toward Olivia, then back to Edward. "Child? Whose child? What did you do to her?"

"Nothing, Hugh. Can't you see Olivia is playing some game?" He looked toward the kitchen, blocked by Olivia, then back at the front door, where Del waited. His eyes darted around the room like those of a trapped animal.

"Did you *kill* her?" The voice was barely recognizable, but it was Hugh's. His hands reached toward Edward's throat.

Edward ducked and backed into a corner. "It wasn't my fault, Hugh. Jasmine was mine first, I loved her. You already had everything, you didn't need her. I would have taken care of her and the child, but she wouldn't listen."

"So you killed her," Olivia said, deliberately goading him.

"*No*. Don't listen to her, Hugh. It was an accident. I was trying to make her listen, make her see how much I still cared for her when she lost her balance and fell down the stairs. I didn't mean to . . ."

"Jasmine died of exposure," Olivia said. "She was still alive when you dumped her body in Patuxent River State Park on a cold March day. That was no accident. Your mother found out, didn't she?"

Hugh let out a yell and leaped at his brother. Edward sidestepped, and Hugh hit the wall.

As Edward sprinted for the kitchen, Olivia shouted, "Cody!" She heard a crash, coming from behind the kitchen door, followed by a deep bark. Edward skidded to a halt and spun around. Hugh tried to block his way, but Edward shoved him so hard, he lost his balance. He twisted and fell sideways. Hugh winced as he used his left arm to sit up. Jason knelt beside him.

Edward barreled forward, and Lucas tried to block him as he neared the antiques cabinet. Edward grabbed the thirty-six-cup coffeemaker and hurled it at him. The metal container bounced off Lucas's shoulder and smashed open, spewing hot coffee down his side.

Del guarded the front door, ready to fight. Powerful muscles strained against the sleeves of his shirt. But he didn't have a weapon. It would be all right, Olivia told herself. Del was the stronger of the two and far more experienced.

Where was Cody? Olivia skirted the sales desk and shoved open the kitchen door. She saw nothing but over-turned chairs and spilled sugar. The door to the alley hung open. She heard a rattling sound and twirled around in time to watch her antiques cabinet rock forward. As it crashed to the floor, she tried not to think about the innocent cookie cutters trapped inside.

When the cabinet fell, the loud crash distracted Del long enough for Edward to dart toward a table in the corner, to Del's left.

What was a table doing in that corner? Olivia's mind flashed back to their preparations for the memorial. Hadn't Maddie moved the pie-baking equipment out of the nook and into the main room to make room for a cookie tray? Cold dread shot through her as she remembered one item in that display—her beloved gray marble rolling pin.

With the quickness of a threatened squirrel, Edward snatched the rolling pin and swung it at Del's stomach. Del doubled over, collapsed. Edward leaped over Del's prone body and escaped into the foyer.

Mr. Willard had herded the remaining guests as far away from the doors as possible, so Olivia didn't have to run anyone down as she raced toward Del. By the time Olivia reached him, Del was sitting up. He grasped her arm and rolled to his knees.

Olivia squatted beside him, an arm around his shoulders. "Del, don't try to move. I'm so, so sorry, I should have known that rolling pin could be used as a weapon, I—"

Del put a shaky finger to his lips, and Olivia realized he was trying to catch his breath. Then she heard a familiar sound from behind the partially open door to the foyer. A growl. A yappy sort of growl.

"Spunky?! Oh my God." He must have escaped when Jason went to get her cell. She reached behind Del and pushed the door open. Edward had cleared the front door, with Spunky nipping at his heels. She stood up and ran after them. The Chamberlain family car, a roomy Ford van, was parked right in front of the store. Edward beeped open the lock before he reached for the door. Spunky jumped inside a moment before the door slammed shut.

"Oh no." She was too late. Edward was about to drive off with her puppy and get away with murder. She heard sirens coming nearer, but would they be in time? She kept running.

Edward was being unusually slow about starting his car. When she got close enough, she heard Spunky's distinctive bark. He'd jumped into Edward's lap. When Edward tried to shove him off, Spunky dug his teeth into Edward's shirt sleeve and tugged, as if they were playing a game. Edward lifted his arm and tried to shake off the tiny dog.

Olivia reached the van first and grabbed the door handle. It was locked. Spunky spotted her outside. He let go of Edward's sleeve, plopped down on the seat, and began to yap excitedly. Edward aimed his key toward the ignition.

"No!" Olivia banged on the driver's-side window. She stopped when she heard a loud thump to her left. Edward's key was in the ignition, but he froze. He stared out the front windshield, where eighty-five pounds of black Labrador balanced on the hood, barking at his little friend inside.

Edward recovered, turned the key. Someone yanked Olivia aside right before she heard a brief explosion. Cody stood in front of the van, holding his revolver. Air hissed out of the left-front tire. The ignition caught, and Edward shifted into drive, flat tire or no flat tire. Dogs or no dogs.

Del appeared. "Sorry about this, Livie," he said. Olivia thought he was talking about her puppy. Then she noticed what he held in his hand—her lovely gray marble rolling pin. Del swung it at the driver's-side window.

Marble isn't the hardest stone on the planet, and Del didn't swing as hard as he might have, but it did the trick.

Edward ducked sideways as Spunky leaped into the back-seat. Buddy the Lab skittered off the hood, taking some of the car's finish with him. A maze of cracks spread across the glass. Del held the marble rolling pin like a baseball bat, ready to smash the window again, if he had to. Cody aimed his revolver at the windshield.

Edward sat up and switched off the ignition. He sat very still, one hand tight on the steering wheel. After a few moments, his hand slid to his lap. Olivia heard the van's locks snap open as Edward Chamberlain, for perhaps the first time in his life, gave up.

Chapter Twenty-five

Olivia and Maddie sat cross-legged on the floor of The Gingerbread House, lights dimmed, mourning over the crushed remains of their antiques cabinet. It lay where it had fallen the afternoon before, facedown, vintage cookie cutters snug inside.

"Like a mommy protecting her babies," Maddie said.

"Let's hope so." Olivia stroked Spunky's ears as he snuggled beside her. "From the size of those cracks in the side, I doubt the poor thing is reparable. I suppose we should turn it over and assess the damage to our cutters." She took her time getting to her feet. The pain from her injuries had lessened, but her muscles felt stiff and tight.

Maddie hopped up and offered a steadying hand. Together, they pulled the cabinet onto its side. The contents clattered and tinkled into a heap on the floor. Maddie turned up the lights, while Olivia closed Spunky into the kitchen to keep his little paws off the glass shards. When she returned with a whisk broom, Maddie was already sorting vintage cookie cutters from broken glass.

After a half hour of work, interrupted only by whining from the kitchen, Maddie asked, "What time will everyone start arriving?"

"I suggested anytime after two." Olivia checked the Hansel and Gretel clock on the wall. "We have somewhere between fifteen minutes and half an hour to get this cleaned up. Del called and said he'd come later. So will Hugh and Tammy. Mom and Jason will probably be on time, and Mr. Willard will bring Bertha along shortly. Del called this morning and filled me in on a few details from Edward's confession. It seems Edward was getting desperate. Clarisse had found out from Faith's letter—the part we didn't see—that Jasmine died soon after giving birth to Hugh's child."

"But not that Edward killed her?"

"Not something you add to a letter asking a stranger to come rescue a grandchild she didn't know she had."

"Good point," Maddie said. "Clarisse would have become very suspicious of Faith's motives. So who was Faith?"

"Faith Kelly, Jasmine's closest friend. Jasmine went to live with her after disappearing from Chatterley Heights. Apparently, Faith grabbed baby Lily and ran when Edward showed up. I wouldn't be surprised if Jasmine told her to. Jasmine was smart; she probably began to suspect that Edward had lied to her about Martin wanting her to disappear forever."

"One thing I don't understand," Maddie said. "If Faith wrote this letter saying she was dying of cancer, why did Clarisse hire a private detective agency to find Lily? Why not just get her from Faith?"

"Ah, because Faith collapsed and was rushed to the hospital before she could post the letter. Social Services took Lily. Faith never went home again. After she died, her landlady found the letter, already stamped and addressed, so she dropped it in the mail. It reached Clarisse nearly a month after Faith wrote it."

"But if Clarisse never actually met Faith, how did she find out that Edward killed Jasmine?"

Olivia picked up a gingerbread man with a tilted hat and a red aluminum handle. She smoothed her fingers over the cool metal. "The same way we did: she searched the Internet. Clarisse had the advantage of knowing about when Jasmine died. She was so upset, she called Edward at that conference in Baltimore and said she was thinking about contacting the police. She couldn't have been completely sure at that point which of her sons killed Jasmine, but she knew one of them was guilty, and I think she suspected Edward. He begged her to wait until he could talk to her. That's why she asked Bertha for a full bottle of wine: she was expecting Edward."

Maddie balanced on her rear and stretched out her arms and legs. "Pilates," she said. "Your mom taught me."

Olivia spotted a small crack in a plastic Hallmark Lucy and reluctantly added it to the pile of damaged cutters. Lucy still had value. Someone would love her, crack and all. As much as one could love Lucy. "It's sad, really," she said. "Because of his drive and intensity, Edward was a successful businessman, but he felt trapped in Hugh's shadow. Then Edward met Jasmine and fell in love. And Hugh won again."

"Love isn't business," Maddie said.

"So right," Olivia said. "Love isn't coolheaded and rational. Hugh would have defied his father to marry Jasmine, and of course, Clarisse would have been thrilled. But Edward couldn't let go. He thought he could convince Jasmine that Hugh cared more about what their father thought than for her and her child. He wanted to look like her knight in shining armor. Edward was only trying to convince Jasmine to marry him instead of Hugh, but his lies about Martin's disapproval frightened her into hiding. He still managed to keep tabs on her and tracked her down probably thinking he had one last chance to get her back into his life. But when she refused him, things turned violent."

Maddie began filling two boxes, one with unscathed vintage cutters and the other with damaged ones, while Olivia whisked up the glass shards.

The Gingerbread House door opened, and Ellie Greyson's head appeared. "Are we early? We brought food and drink, in the form of pizzas and wine. Jason brought beer, of course. I'll warm some pizza in the oven, shall I?"

Lucas arrived, followed by Mr. Willard and Bertha with more wine and a sweet potato pie. "My mother's recipe," Bertha said. "And sweet potato is so good for you, too."

"I'm not much of a cook," Lucas said as Maddie took his offering of potato chips and a carton of onion dip.

"I love a man who can shop."

Two pizzas and a bottle of wine later, Olivia had shared what she'd learned from Del. Ellie was emerging from the kitchen bearing a third pizza when the front door opened and Del poked his head inside.

"We have someone we want you to meet," Del said. He held the door as Hugh and Tammy entered. Hugh had one arm in a cast. In his good arm, he carried a lovely little girl with sapphire blue eyes and black curls falling loosely to her shoulders. She looked sleepy and a bit dazed. Hugh and Tammy didn't appear to have slept much, either.

"We won't stay for long," Hugh said, "but I wanted all of you to meet Lily Chamberlain. My daughter. And while I'm at it, let me introduce my new wife, Tammy Deacons-Chamberlain."

Lily hid her face against Hugh's shoulder as well-wishers stampeded toward them. Olivia went right to Tammy. "I'm so happy for you," Olivia said. "But when . . . how . . . ?"

"Oh, Livie, I wanted to tell you, but Clarisse was so against us being together. We thought if we got married and then told her, she'd have to accept it. But Clarisse died at the very worst moment. . . . I didn't mean that the way it sounded. Hugh was worried about how it might look if we announced we'd gotten married the same day his mother died."

"The same day?" So the argument she and Maddie had heard from Tammy's bathroom when they'd announced their "engagement" had really been about revealing their marriage.

"Looking back," Tammy said, "I wish I had told you. It would have cleared everything up more quickly and without . . ." She nodded toward the ruined antiques cabinet, lying splintered on the floor like the body in a murder mystery game.

"What you're saying," Olivia said, "is that you and Hugh had alibis?"

"Ironclad. Some of Hugh's friends in Baltimore witnessed our marriage and then gave us a party. We stayed with them that night. We'll have a real honeymoon later, of course." Her eyes strayed toward Hugh. "We're thinking we might take Lily with us. She has lost too many mothers; she needs stability."

Our little Tammy is growing up. Olivia could almost hear those words coming from Maddie's mouth.

Hugh, Tammy, and Lily left a few minutes later, followed by Mr. Willard and Bertha, then Ellie and Jason. Maddie and Lucas retired to the kitchen to clean up. Which left Olivia and Del. They settled into the nook armchairs.

Del refilled their wineglasses and answered her last few questions. "Roberta traced the disconnected phone number on Faith's note. It led her to a small apartment, rented up until a month ago by Faith Kelly. She'd never reported Jasmine missing, probably to avoid losing Lily. Faith must have lived in fear while she raised Lily as her own."

"But how exactly did Edward kill Clarisse?"

Del paused before answering. "He snuck into the house after rushing home from Baltimore and was careful to make sure that Bertha didn't see him. He found his mother's pills before heading up to her study. He confessed that he was trying to convince her not to go to the police with what she knew but he was sure it was useless, so he'd begun crushing up her pills into the wine he was pouring for her. Clarisse was pacing and too upset to notice."

"Poor Clarisse. At least now her granddaughter is back with her family and Clarisse can be at peace. Thanks for keeping me in the loop." Olivia sighed as the weight on her chest and the knot in her stomach began to dissipate for the first time since her friend was killed. "I know you didn't have to. Oh, but wait, what about Sam? And my car?"

"Edward was checking in at Chatterley Heights pharmacy, which is owned by Chamberlain Enterprises, when Sam dropped off the mail. He heard Sam boast about knowing what was in the letter Clarisse received from the private investigator she'd hired to search for Jasmine. Edward claims he only wanted to put Sam out of commission for a while, not kill him. Edward had dropped off a check for the bequest his mother had left the food shelf, and he had seen the decorated cookies Olivia delivered earlier. He moved fast once the whole idea occurred to him. He managed to swipe some cookies from the food shelf without being seen, then laced them with a high-powered insulin enhancer he'd taken from the pharmacy. He just wanted Sam to back off." Del leaned toward Olivia. "On the other hand, I think he was trying to do some serious damage to you when he punctured your brake line. He recognized your car while you were gathering those cookie cutters from the Chamberlain house. He really viewed you as an outsider meddling in 'family affairs.' He was also still resentful of your close relationship with his mother."

Del stretched out his legs and yawned. "So have I answered all your questions?"

"Actually," she said, "I do have one more."

"Fire away." Del leaned his head back and closed his eyes.

Olivia drained her glass in one large gulp. The loss of her friend and her own near-death experience combined with all of the chaos she had endured suddenly made Olivia realize that she wanted something more in her life, maybe someone . . .

"So," she began and then paused to clear her throat. "Maybe, when our respective injuries have healed, we should go on a real date sometime."

Del's face reddened a bit as he sat up and said, "Livie Greyson, it's about time you asked me a question I can gladly say yes to."